JOSEPH COVINO JR

EDGAR ALLAN POE'S
SAN FRANCISCO

TERROR TALES OF THE CITY

AN EPIC PRESS BOOK

Published by *Epic Press*
PO Box 30108
Walnut Creek, CA 94598
First *Epic Press* Edition published 2005
Special thanks to *Wayne Harada* for his painstaking proofreading!

CONTENTS

For Megan,
the young maiden,
who bore me the soul of
Annabel Lee,
one sweet summer,
in 1996,
in the kingdom,
close by the sounding San Francisco sea

PROLOGUE:

BURIED ALIVE

*"There are moments when, even to the sober eye of Reason, the world of our sad Humanity may assume the semblance of a Hell—but the imagination of man is no Carathis, to explore with impunity its every cavern. Alas! the grim legion of sepulchral terrors cannot be regarded as altogether fanciful—but, like the Demons in whose company Afrasiab made his voyage down the Oxus, they must sleep, or they will devour us—they must be suffered to slumber, or we perish."—**The Premature Burial**

JOSEPH COVINO JR

To be buried alive is no doubt the most horrific and frightful extreme of torment ever to befall the fortune of sheer humanity. At best the borders separating life and death are nebulous and obscure. Who will say where one ends and the other begins?

Upon awaking I found myself the captive of a grave. Footfalls heard overhead awakened me from a deep sleep. In turn I struggled ferociously to make myself heard. No sooner was I awake did I become completely conscious of the dreadful terrors of my predicament.

"I am alive," I muttered to myself, "but I am trapped."

No situation is so horribly well suited to incite the height of physical and mental torment as burial before death: the insufferable oppression of the lungs; the suffocating smell of the moist dirt; the sticking of the grave clothes; the stiff confinement of the cramped coffin; the darkness of the consummate night; the overpowering ocean of tomblike stillness; the imperceptible but perceived presence of the ravenous worm—that our desperate lot is that of the fatally dead.

Your heart still beats with a pitch of petrifying and insupportable terror. You conceive of nothing so excruciating in all the world—you can imagine nothing half so horrible in the nether regions of the most infernal hell.

There came a time—as commonly before there had come—in which I found myself coming forth from complete sleep into the first faint and vague sensation of being. Gradually—by slow degrees—I neared consciousness. A listless trepidation. An indifferent sufferance of blunt pain. No concern—no contemplation—no exertion. Then after a long interlude a ringing in the ears; then after an interim still longer a prickling, stinging sensation in the extremities; then a seemingly infinite interval of pleasant repose during which the awakening sensations are striving into consciousness; then a fleeting relapse into nothingness; then a sudden revival. At length the slight flitting of the eyelids, and instantly after that a severe shock of a horror, lethal and unclear, which pumps the blood in spurts from the temples to the heart. And then the first attempt to think. And then the first effort to recollect. And then a partial and evaporating accomplishment.

And then the recollection had so far recovered its control that to some extent I was conscious of my condition. I sensed that I awoke from no simple sleep. And then finally, as if by the surge of a sea, my shivering soul was overrun by the one ghastly menace—by the one ghostly and ever pervading impression.

For some moments after this impression preoccupied me I remained motionless. But why? I could not summon up courage to budge. I dared not make the attempt which was to assure me of my doom—and still there was something in my soul which murmured me *it was assured*. Desperation—such as no other race of misery ever brings into existence—desperation alone spurred me, after prolonged indecision, to raise my heavy eyelids. I raised them. It was black—all black. I knew that I had then completely regained the use of my visual powers—and still it was black—all black—the acute and sheer lightlessness of the night that lasts eternally.

I struggled to scream; and my dry lips and tongue fluttered spastically together in the effort—but no voice emanated from the hollow lungs, which oppressed as if by the pressure of some weighty burden, panted and pulsated with the heart at every labored and erratic breath.

In this attempt to cry out loud the movement of the jaws confirmed for me that they were locked as is normal with the dead. I sensed also that I lay on some rigid surface; and by something like it my sides were tightly constricted as well. So far I had not dared to budge any of my limbs—but then I wildly flung up my arms which had been lying lengthwise with the wrists crossed. They hit a hard wooden surface which stretched over my body at a height of mere inches from my face. I could no longer deny that I rested inside a coffin finally.

I wriggled and strained every convulsive nerve to forcibly

break open the lid: it would not budge. And then also there came abruptly to my nostrils the potent unnatural stench of damp dirt. Irrevocable was the conclusion. I was *not* inside the tomb. I was buried alive—nailed up in some ordinary coffin—and plunged deep, deep and eternally into some common and unnamed grave.

As this dreadful certainty forced itself so into the innermost bowels of my soul I once more strove to cry out loud. And in that subsequent attempt I succeeded. A prolonged, uncontrolled and unremitting scream or shriek of anguish resounded throughout the regions of the unfathomable night.

I had fainted; but yet not all of awareness was gone; no, all was not gone. In the deepest sleep—no! In dementia—no! In a trance—no! In a coma—no! In death—no! Even in the pit all *is not* gone. Otherwise for mortals there is no immortality. Awakening from the deepest of sleeps we shatter the delicate web of *some* dream. But in an instant afterward—so flimsy may that web have been—we do not recollect that we have dreamed. In our return to wakefulness from sleep there is first the perception of the spiritual and then that of the physical reality. If upon attaining the physical we could recollect the perceptions of the spiritual we should find those perceptions fluent recollections of the abyss beyond. And that abyss is—what? How at least will we tell apart its shadows from those of the crypt? But if the perceptions of the spiritual are not by choice recollected still, following a lengthy interim, do they not approach uninvited while we wonder from where they come? If you have never fainted you have not perceived peculiar places and freakishly familiar faces in smoldering embers aglow; have not watched floating in mid-air the dismal sight of your own dead body lying lifeless beneath you.

Amidst repeated and pensive attempts to recall; amidst diligent efforts to recollect some sign of the condition of apparent nonexistence into which my spirit had reverted there have been moments when I have imagined triumph; there have been fleeting, extremely fleeting times when I have summoned up memories which the clear logic of a later era satisfies me could have had relation solely to that state of apparent unawareness. These ghosts of remembrance recount vaguely the tall, hooded figure cloaked in crimson red who raised and removed me in stillness down—down—down—yet down—until a frightful vertigo afflicted me at the sheer notion of the endlessness of the fall. They recount too the uncertain terror at my heart by virtue of that heart's aberrant quiet. Then approaches a perception of startling stillness throughout everything; as if he who conveyed me—a ghostly figure—had overtook in the fall the ends of endlessless and idled from the fatigue of the task. Following that I recall flatness and dankness; and then everything is insanity—the insanity of a recollection which preoccupies itself amongst things taboo.

Most abruptly there returned to my spirit movement and sound—the convulsive movement of the heart, and to my ears, the noise of its throbbing. Then a lull in which all is hollow. Then again noise, and movement, and feeling—a tingling sensation permeating my form. Then the sheer awareness of being without thought—a state which lingered long. Then most abruptly—*thought*—and shivering horror and determined effort to understand my actual condition. Then a powerful longing to revert to oblivion. Then a surging resuscitation of spirit and a triumphant attempt to stir.

So far I had not opened my eyes. I perceived that I lay upon my back unconfined. I stretched out my hand and it dropped weightily upon something moist and rigid. There I endured it to linger for many moments while I struggled to conceive where and *what* I could be. I yearned but ventured not to exert my eyesight. I feared the first glimpse of things about me. It was not that I was afraid to behold things terrible but that I grew alarmed for fear that there should be *nothing* to see. At last, with a frenzied futility of spirit, I abruptly opened my eyes. My worst speculations were then confirmed.

The darkness of perpetual night enveloped me. I strained for breath. The depth of the blackness appeared to oppress and smother me. The space was insufferably snug. I yet lay still and exerted myself to employ my rationality. I carried my thoughts back and strove from that time to work out my true state; and it seemed to me that a decidedly prolonged lapse of time had since passed. But not for an instant did I presume myself really dead. But where and in what condition was I?

Then I heard a sharp scraping sound like solid steel grating across gritty ground. Then onto my face shone a small but dim speckle of light shed suddenly through a narrow and dull glass opening—a kind of window—which even though cleared of murk now clouded over with misty vapor from my quickening, gasping breath. Showing through the foggy haze before my face I saw gliding over me the slow, languid and rhythmic movements of the tall figure shrouded in red: and wielding what looked like—yes, it was—a grave-digger's iron spade! Out of nowhere he was scooping up shovelfuls of crumbly dirt and heaping them on top of the coffin. And outside I could hear the lumpy dirt clumps thudding over its wooden lid.

But how did I come to be here? Try as I might, try as I must I could barely remember. But as sure as I was now being buried alive I was beginning to dig up deeply dark and murky memories. Exhumed were familiar but blurred pictures and images which, gradually, flashed across my memory and recurred to my mind. And at last deep reflection lent its aid. Let me then recollect.

JOSEPH COVINO JR

ONE:

FLIGHT FROM DEATH

"Alas, I cannot feel; for 't is not feeling,
This standing motionless upon the golden
Threshold of the wide-open gate of dreams,
Gazing, entranced, adown the gorgeous vista,
And thrilling as I see, upon the right,
Upon the left, and all the way along,
Amid empurpled vapors, far away
*To where the prospect terminates—**thee only**."*—Poe
poem: ***To — —***

JOSEPH COVINO JR

S ade kept on reminding me, her smooth, silken voice and her sonorous, sensuous song resounding in my ears through my music player headset: mine was no ordinary love. Over and over again she reminded me, jogging my memory at the very same time my laboring legs were making long and rapid strides jogging on so vigorously southbound.

Far off behind me—their ocher and olive layers at once rising and falling away in the distance—hovered the bunchy and lumpish hills of the *Marin* headlands. A long way off before me loomed the woodsy bluffs of the San Francisco *Presidio*. Far off below me, surging through the broad strait which narrowed to less than a mile between the facing points of land, ebbed and flowed the powerful, churning tidewater, running robustly back and forth between the Pacific Ocean and the San Francisco Bay: the *Golden Gate*. And across the great and grand *Golden Gate Bridge* I was running in earnest.

For neither the sublimely beautiful young woman whose resplendent face kept on flashing across my memory, nor the magnificent bridge I was running across, nor the splendid city I was bound for—for them mine was no ordinary love.

Past the leftward, low-set balustrade I could see from the lofty walkway I was crossing the icy, windswept waters of *San Francisco Bay* spreading far and wide, looking as if blustering breaths of air were fanning them to the faraway horizon—and farther to the very edge of the world. Looming ahead on the horizon, clouded over by a somber, muzzy haze the craggy outline of *Alcatraz* island jutted out of the waves. And beyond, where the stirred sea line met the hazy skyline, shot up the distinct and distinctive silhouette of America's most beautiful and bewitching cityscape*: San Francisco* herself.

All around me the outstretched neck of land, the marble blue sea and the shady gray sky all came together at this spectacular suspension bridge I was grimly running across. Stormy blasts of air blew up from those turbulent, tumultuous waters

17

sunk more than two hundred feet beneath the broad and busy bridge roadway rolling on alongside me—thick with all manner of moving, motorized traffic. Only I heard or saw precious little of what sped by me.

Gusty crosscurrents whipped up and down my hardworking body, drowning out most sound except for the pulsating, sensuous song falling upon my ears in concert with my own panting breath—or perhaps the breath of the bridge herself: for with truth the *Golden Gate* has been called the bridge that sighs. Fast and furious is the wind blowing so incessantly through the *Golden Gate*: and the bridge's sole safety valve is her ability to sway—and sigh—along with it. Back and forth, sometimes as much as twenty feet, will more than eighty thousand tons of structural steel swing and shift with the wind.

What I did see pass by me as I passed on were the bridge's familiar, fibrous looking lines. Obscurely they whisked by—their warm, tempered, terra cotta color growing dim as my pace quickened.

From shore to tower, tower to tower and tower to shore the bridge's giant circular cables—their scores of strands spun from thousands of entwined wires—sweep gracefully across the gate in gently curved crescents. From the main cables hang the straight suspender cables which fasten vertically to the roadway at separately spaced intervals. And suspended between these sidelong steel draperies are the bridge's slender but soaring twin towers.

Coming at me and shooting up majestically almost five hundred feet above the roadway was the bridge's north tower; its vertical fluting and huge, gaping portals—four massive frames fringing sky, clouds and fog—slimming and tapering off aloft, piercing the very heavens. Only the whole colossal superstructure, along with all its whizzing automotive traffic, began to blur and cloud over into a single, solitary veil of orange-vermillion shade and shadow.

In fairness of face few youthful females were equal to my

lovely Lenore. Hers was the splendor of an unreal, unworldly dream—an ethereal and exhilarating vision more impetuously unearthly than even the flightiest and most fabulous fantasies of sleeping spirits. But her countenance was not of the conventional, classical cast. But although I perceived that the countenance of Lenore was not of a classic convention—although I discerned that her beauty was in fact superlative and sensed that there was ample peculiarity permeating it—but I have attempted to no avail to disccover the peculiarity and to deduce my own impression of its unusualness. I lost myself in the outline of her high and pallid forehead—it was flawless—how frigid indeed a word when alluding to a grandeur so heavenly!—her flesh surpassing the purest alabaster, her powerful intensity and composure, the graceful conspicuousness of the parts over the temples; and then her sable-black, her sleek, lush and naturally wavy locks! I marveled at the delicate contours of her faultless nose. There were the same sumptuous smoothness of texture, the same barely discernable inclination to the Roman, the same congruous arcs of her nostrils denoting her liberated spirit. I admired her luscious mouth. There was indeed the victory of all things divine—the fine curl of her little upper lip—the supple, sensuous repose of her lower—the dimples which frolic and the pallor which bespoke—her teeth glimpsing back with a radiance almost dazzling, every beam of hallowed light which reflected from them in her calm and tranquil, but most jubilantly brilliant of all smiles. I fathomed the configuration of her chin—and there also I found her gracefulness of form, her silkiness and stateliness, her sensuality and sanctity. And then I gazed into the large eyes of Lenore.

Lenore's eyes were, I must take for granted, much larger than the average eyes of our race. They were even larger than the largest of doe eyes. But it was merely at interludes—in moments of passionate arousal—that this idiosyncrasy became more than slightly conspicuous in Lenore. And at such moments was her comeliness—in my fertile imagination so it seemed perchance—the comeliness of creatures abroad or beyond this world. The color of her eyes was the most lustrous of black, and far over them laid jet-black lashes of full length. Her brows, slightly inconstant in contour, had the same shade. The unusualness though which I found in her eyes was of a quality different from the cast, or the color or the radiance of her countenance and must at most be ascribed to her *expression*. Ah, term of no import! behind whose infinite extent of sheer sound we entrench our incomprehension of so much of the supernatural. The expression of the eyes of Lenore! How for prolonged hours I have contemplated it! How have I, during the dead of night, striven to penetrate it! What was it—that something deep as a well—which lurked unfathomed inside the eyes of my darling? What was it? I was seized with a fever to fathom it! Those eyes! those large, those gleaming, those heavenly eyes! And so how often in my passionate probe of Lenore's eyes have I sensed looming the complete comprehension of their expression—sensed it looming—but not quite become my own—and so completely disappear!

When I made love with Lenore, whose aquiline face even now haunted me in my head, everything around us—even a room's most prominent objects—would fade and grow dim until all else passed and melted away with nothing left over but a murky haze enveloping us both. Haunting she with truth once called it.

All I would see beneath me would be her resplendent, prepossessing face—her brow deeply furrowed; her eyes contentedly closed; her flushed cheek nuzzling my palm, fervidly warm to my touch; her parted, panting lips inviting mine to fall upon them. Her hands all over me, caressing gently my shoulders, chest and arms. My hands all over her, feeling warmly her soft, satiny skin and filling with her supple, swelling bosom. Our ravenous mouths, our gasping breaths, our grasping fingers, our heaving bodies, our throbbing hearts, our merging souls—all joining and coming together: embracing, undulating, fuming.

And Sade sang on—her song running in my head along with the recurring, reeling image of our last lovemaking: ours was no ordinary love.

"God!" I heard my beloved murmur, giving a squealing cry of rapture and pain under her breath.

And in the very same breath I passed beneath the north tower, looking up appreciatively and catching purely a passing glimpse of its steel fascia plates and fluted portal brackets when most rudely interrupted by the rapidly blurred sight of a strange, unfamiliar and uncontrollably frantic face—that of a wild-eyed, wildly flailing young man gone berserk—who like a bolt from the blue abruptly bore down upon and collided headlong with me at full tilt, plowing into me and knocking us both violently off our feet!

§

Knocked down and laid out flat on my back on the bridge walkway, feeling hit hard between the eyes, I raised up on one arm, shook my stunned head and struggled sluggishly to regain my senses. I strained my eyes to bring my blurred vision into focus. And what slowly stood out and showed through my bleary eyesight was apparently an equally stunned, supine but reviving *sailor*—a tall, stalwart, wiry young man with a decisively devil-may-care demeanor of face not entirely unengaging. His perceptibly sunburnt countenance was more than half covered by a bristly mustache and whiskers. Frantically he fumbled, groping the ground desperately to snap up a large oaken cudgel he had dropped upon impact at our collision.

"What the devil's the matter with you?" I exclaimed through my staggered, perturbed breath. "Have you lost your wits?"

Suddenly the sailor turned black in the face as if he were straining from strangulation. He stumbled to his feet and tightly gripped his cudgel; but at the same instant he dropped back down onto the ground, shuddering convulsively and with the pale complexion of death itself.

"The devil stalks me!" he exclaimed inexplicably. "It chases after me—even now!"

"What?" I gasped, utterly agog.

"It treads on my heels right behind me! It draws near, I tell you—even now!"

Looking aghast, I glanced around anxiously but caught only a vague glimpse of just the most proximate of perplexed and apprehensive pedestrians beginning to congregate at a discreet distance at that troubled spot on the bridge walkway.

"Who chases after you?" I asked falteringly, flinching from the sheer licentious terror of the sailor's panicky reply.

"Not who—*it!*" he cried out aloud at the top of his voice. "The brute beast! The butcher! The bloodthirsty, murderous monster!"

"Where?" I stammered in my own halting voice. "I don't see anyone—"

"*Thing!*" he stressed repeatedly, frightfully panic-stricken. "The *thing!* It's not human!"

"I don't see any...*thing*—threatening."

There was a breed of maddened mirth in his eyes—a seemingly constrained *hysterics* in his entire deportment. His manner alarmed me.

"Are you blind?" he asked abruptly after having glared about himself for some moments in stillness. "Can you not see? And have you not seen it? Have you not seen it then?—but, wait! you will."

"See *what?*" I cried, raising my irritable voice out of frightful frustration.

"*That!*" he shrieked in sheer hysterics, cringing and shrinking back against the pavement at the base of the bridge guardrail. "*That! That!*" he repeated, pointing fanatically and frantically at an adjacent curtain of straight suspender cables stretched taut from the main cables to the roadway at regular intervals—but through which nothing showed but open air, gray clouds and overcast sky!

What the mortally appalled sailor saw lurked unseen and was indiscernible to any other seeing observer or onlooker: a mighty and monstrous orangutan of gargantuan stature, prodigious strength and staggering agility swinging from the suspender cables—and wildly wielding a glinting barber's razor steeped and dripping with curdled droplets of blood!

Paralyzed with fear the sailor gradually got to his feet by excruciatingly slow degrees, groping with his trembling free hand and laying firm hold of a single suspender cable. He stared insanely, riveting his distraught eyes on some imperceptible apparition. Slowly I stood up myself.

"What is it?" I finally relented, taking belated pity on the frightfully distracted sailor. "What do you see?"

What the terror-stricken sailor saw was the supernatural specter of the gigantic orangutan—ferocious, frenzied and infuriated, bristling with tawny tufts of ruffled hair, glowering with fiery eyes ablaze with rage, snarling and rabidly baring his spiked and grindingly gnashed teeth. Inflamed with fury the wrathful orangutan reeled to and fro from the lofty perch atop the suspender cables, wildly waving the glistening, spurting, blood-red razor. Trembling, the sailor irresolutely heaved and threw his oaken cudgel straight at the fearsome, menacing, maniacal apparation, and watched dejectedly as the rageful creature deftly dodged, and the twirling projectile hurtled past and disappeared into open space. Fidgeting for a grip, the sailor clutched the single suspender cable with both hands and handily hoisted himself atop the walkway's sidelong guardrail, holding fast amidst the stiff, boisterous sea breeze.

"What are you doing?" I ejaculated, intensely startled. "Come down from there before you fall and kill yourself."

His soles squeaked atop the guardrail as he held tight and swung himself round the suspender cable, turning on his toes. He stared straight down at me—his frightened eyes darting about distractedly.

"I would rather kill myself than get slaughtered by that savage beast!" he snapped back—his touseled hair blowing up in the blustering wind.

"Then you would die for nothing," I shouted irately, "because there is most certainly *no beast!*"

§

By that time another spectating bystander, who was in turn amused and alarmed, hustled toward a tall pole supporting one of the sodium and mercury vapor lamps lighting up the bridge's roadway. To the side of the pole a small yellow box was attached beneath a blue sign picturing in white a telephone receiver along with the printed words: *EMERGENCY PHONE*. Stepping up promptly to the pole the anxious bystander wrenched the receiver from the phone box and pressed it to the ear to speak urgently.

Perched at the southwestern end of the *Golden Gate Bridge* was its beige toll plaza office. Inside its wide, reflecting bay windows a complex control center—looking like the instrument panel of a jet aircraft—pulsated with chaotic light and noise. All around the crowded console, aglow with closed circuit television and computer monitors, alarm-activated beeps and flashes mingled with the sporadic squelching of police intercoms and radios.

A stocky, balding bridge officer twitched his bushy black mustache with mild imperturbability as his surveillance camera zoomed in on the tall, stout sailor standing atop the guardrail, holding on to one of the bridge's thin and taut suspender cables. Presently his camera brought into clear focus the sailor's shaky, wind-whipped shape. At the same instant he dispatched a summoning call over his radio transmitter.

"Units 51 and 52," he announced stoically. "We have a possible 10-31 in the area of light pole 69 on the east side. He's a white male wearing a sailor's uniform..."

In minutes two four-door, Ford LTD Crown Victoria patrol cars, each displaying bridge insignias on their sides, their rear red and white sequential lights flashing on their way, were speeding toward the potential suicide scene.

§

"My friend," I said in a solicitous tone, "you are frightening yourself needlessly—you are indeed. No one means you any harm whatever. I give you my word of honor that no one intends you any injury."

"You cannot answer for the foul fiend that means to butcher me!" the edgy sailor exclaimed, adamant.

"What primitive brute beast could strike so much terror into you—except perhaps some deranged, escaped lunatic?"

"It's far worse than any raving mad *man!*" he spouted. "It's a mad, maniacal demon run amuck! It's possessed of a devil and means to brutally mutilate me! It wants to tear out my hair by the roots! It wants to throttle me to death. It wants to bite my choking tongue clean through. It wants to cut my throat with its razor until my head is completely severed from my body! It's the savage and sadistic ape! It's the bloodthirsty, rampaging *murderer in the Rue Morgue!*"

Taken aback by the discernibly disturbed sailor's demented pronouncements I was for some moments at a loss how to react.

"Why then let that brute beast terrorize you?" I asked, collecting my thoughts and holding out my hands to him with a placating gesture. "Why can you not control it rather than let it control you?"

Momentarily the jumpy sailor looked mindful of my sympathetic suggestion as if it had made some slight impression upon him.

"I have been in the habit of taming the beast—even in its

25

fiercest temper—with the aid of a whip! he finally conceded, gesturing suggestively to the ground. "Now you could resort to it!"

Glancing around, I stood aghast at the unexpected sight of the leather whip that I spotted discarded—cast aside unnoticed upon impact at our collision—and lying untouched upon the bridge walkway.

"It deathly dreads the whip," the fidgety sailor said, undespairing, spurring me to snap it up, "which would no doubt immediately transform the fiend's frenzy into fright!"

Hesitantly—and somewhat awkwardly—I gripped the whip and attempted to snap it repeatedly at the vacant spot admidst the vertical suspender cables where the menacing ape apparition reputedly appeared—much to the addled sailor's conspicuous if passing relief.

"Keep at it!" he bellowed. "Aware of deserving punishment it looks wishful of covering up its gory outrages! It swings from the cables in an anguish of tense trepidation!"

By then the two bridge patrol cars had raced through the dark, narrow, yellow-walled tunnel linking the toll plaza office to the bridge's access. Along the active roadway the cars sped, one behind the other, screeching to a stop at the bridge's midmost section. Once parked in line at the roadway's retaining wall two tall, burly and graying bridge patrol officers stepped purposefully out of their cars, their red and white top lights left flashing. Signaling his sergeant to lag behind, the ranking lieutenant strode forward to post himself ahead of the potential suicide scene. Silently both officers waved away some loitering bystanders. From front and back they crept slowly toward me and the jittery sailor poised so precariously atop the spare bridge guardrail.

Skittishly the sailor's eyes darted back and forth between the two approaching officers. Step by step they inched nearer to close in on us from either side. Silently I motioned for them to stand away but they ignored me and abruptly barreled ahead.

Impossibly I tried to reattract the restless sailor's attention.

"The whip worked!" I heartened him, nodding reassuringly. "It beat back the beast! I drove it off!"

Step by step the two bridge patrol officers drew nearer to us from either side.

"Far from it!" the sailor shrieked, shaking his head emphatically and swinging from side to side about the suspender cable he clung tenaciously to. "The ape approaches! It's coming at me—wildly brandishing the razor!"

"Freeze!" the police lieutanant abruptly barked at me. "Stop where you are and slowly put down the whip!"

Both officers had their pistols drawn and aimed straight at me. I froze, stopping cold in my tracks and turning just slightly toward the lieutenant to look him seriously in the face.

"It's not what it seems," I pleaded. "He needs help! He sees something that frightens him and wants me to ward it off with the whip!"

"Put down the whip—*now!*" the lieutenant repeated, predictably ignoring my plea.

Slowly I complied and put down the whip onto the walkway and stood aside, throwing up my hands in stoic surrender.

"If your friend's hallucinating," the lieutenant sneered, barging ahead to kick away the ungathered whip, "dropping off this bridge will definitely cure him."

Petrified, the agitated sailor suddenly recoiled, shrinking agape along the suspender cable—his slippery grip sliding!

"What's your problem, pardner?" the lieutenant challenged him, holstering his pistol. "Nothing could be so bad that you'd really want to kill yourself."

"I dread the consequences of the beast's butchery!" the sailor cried clamorously. "I happily relinquish all responsibility for the fate of the beast!"

"If you really mean to kill yourself," the lieutenant scoffed, heaving a resigned sigh, "there's nothing we can do about it. You'll just keep trying until you do it anyway. If you do manage to do it people will just think you're crazy."

"What are you doing?" I blurted out, shocked. "He's not trying to kill himself! He's fleeing some horrific apparition!"

"Same thing!" the lieutenant growled, riveting his perturbed eyes directly on me. "Now look—quit interfering and keep out of the way! We can't coddle these characters or they'll be jumping off the bridge all the time. We have to charge them with something to discourage this foolishness."

"Come down from there!" he snapped impatiently, directing his eyes back to the unsteady sailor hanging over the guardrail. "You're trespassing! It's illegal to climb the rails without permission. You can jump. You just can't jump off the rails. We don't have time to waste with talkers. If you were really going to jump you would've done it by now."

"So help me God!" the sailor said after a crisp pause, reclaiming some soundness of mind; but his habitual daring was missing. "I would tell you everything I know about this episode;—but I would not expect you to believe half of what I said—I would be an idiot indeed if I did. Yet, I *am* innocent, and I will make a clean slate if I die for it."

"Stop—hold him back—grab him—he's about to jump off!" I warned. "There—I knew it—he's jumped!"

Slowly, sadly, knowingly—he lifted up his eyes to meet mine. Both officers bustled forward. We all heard the sailor's ghastly, spine-chilling scream. Then he was gone.

"My God!" I yelled, rushing to the guardrail and looking over. "What have you done?"

Then just as hastily I looked away, shutting tight my eyes— unable to bear watching his body plummet helplessly some two hundred sixty-five feet to the unyieldingly hard waters below.

"I don't believe this!" I railed. "I was getting through to him!"

"Shut up!" the lieutenant snarled. "Amateur psychology doesn't cut it. He belongs to the Coast Guard now."

Abruptly he stretched out his arm, snapping his fingers.

"Sergeant!" he ordered. "Drop a flare marker!"

Right away the sergeant hurried to the rear of his patrol car and opened up its trunk. From inside he pulled out a long gray metal cylinder marked: *CCC FLAMMABLE*. Carrying the cylinder back to the guardrail he pulled its pin and hurled it into the water. Once it plunged into the bay an orange flame activated by salt water shot up some four feet and blazed in the thick of billowing smoke.

"You must really get off on that!" I jeered angrily.

"Look!" the lieutenant scowled. "Move on before I arrest you for something!"

Stoically I moved away, stopping farther along the guardrail to watch the two patrol officers rejoin one another and huddle over a car radiophone. Then I looked back down at the crooked pillar of smoke rising so far off from below.

Unexpectedly from behind I heard a man's serene, soft-spoken and articulate voice.

"They don't understand," it asserted.

Turning around abruptly I cast my surprised eyes on a tall, slender and elegant older man: his deeply etched features wrinkled but venerable; his brushed back hair and mustache silvery but tidy; his manner courteous but courtly.

"What's that?" I asked, flustered.

"They don't understand," he repeated softly but distinctly. "To deny what exists is to accept what doesn't."

Of this strange and mysterious old man I could only stand in awe.

TWO:

IMAGE OF DEATH

"Be silent in that solitude,
Which is not loneliness—for then
The spirits of the dead who stood
In life before thee, are again
In death around thee—and their will
Shall overshadow thee: be still."—Poe poem:
Spirits of the Dead

JOSEPH COVINO JR

Out of the night's dark and drenching downpour San Francisco's distinctive cityscape loomed ahead a long way off—a blurred and misshapen haze spread irregularly across the shadowy and somber skyline. Through the pendulous, squeaking sweeps of my windshield wipers I saw only an occasional car pass and repass me as I cruised cautiously south down the *Waldo Grade* toward the *Golden Gate Bridge*. Receding red tail lights grew dim and faded away in the wide, showery swaths cut by the low beams of oncoming headlights skimming along the wet and watery road.

Right ahead on the road's sodden shoulder stood a disheveled girl, looking solemn and deathlike as she limply held out her hand to thumb a ride. Unthinkingly I pulled over and stopped, reaching across my front seat to open up my passenger door for her. Facing front she stepped in and sat down, drenched and dripping. Pulling her door shut she sat still and silent: her moist skin looking pale and bloodless; her sad eyes swollen and circled by darkened rings; her thin lips lifeless and leaden.

A foghorn moaned mournfully as I pulled away and resumed driving along the rain-soaked roadway. And a lurid, murky fog overran the road surface, clouding over my field of view as it ooozed and seeped through the very cracks and crevices of the car itself.

"Where are you headed?" I asked my strange and speechless passenger.

Only I heard her give no answer. Large-eyed, I looked back over to her but saw she was gone, having melted away with the overflowing fog. Where she sat my fingers reluctantly touched a puny puddle of water—very wet and very, very cold.

§

My eyes were shut tight. I shook my head and came to

myself, shuddering. I was never driving toward the *Golden Gate Bridge* at all. I was still standing on it about center span, listening to the old stranger's story—his deep, resonant voice falling upon my ear with an ominous tone.

"That's some traveler's tale," I said, rubbing open my eyes. "I could see it vividly as if right in front of me."

"That's the greatest tribute you can pay a practicing hypnotist," he said with a grateful bow, leaning forward with crossed hands on a rosewood cane. "Thank you, young man."

"You're a hypnotist?" I asked, raising my eyebrows.

"Hypnotherapist—to be precise." He nodded slightly and held out his hand to press mine. "Permit me to introduce myself: I am Dr. Vincent Valdemar."

"Nicolino." I recited my name as an afterthought as I took the measure of this elegant old gentleman—so simply dressed in a bone-buttoned tweed jacket worn over a V-necked cashmere sweater, corduroy pants and cream-colored shirt brightened by a pink, shantung bow tie.

But the personality of his countenance was doubtless extraordinary. A corpselike aspect; an eye large, fluid and lucid beyond compare; lips rather thin and very pale but of a superlatively refined arc; a nose of a delicate cast but with a broadness of nostril uncommon in comparable shapes; a sharply cast chin; hair of a more than feather-like softness and thinness; these contours—with an excessive space above the areas of the temple—composed entirely a face not simply to be forgotten. The deathly paleness of the flesh and the mysterious lucidity of the eye above all else alarmed and even appalled me. The satiny hair also had been indulged to grow all unattended to and—as in its untamed flimsy texture—it drifted rather than tumbled about the face.

"But the girl looked so real as if she came to life right before my eyes," I thought aloud. "Who was she?"

"Legend has it that she is the spirit of a suicide—doomed to repeat her deed for all eternity—forever wandering and forever leaping from the bridge. This kind of legend is told all over the world. But as they say truth is stranger than fiction."

"How do you mean?"

"This bridge has a long and intimate relationship with death," he said gravely. "Come. Let me show you."

§

Together we strolled to a site near the bridgehead on the bayside just below the toll plaza. Before us—atop a modest pedestal hedged round by multi-colored blossom beds—stood a large-as-life bronze statue of a man clenching in one hand a rolled set of blueprints—a little man who dedicated himself to building a masterwork far greater than bigger men would ever dream of: *Joseph Strauss.*

Inscribed on the pedestal's plaque are the words:

> *The Man Who Built the Bridge*
> *Here at the Golden Gate is the eternal*
> *rainbow that he conceived and set to form.*
> *A promise indeed that the race of man*
> *shall endure unto the ages.*
> *Chief Engineer of the Golden Gate Bridge.*
> *1929-1937*

"Joseph Strauss once said that suicide from the bridge was neither possible nor probable—although it's known that well over a thousand people have leapt to their deaths from the bridge," Dr. Valdemar recounted grimly, gesturing to the tall-standing monument. "But as another memorial to the bridge reveals—a memorial rarely seen much less publicized—the bridge was a site of death long before its construction was ever completed."

§

Along an uphill bike path marked by signposts we sauntered beneath the bridge to another site raised and nestled seaside near the toll plaza office. Cast in a bronze plaque embedded in concrete above the bridge's bikeway—along with the names of eleven dead bridge builders—are inscribed the words:

> *For forty-four months out of a total*
> *construction period of fifty-two, tragedy*
> *passed the Golden Gate Bridge. By then*
> *death struck twice claiming the lives of*
> *eleven builders of the bridge. Here in*
> *memory of their tragic passing we inscribe*
> *their names so that posterity may know how*
> *much they rendered.*

> *To these dead who made the supreme*
> *sacrifice, we the living pay tribute for their*
> *contribution to California and that which*
> *she has achieved. They gave their all. None*
> *could give more.*

"Posterity can know very little of what these men gave when their monument is closed to walkers of the bridge," Dr. Valdemar lamented, riveting his eyes on the graven words, "remaining open only to transient cyclists who race by it—utterly oblivious if not indifferent."

Looking blank I kept silent.

"Do you know how these men came to make the supreme sacrifice?" he asked me pointedly.

I shook my head.

"They never gave their lives willingly." He made a wry face. "Their lives were taken—and horribly. Picture in your mind their terrible calamity."

Then he proceeded to tell me the ghastly story of the man-killing *Golden Gate Bridge.*

"As a precaution to make work on the bridge safer," Dr. Valdemar recounted, "Joseph Strauss hung a web-like safety net made of manila mesh beneath the suspended steel structure under construction. Before work on the span was finished the net had saved the lives of nineteen men from falling to their deaths. So bonded together did the survivors feel that they formed an exclusive fraternity which their members called *The Half-way to Hell Club*. Their sole membership requirement was an accidental fall into the net."

"It's not a club I'd sign up for."

"Ah," Dr. Valdemar sighed. "To join this club you had to respect the law of high steel."

"A club bylaw?"

"An old adage which said that for every million dollars spent the bridge would take one human life. So the bridge demanded its life."

"Was the law respected?"

"The law was broken but the bridge cost thirty-five million dollars and eleven human lives."

He pointed his cane toward the nearby bike path.

"Come. Let me tell you more."

Dr. Valdemar led the way back along the shadowed and sandy bike path winding beneath the crown of the roadway—buttressed high up at the southern San Francisco abutment. He led me to an elevated spot on one side of a sagging chain link fence looking out on the old historic red brick stronghold: *Fort Point*.

Arched over the fort like some colossal erector set was a matchwork maze of unsightly X-braced steel—built deliberately beneath the bridge and put out of sight. Flanking the fort two 50,000-ton anchorages spread the powerful pull of each of the bridge's main cables—some 63 million pounds—across a giant concrete anchor block weighing 240 million pounds.

"Up there," Dr. Valdemar pointed his cane toward the bridge's raised roadway. "The bridge took its first life when a moving derrick was lifting the steel beams to be laid for the bridge's decking. While a man working on the roadway hooked up the beams as they were put into place, the derrick toppled over and crushed him to death—decapitating him as it fell."

"Horrible," I said, shaking my head in sad disbelief.

"Even more horrible perhaps was the way the bridge took the lives of the other ten men," he grimly related. "Eleven men were working on a moving scaffold called a stripper suspended below the bridge deck. There they tore out and stripped away the wooden forms from the concrete pourings of the main-span roadway. From their platform they threw these boards into the safety net below where two more men picked them up. Suddenly the whole scaffolding tilted way out of kilter. There was a sickening sound of wrenching steel and timber as the whole scaffold—all ten tons of it—tore free from the bridge's underbelly and dropped down into the safety net."

"No way could the net hold up under that load."

"For a few agonizing seconds the net *did* hold—and the stripper hung there, momentarily suspended in time and space, but it was designed to catch men—not tons of heavy equipment."

"And then?"

"There came a thunderous noise which sounded as if the fabric of the sky had torn in two. The safety net sagged deeply—as over two thousand feet of heavy manila rope tore away with explosive snaps—which went flying as the net ripped loose all around. Twisted and tangled in the mesh the entire ten-ton scaffolding tumbled down long and far, plunging over two hundred feet into the surging strait of the *Golden Gate* at one of its deepest points—and taking twelve screaming men with it. They landed in the waters of a roaring riptide as if they had fallen from a twenty-two story building with an impact which raised whitewater waves. Ten of them died."

"I'm sorry," I said, curious. "Is there some special reason why you're telling me all this?"

"Guilt and fear," Dr. Valdemar reiterated. "They can drive a person to the point of sheer, unadulterated terror—and even death."

"Did guilt or fear drive that poor soul who jumped from the bridge to take his own life?"

"Perhaps." Dr. Valdemar raised his eyebrows sedately with a slight shrug. "Fear alone can deaden a person from inside out. Certainly the men who built the bridge labored under some measure of fear. As they risked their necks to successfully complete their task they had no alternative but to master their fear—or else capitulate and succumb to it."

"Could succumbing to fear make him kill himself?'

"If fear overpowered him so much that it fully engulfed him—his mind, his soul, his whole being—until finally it compelled him to go unwillingly to his untimely end."

"What kind of fear could force him to commit suicide?"

"An indomitable and irresistible fear—as mighty and unconquerable as any army of demons could ever be."

"Hell-born demons?"

"My dear fellow," Dr. Valdemar said assuredly with an all but demonic grin. "Aren't the most harassing and oppressive of demons those whom we conjure up for ourselves out of our deepest and innermost fears? They are doubtless the most devilish and bedeviling ones."

Gazing out over the spacious and smooth sheet of acquamarine water spreading itself far and wide beneath the graceful *Golden Gate Bridge*, rippling at its edges with gentle breakers which rolled awash onto the stony shores of *Fort Point*, I was turning over in my mind the doctor's words.

"Come." He abruptly interrupted my deep reflection. "I must go. Tonight I'm giving a hypnotic demonstration at the *Palace of Fine Arts Theater*; and I must prepare for it."

"I'm headed for the Palace myself—to meet my girlfriend," I said, stupefied. "She's the house manager. Now that's quite a coincidence!"

"Or fate," he suggested portentously. "Perhaps you would care to accompany me."

"With pleasure. Did you drive?"

"No. I'm walking over the bridgeway. Except for some stretches broken by the oncoming traffic I find it quite a pleasant path to take. And the walk does me a world of good. Shall we go?"

§

Together we made our way back to the toll plaza and headed for the *Merchant Road* access to the northbound extension of Highway 101 leading onto the *Golden Gate Bridge*. Bending our steps southward over a crosswalk which cut the access road we set foot onto a drab concrete sidewalk with curbed edges skirting the highway. Already the rush of motorized traffic whisked by us, blowing up boisterous breaths of air into our faces. Underfoot crunched little brown leaves. On our left stretched a tall, green chain link fence topped off by slanting lines of barbed wire and overhung by all manner of dense brushwood.

"What kind of fear could overpower someone so completely?" I asked finally.

"A morbid fear," Dr. Valdemar answered solemnly, "which we who move in psychiatric circles call a phobia."

"Phobia?"

"A condition of extremely intense but largely imaginary fear. An abnormally exaggerated fear of particular things or situations."

"Such as?"

"Look around you."

He stopped and faced about to gesture back at the soaring towers of the *Golden Gate Bridge* drifting away behind us.

"Phobic people can fear almost anything and everything— driving, heights, crowds, open spaces, closed spaces, water. Or certain creeping things like spiders, rats or cats. They can fear being alone, in the dark, in a graveyard, or being touched. They can even fear the opposite sex."

"Tragic," I said. "And death?"

"Death, disease, decay—even fear itself."

Soon we came up to a sidewalk sign propped by a single gray metal pole overtopped by a lamp and displaying a leftward pointing black arrow which read:

PEDESTRIANS USE SUBWAY

There the highway-skirting walkway was hedged about with denser thickets.

"Morbid fears are frequently responsible for many real physical pains—and sometimes: even deaths."

Dr. Valdemar paused to lean on his cane and look back toward the *Golden Gate Bridge* before it was lost to sight.

"In cases where they exist beneath the level of conscious awareness these morbid fears can go dangerously undetected."

"Phobic people are disturbed?" I asked.

"Phobic people are perverse, so to speak, and possessed of some unseen and inexplicable devil."

Dr. Valdemar gestured for us to turn off onto a branching cement footpath descending and winding through heavily overgrown foliage and underbrush.

"Strictly speaking, however, the phobia itself is more perverse than the person suffering it. But people afflicted with phobias often fail to recognize them as such."

"How's that?"

"Phobic people tend to rationalize deviant conduct which strays from the accepted norm—that is to say, whatever society at large deems to be the norm. Phobias habitually display themselves in abnormal behavior."

"How so?"

"Countless innocuous objects or harmless situations can

become the focal points of acute phobias in people who otherwise appear to be comparatively normal."

"Like what?"

"Crossing the bridge we just passed. Because they are so commonplace, and because they can escape detection, such phobias expose their prey to the most peculiar dangers."

"A phobia inspired by inoffensive things is all in the mind?"

We came up to a short and narrow cement tunnel overlaid with leafy creepers and vines—its crowning slab engraved with the year: *1939*. We stepped inside its foursquare whitewashed walls.

"At the heart of any phobia is its irrationality." Dr. Valdemar's voice echoed off the tunnel's close and confining walls. "The actual condition feared need not necessarily be innocuous. Consider the phobic fear of deadly disease. Should the phobic person know full well that he hasn't the slightest rational reason to suspect that he's afflicted with the condition—or disease—then conscious awareness of his own irrationality only adds torment to his fear."

Dr. Valdemar stopped in the middle of the tunnel, nodding his head in accord as he gestured at a wall defaced by some graffiti scrawled in red:

We scatter the Future to the winds, and slumber tranquilly in the Present, weaving the dull and dead world around us into dreams.

"Quite a perceptive poet for a vandal," he remarked, "as the state of hypnosis is a waking dreamlike escape from our dreary world of reality."

"How can something that exists only in the mind actually harm you?" I asked, sidestepping the subject.

"Never underestimate the power of the human mind," he said in deathly earnest. "It is a profoundly powerful thing."

Going out of the tunnel we came back to daylight and climbed a rising, winding cement footpath leading up to the merging intersection where extensions to Highways 1 and 101 crisscrossed. Along the busy and noisy highway we walked just a short stretch before stepping up to another pedestrian subway sign.

"As times goes on," Dr. Valdemar elucidated, "even the most innocent object or situation of dread can become utterly terrifying. Every time it crops up it can affect the person physically and conspicuously: his heart beats faster, his skin sweats, his stomach cramps and he flies into such a frantic panic that he can't tolerate even being in close proximity to the thing— whatever is so intensely fearsome. So phobic fear is not only irrational but obsessive as well."

"How severe can phobic fear be?"

"Purely physical reactions can vary in severity from mild to violent."

Dr. Valdemar paused to lean on a low-set reddish brown metal barrier blocking forward passage.

"Typical symptoms are rather obvious: blurred vision, erratic heartbeat, sweaty palms, rigid muscle tension, shortness of breath, nausea, even fainting. These are all suggestive of a very morbid and deep-seated fear."

"What provokes phobic fear?"

We turned off onto a falling footpath turning and twisting through snug hedges of bulging shrubbery. Then the tall green barbed wire fence—jagged limbs of bushes and shrubs jutting out through its chain links—hemmed us in on both sides.

"A phobia is the product of a specific stimulus which excites it," he explained. "It can be inspired by severe stress or some severe shock from a person's past—or by a series of experiences or events taking place over a particular period which precipitate an extreme and excessive phobia. Like a contagious disease a phobia can be transmitted between people in close contact. Fear of fear itself might inspire it. Whatever its source a phobia can take such a tenacious grip on a person's psyche that it appears impossible to escape."

"How do you deal with it?"

"To effectively treat a phobia you must first appreciate it," he said stoically. "Hypnotic analysis—or hypnoanalysis, if you will—is the perfect expedient through which to explore and resolve a phobic fear."

"How would a person know for sure if he were possessed by a phobic fear?"

"Most conspicuously by his deliberate avoidance of the dreaded object or situation."

Dr. Valdemar stopped and turned to confront me directly.

"What might strike terror deep into your own palpitating heart?"

"Heights," I admitted with a start. "You won't catch me scaling the towers of the *Golden Gate Bridge*."

"Hypnotherapy can work to cure that affliction through the method known as gradual desensitization."

He continued strolling along the littered footpath with a self-satisfied smile.

"It uses hypnosis to induce in the subject a state of deep relaxation combined with vividly-evoked imagery."

In a hedged niche the fenced in footpath ended. We turned a corner and Dr. Valdemar pointed his cane toward another tunnel block ahead. Through the narrow concrete tube we passed to reach the green metal railing in sight at its opposite end. We stepped up to the railing and stopped, pausing to look out through tall and willowy trees commanding a vast view of the Fort Point Coast Guard Station and *Crissy Field* sprawled along the far off shore of *San Francisco Bay*. A cool and gentle bay breeze blew up across our faces. Dr. Valdemar suddenly fixed his penetrating eyes on my expectant expression.

"Might I be permitted to demonstrate my point?" he asked sedately.

"Why not?"

Dr. Valdemar led the way up another crooked cement footpath which sloped to an expansive overpass where the Highway

101 extension crossed *Lincoln Boulevard*. From that prospect the orange red-roofed barracks of *Crissy Field* and the gently tossed waters of San Francisco Bay stretched out spaciously before us. Highway traffic rumbling by beside and beneath us visibly vibrated the concrete supports buttressing the bridge walkway.

"Look at Alcatraz."

He pointed toward the stony island silhouette lying on the distant horizon.

"Empty your thoughts and shut out the outside world. Close your eyes and relax. Be wholly at ease. Concentrate your mind. Give play to your imagination."

Slowly, reluctantly—I shut my eyes and felt Dr. Valdemar move toward me as I listened intently to his softly intoned but resonant voice fall upon my ears:

"With great difficulty—and at the impending danger to your life—you are harnessing the violent flaring of an enormous and flaming-colored horse.

"You captured him fleeing—all smoldering and frothing with fury—from the burning stables at *Golden Gate Park*, which is mysterious since he sustains obvious signs of having made a narrow escape from the blaze.

"Exceptionally peculiar! you say with a wistful air but seemingly unaware of the import of your words. He is, as you say, an extraordinary horse—a monstrous horse!—although as you rightfully remark of a dubious and unruly nature. Let him be my own, nevertheless, you add following a lull: perchance a horseman like myself might break even the demon from the stables at the Park.

"But the mighty mount which you had embraced as your own reared and curveted with heightened frenzy.

"It was likewise to be remarked that although you had captured the mount as he bolted from the blaze at the park, and managed to halt his flight with the aid of a chain-bridle and noose—you could not with any conviction assert that you had, throughout that perilous struggle or at any time after that, positively put your hand upon the body of the brute.

"Cases of idiosyncratic temperament in the bearing of a stately and high-spirited steed are not to be presumed able to attract immoderate attention, but there were singular situations which forcibly imposed themselves on even the most suspicious and apathetic; and it is stated there were times when the beast provoked the awestruck gathering who loitered about to shrink in terror from the profound and imposing implication of his terrifying stamp—times when even you blanched and recoiled from the fleet and penetrating aspect of his humanlike eye.

"Among all your entourage, nevertheless, none were found to dispute the fervor of that unnatural attachment which persisted on your part for the tempestuous traits of your steed— the fiery steed of *Metzengerstein!*; at least none had the audacity to affirm that you never leapt into the saddle without an inexplicable and almost indiscernible shudder—"

My shuddering hand was indeed outstretched and reaching for the pommel of the saddle and I was all set to vault for a foothold in the stirrup when something—or someone—abruptly laid a firm hold on it, staying it and roughly wrenching me aside! Widely my eyes burst open! In a fright I found myself not leaning on the handrail but reaching right ahead into the traffic-congested highway—about to step completely off the curb and into the path of onrushing cars! At the chilling sound of one car's prolonged blaring horn and screeching tires I lurched backward, breathless, into Dr. Valdemar's faltering grasp! Shakily I fell back panting against the bridge handrail!

"Conjuring up a vision that real can't be possible!" I gasped.

"When the unreal becomes real," Dr. Valdemar said with alarming assuredness, "anything is possible: too much fear, too much danger—even death!"

THREE:

A ROMANTIC RUIN

"But evil things, in robes of sorrow,
Assailed the monarch's high estate.
(Ah, let us mourn!—for never morrow
Shall dawn upon him desolate!)
And round about his home, the glory
That blushed and bloomed
Is but a dim-remembered story
Of the old time entombed."—Poe poem:
The Haunted Palace

JOSEPH COVINO JR

Together we crossed *Marina Boulevard* and stepped into the paved parking lot of the *Exploratorium* in sight of the *Palace of Fine Arts*. Dr. Valdemar gestured to the majestic Corinthian columns at the northern end of the curved colonnade towering before us. Atop mammoth planters sculptured maidens reposed at their corners, weeping over the city's rooftops.

"Magnificent, isn't it?" he marveled.

"Incredibly so."

Then he turned to deliberately direct his eyes to me.

"Before I go," he suggested seriously, "let me leave you to consider a special proposal."

"What's that?"

"I'm presently making preparations to carry out a most exceptional hypnotic experiment for which I will require a most exceptional hypnotic subject."

"Exceptional in what way?"

"I require a very special subject—someone with an acute ability to concentrate his mind who can at the same time give full play to his imagination."

"You mean you need a guinea pig."

"Perhaps you could be persuaded to participate in my experiment."

"You think I would make a desirable subject?"

"You treated that tragic man on the bridge with remarkable creativity and compassion," he said approvingly. "Abundant imagination was needed for that sympathetic act. I've found that highly imaginative people make the most excellent subjects."

"I thought being a hypnotic subject was more a matter of submission than imagination."

"A common misconception. Hypnotists possess no preponderance of power over their subjects. Hypnosis itself is no struggle for power—no war of wills. Hypnotic subjects are not weak-minded puppets."

"You think I'm capable of being successfully hypnotized?"

"The ability to be hypnotized is quite a natural trait. Any-one—rational, neurotic or psychotic—can be hypnotized if he's willing and able to concentrate his mind on the induction stimulus being suggested."

"Some outside stimulation of the mind is needed to induce hypnosis?"

"In hypnotism we exploit and resort to the imagination," Dr. Valdemar explained. "Or more precisely the manipulation of the imagination. Contrary to popular misconception the hypnotist possesses no power whatever—the sole power em-ployed is actually the subject's own imagination. The hypno-tist simply persuades the subject to exert his imagination to its fullest extent through simple suggestion. The best hypnotic subjects are ordinary, normal people—the more intelligent, in-ventive and imaginative they are the better. You could be made to order."

"Is the experiment safe for the subject?" I asked, skeptical.

"Perfectly," he assured me. "Into the bargain I plan to pay my subject handsomely for his services."

"How handsomely?"

"Quite handsomely," he answered dismissively. "Think it over awhile before we discuss details. Tomorrow I'm delivering a lecture at the *Herbst Theatre*. If you can attend we'll talk to-gether then. Until then I thank you for keeping company with me. I look forward to seeing you again."

Dr. Valdemar held out his hand to gently squeeze mine.

"Until we meet again."

"Goodbye."

§

Lenore stood staidly in front of the midmost arched double-glassed doors of the drab facade of the *Exploratorium*, running her eyes over our clasped hands from afar. As I stood watching

Dr. Valdemar shuffle on and tread a path around the side of the building she slowly started to move toward me.

§

With a fondness of profound yet most exceptional tenderness I revered my beloved Lenore. Cast by chance into her company several years ago my spirit, from our first encounter, blazed with flames it had never before felt; but unpalatable and torturous to my soul was the slow persuasion that I could in no way explain their uncommon import or moderate their obscure acuteness. But we met; and destiny joined us together; and I never declared love nor contemplated passion. She, nevertheless, shirked society and clinging to me solely made me content. It is a contentment to marvel at;—it is a contentment to conceive.

Several years have since passed and my remembrance is infirm through profuse misery. Or perchance I cannot *now* call these particulars to mind since with truth the nature of my beloved, her singular erudition, her exceptional but serene comeliness of form, and the exciting and fascinating fluency of her mellow and melodic vernacular, found their way into my spirit by steps so steadfast and surreptitiously advanced that they have been overlooked and unseen.

There is one precious subject, nevertheless, about which my recollection falters not. It is the *form* of Lenore. In height she was tall, rather thin and in her later time even wasted. I would to no avail try to picture the stateliness, the gentle grace of her bearing or the unfathomable softness of her footstep. She came and left as a ghost. I was never made conscious of her admittance to my shut study except by the precious tone of her soft lush voice as she put her pale hand upon my shoulder.

An acuteness in thought, deed or expression was perhaps in her a consequence or at least a characteristic of that colossal will which, throughout our lengthy intimacy, failed to lend other and more precipitate color to its being. Of all the women whom I have ever experienced she, the outwardly tranquil, the ever-calm Lenore was the most violently a victim of the tempestuous predators of grim emotion. And of such emotion I could take no measure except by the mysterious enlargement of those eyes which at once so thrilled and alarmed me—by the almost mystical tone, timbre, distinction and serenity of her extremely soft voice—and by the fiery intensity—made doubly potent by contrast with her way of pronunciation—of the intemperate words which she habitually spoke.

I have mentioned the erudition of Lenore; it was vast—such as I have never experienced in a woman. I perceived not then what I now plainly discern—that the attainments of Lenore were astonishing; yet I was amply conscious of her immense mastery to surrender myself, with trustful assurance, to her direction through the disordered world of metaphysical inquiry at which I was most actively engaged throughout the earliest times of our intimacy. With how immense a victory—with how vibrant a rapture—with how much of all this is unearthly in faith—did I *sense* as she hovered over me in researches but scarcely explored—but less recognized—that delectable prospect in some measure extending ahead of me—along whose lengthy, beautiful and entirely untrampled trail I might finally press on to the end of an understanding too heavenly dear not to be taboo.

How painful then must have been the sorrow with which after some time I watched my well-settled prospects take flight themselves and steal away! Without Lenore I was but a boy fumbling in the dark. Her attendance, her renditions alone, made vibrantly radiant the many secrets of the transcendentalism in which we were submerged.

Lenore's learning was deep. As I wish to survive her gifts were of no ordinary kind—her faculties of intellect were immense. I sensed this and in many matters became her student.

In all this if I lapse not my logic had little to do. My persuasions, or I forgive myself, were in no way influenced by the ideal, nor was any trace of the mysticism which I read to be found unless I am mightily mistaken either in my actions or in my thoughts. Convinced of this I resigned myself expressly to the direction of my beloved and took up with an unshrinking spirit the complexities of her researches. And then—then, when mulling over forbidden folios I sensed a forbidden specter inflaming inside me—would Lenore put her frigid hand upon my own and dredge up from the cinders of a dead doctrine some dim, peculiar words whose mysterious import seared themselves upon my memory. And then hour after hour would I remain by her side and brood upon the melody of her voice—until finally its tone was tarnished with horror,—and there spread a shadow upon my spirit—and I became bloodless and shivered internally at those too ethereal tones. And so jubilation abruptly evaporated into terror and the most sublime became the most loathsome.

§

"Rebirth?" I asked curiously.

"Yes, my love, rebirth," Lenore said with a mild nod of accord. "This is the word upon whose mystical import I have so long contemplated, repudiating the strict interpretation of the cloth until Death himself resolved for me the mystery."

"Death!" I stood aghast.

"How curiously, darling Nicolino, you repeat my expression! I notice too an uncertainty in your step—a joyful uneasiness in your eyes. You are baffled and afflicted by the stately novelty of Life Everlasting. Yes, it was of Death I spoke. And here how curiously sounds that word which long since was given to strike terror into all hearts—casting decay upon all comforts!"

Together we went to the shady and shadowed edge of the

spacious blue water lagoon spreading at length before the classical ruin known as the *Palace of Fine Arts*. Over its winding brown footpath, fringed by tall and lusty eucalyptus trees, we strolled side by side along its placid reflecting pool—stirred solely by the gentle gliding of graceful ducks and swans. We mostly stared down at the ground as we made our way slowly and solemnly from end to end of the palatial colonnade.

"Ah," I said knowingly. "Death—the phantom that feasts at all banquets! How frequently do we preoccupy ourselves with speculations about its nature! How mysteriously does it serve as a block to mortal delight—admitting only so much and no more! That passionate mutual love which blazes within our hearts—how conceitedly do we flatter ourselves, being pleased at its early upsurge, that our pleasure would intensify with its intensity! Alas! as it deepens so deepens in our hearts the dread of that wicked hour which rushes to sever us forever! So in time it becomes hurtful to love. Hate will be a favor then."

Straight across from the expansive lagoon the Palace's 18-story rotunda soared from the facing shore. As we passed on beneath a lone cluster of trees we rounded a bowed turn in the twisting footpath which stretched to the far off end of the lagoon.

"Talk not here of these regrets, darling Nicolino—mine, mine forever now!"

"But the recollection of past heartache—is it not present bliss?" I persisted. "I have plenty to say yet of the things which are past. Above all, I long to learn the particulars of your own procession through the valley of the shadow of death."

"And when did my handsome Nicolino ask anything of his Lenore to no avail?"

Nearby a solitary fountain shot up high in a streaming plume, rippling an inward niche of the lagoon. Looming ahead was the southern end of the lofty and imposing colonnade—detached and curved in a stately semicircle about the grand octagonal rotunda.

"I understand you," I told Lenore. "In Death we have both discovered the tendency of man to explain the inexplicable. Then I will not say begin with the instant of life's end—but begin with that dismal, dismal moment when the fever, having left you, you lapsed into a breathless and listless languor—and I pressed down your bloodless eyelids with the affectionate fingertips of tender passion. You languished and slipped into the grave."

"Undeniably," she began, "it was in the world's decrepitude that I died. Spent at heart with worries which had their source in the widespread confusion and corruption I surrendered to the violent fever. After some few days of malaise and many of dreamy delirium sated with ecstasy—the symptoms of which you misconstrued as malaise while I aspired but was powerless to disabuse you—following some days there fell upon me, as you have said, a breathless and listless languor; and this was designated *Death* by those who hovered over me."

Our footpath divided and we sauntered quietly onto its narrower branch as it forked off toward the sky-high colonnade, hugging close to the shore of the tranquil lagoon, acacias and willows skirting its damp banks. Hovering over us along the dirt path were the colonnade's colossal columns—ivy vines creeping and overrunning their weathered and withering piers, plinths and cornices. High up the dome of the great rotunda arose above the treetops as we drew near to its vast open gallery. Soon we came up to an open, gravelly and grassy space facing the lagoon shore.

"Words are ambiguous things. My state did not strip me of sensation. It seemed to me not profoundly different from the intense tranquility of him, who having slept long and deeply, lying still and totally flat on a midsummer noonday, starts to revert gradually back to awareness through the sheer satisfaction of his slumber, and without being aroused by outside disturbances."

§

"I breathed no more," Lenore continued. "My pulse was silent. My heart had stopped beating. Will had not left but was paralyzed. My senses were singularly acute but strangely so—taking over frequently each other's faculties at random. My taste and smell were inextricably confused and became a single sensation—aberrant and acute."

Tenderly I patted my moistened fingertips—gently dipped into rosewater—to Lenore's full, luscious lips and was titillated with lush fantasies of flowers—fabulous and exquisite flowers blossoming in explosive profusion all around us.

"My eyelids," she went on, "limpid and pale, presented no total obstruction to sight. As will was in suspension the balls could not roll in their sockets—but all things within the range of my visual sphere were seen with more or less clarity; the beams which fell upon my outer retina—or into the corner of my eye—producing a more vibrant effect than those which struck the frontal surface."

In that particular instance that effect was so far peculiar that I perceived it solely as *sound*—lush or harsh as the materiality manifesting itself on every side was light or dark in shadow—curved or crooked in outline.

"My hearing," she went on, "although sharpened in degree was at once not erratic in function—gauging true sounds with an exaggeration of exactness not less than sensitivity. Touch had experienced a change more strange. Its sensations were felt late but persistently retained and resulted invariably in the intensest physical pleasure."

With my fingertips upon her eyelids I put barely the slightest pressure.

"So," she went on, "the touch of your sweet fingertips—at first purely perceived through my sight, and finally, long after their removal—overwhelmed my whole being with a sensual ravishment limitless. I say with a sensual ravishment. *All* my sensations were purely sensual."

So my uncontrolled outcries fell upon her ear with all their sorrowful rhythms and were perceived in their every variation of somber tone; but they were low melodic sounds and nothing more; they imparted to the lifeless logic no mimicry of the woes which precipitated them; while the profuse and incessant tears which burst out upon my face, apprising the passerby of a heart which burst, stirred every fiber of her being with rapture on its own. And that was with truth the *Death* of which those passerby spoke devoutly in soft undertones—me, chokingly, with clamorous outcries.

They dressed Lenore for the coffin—three or four lurid figures which darted diligently back and forth. As those crossed the straight line of her sight they stirred her as *shapes*; but upon gliding to her side their forms struck me with the notion of screams, moans and other somber expressions of horror, of terror or of misery. I alone, wrapped in a white robe, slid in all directions melodically all around her.

"The day ebbed;" she went on, "and as its light dimmed I became possessed of an ambiguous apprehensiveness—a dismay such as the sleeper senses when dismal actual sounds fall constantly upon his ear—soft remote bell tones, sober, at long but even intervals and merging with desolate dreams. Night came; and with its shades a weighty distress. It oppressed my limbs with the severity of some deadened weight and was touchable. There was also a groaning noise not dissimilar to the remote rumble of breakers but more constant which, starting with the first nightfall, had intensified in strength with the dusk."

Abruptly lights were carried into the chamber and that rumbling became instantly disrupted into incessant uneven outbursts of the same sound but less gloomy and less explicit.

"The heavy oppression was to a great degree relieved," she said.

And emanating from the flames of each lamp—for there

57

were many—there fell unremitting upon my ears a strain of melodic monotone. And when then hovering over the bed upon which Lenore lay outspread I sat gently by her side, panting warmth from my lips and pressing them upon her forehead.

"There arose trembling in my breast, and merging with the purely physical sensations which conditions had summoned," Lenore recounted at the last, "a something like emotion itself—a sensation that, partly perceived, partly responded to your intense passion and sadness; but this sensation took root in the pulseless heart and appeared indeed rather a shade than a reality and melted swiftly away—first into intense stillness and then into a purely sensual rapture as before."

§

As this dreamy vision wholly enveloped us I took Lenore gently by the hand and led her behind a mammoth planting basin at the foot of stone steps rising in massive blocks to buttress the base of the rotunda.

"So I suffer this endless foreboding of my own death—my own extinction," she said sullenly, "from which my sole escape must be...*rebirth!*"

I firmly grasped her hips and lifted her up onto one of the lower ledges of the stone steps.

"What are you doing?" she asked, taken by surprise.

Softly kissing her lips and worming my tongue into her warm, moaning mouth my hands rose from her hips to caress and squeeze through her blouse the smooth curves of her full, shapely breasts. Then I reached through her coat to fold her snug in my arms.

"This was meant to be a romantic but sad place tempered and soothed by beauty," I said under my quickening breath.

"What?" she panted, kissing me softly back.

Then my hands groped to slide her long black slit dress and

slip above her knees and up to her thick and firm thighs, fumbling to pull apart the snaps at the crotch of her black nylons. Discreetly glancing around my fingers gingerly wriggled into the embroidered hole of her panties and plunged joyfully into her lush and syrupy wetness.

"I'm feeling romantic but sad about us..." I whispered excitedly, my voice quivering. "So—"

"Yes?" she gasped.

"I want to soothe my sadness with your beauty!"

"Here?" she gasped again, wide-eyed and heaving.

"Yes! Right here! Right now!"

§

Beneath a faded crimson canopy inscribed in large white letters a procession of people filed through three double-glass doors leading into the *Palace of Fine Arts Theater*. Inside patrons picked their way through the aisles and rows of a crowded arena-style arrangement of scarlet theater seats. All around the theater's high walls were overhung with tall scarlet draperies. And across the spacious and darkened stage stretched an outspread scarlet curtain.

"I just told the stage manager to start the show," Lenore said as she led the way through open metal doors into a red-draped foyer in the rear of the theater lit by downward-facing wall sconces. "Let's watch."

Rounding a curved corridor she showed the way up a short flight of wide red-carpeted steps to a wooden banister atop a raised tier of the theater. High up in the central ceiling a large circle of house lights abruptly grew dim.

"Do you want to tell me what really happened to make you so sad?" she asked perceptively—her eyes still directed to the forestage.

"I saw a man kill himself today," I stammered, glancing around at the sea of patrons silhouetted before us in every quarter of the theater.

"My God!" Lenore exclaimed in a breathless whisper, staring over at me—stunned. "When did this happen?"

"On my way to you from running," I said solemnly. "I saw a man jump from the bridge to escape some invisible apparition which only he could see—but which was too terrifying to endure!"

Just then over the stage's central and sidewise loudspeakers a muffled but big-sounding reverberation filled the air: it was the distinct and resonant sound of a beating heart!

FOUR:

THE TELL-TALE HEARTBEAT

"But when the Night had thrown her pall
Upon that spot, as upon all,
And the mystic wind went by
Murmuring in melody—
Then—ah then I would awake
To the terror of the lone lake."—Poe poem:
The Lake: To —

JOSEPH COVINO JR

"One proverbial picture is worth a thousand words!" Dr. Valdemar's amplified voice resounded throughout the darkened amphitheater.

"The power of pictures and their ability to send vivid images to the human mind has been known and exploited since ancient times. Pictures can evoke certain ideas which in turn can evoke certain feelings and emotions. And emotions sensitize the mind to hypnosis.

"Such feelings and emotions arise from the action of the autonomic nervous system which acts quite automatically and independently of our free will, affecting all the organs and glands of the body in reaction to impulses generated by those ideas.

"The power of the autonomic nervous system and the part it plays in regulating our bodily functions cannot be denied. No organ or gland of the body can work without the proper commands from this system. Nor can it be denied that through hypnosis we have greatly intensified our control over this system.

"This is not a matter of mere supposition, for such control has been scientifically tested and proved. Through hypnosis we have heightened control over our autonomic nervous system and—indirectly—over all the organs and glands of the human body.

"Our autonomic nervous system—although so incredibly efficient at running the human body—is very vulnerable in one crucial respect: it is quite powerless to distinguish between a real and an unreal thing. So real food can make the mouth water and the mere idea of imaginary food can do the very same thing.

"Real danger can provoke the unsavory feelings of fear— and imaginary danger can do the very same thing. It makes no difference what the imagined danger is. Whatever the danger may be: unsavory feelings of fear will result from the action of the autonomic nervous system. From this you will see that a mere idea—an image conceived and visualized in the mind—can induce real physical changes in any organ or gland in the human body.

"Now, word pictures are particularly easy to evoke through hypnosis. Such pictures are always more real in kind than those evoked by simple suggestion in the waking state. So it follows that through hypnosis: an unreal danger can evoke in the human mind a very real and compelling fear—or phobia.

"What is fear?—

"You have heard that faint moan, and you have known it was the moan of deathly horror. It was not a moan of discomfort or distress—oh, no!—it was the soft muffled sound that emanates from the bowels of the soul when overcharged with dread. You know the sound well. Many a midnight—in the dead of night when all the world slumbered—it has welled out from your own heart, deepening with its frightful reverberation the horrors that bewildered you. I daresay you know it well."

By slow degrees the great scarlet stage curtain budged aside. A beamy spotlight threw its bright circle upon a balding and bloated man wearing a white hospital gown and sitting upright in an armchair facing the theater audience. Set beside him was an activated electrocardiograph. Floating-disc electrodes hooked up the man by metal contacts to the monitor displaying his heart's electrical activity.

"Fear!" Dr. Valdemar's voice bellowed along with the softly pulsating heartbeat all throughout the theater. "Fear—no matter of what it may be—can provoke a severe disturbance of the autonomic nervous system. Physical symptoms resulting from this disturbance can frighten a person even more until a vicious cycle is created and perpetuated: a cycle of fear! Its victim quite literally grows afraid of the very symptoms of fear until, finally, he comes to fear fear itself.

"This unfortunate man sitting before you suffers such a

fear. It is an aberrant and abnormal fear known as a phobia. It is a fear which turns into an obsessive and compulsive anxiety—a distressing disorder in which the victim feels compelled to dwell upon distressing worries which he admits to being completely pointless."

At the same instant another spotlight lighted up a strange and spectral figure standing at the far off end of the stage, wrapped up from top to toe in a deep crimson cloak and hooded cape.

"Good evening." The figure hailed the audience and stepped up stoically to the forestage. "I am Dr. Vincent Valdemar. And I am here to demonstrate—no matter how fanatically skeptical you may be of what you will see—that through this mysterious craft of hypnotism we possess the most powerful and potent method of controlling the human mind—and through the mind—the whole human body.

"When a few mere words—by suggestion paralysis, for example—can make the hypnotized person powerless to move—even though fully conscious and aware—who can truly doubt the power of hypnotism? When hypnotic suggestion can make the mouth water, quicken the heart rate or force the sweat glands to perspire—who can fail to be impressed with its potential in manipulating the mind and harnessing all its unexplored and untapped power?

"Anyone who doubts the idea that mere words can affect bodily functions should bear in mind that even waking suggestions can elicit changes in organs and glands in any part of the body which can be affected by emotion. So even in the normal waking state most people are open to simple suggestion.

"A single word or phrase can make a person feel happy, sad, angry or afraid and often excites the physical symptoms which accompany such feelings. Yawning is infamously infectious. One person faints in a crowd and others do the same. Words working through the emotions can have definite effects. And emotions sensitize the mind to hypnosis.

"The specific organ or gland of the body affected will depend on the idea evoked. And one of the simplest and most powerful methods of evoking an idea is by means of painting a word picture through hypnosis."

Dr. Valdemar stepped up to the man seated still and silent in the armchair.

"Consider the human heartbeat." He gestured to the man connected to the electrocardiograph. "In everyday life heartbeats are perceived only when their rhythms fluctuate—and severely only when a disturbance occurs. It is well-known that hypnotism can affect even the human heartbeat which can be controlled by hypnotic suggestion. In fact the human heart can be worked just as hard and just as fast—as a danger to the body as a whole—from an armchair as from a rower's bench.

"Behold!"

Dr. Valdemar turned to the man seated, slumped in his armchair as if he were dozing. He remained immobile. His fleshy facial muscles looked relaxed. His breathing sounded dull and deep. Glowing on the side of the electrocardiograph was a fluorescent oscilloscopic viewing screen across which flitted the pulsating waves of light corresponding to the man's heartbeat.

"You are still resting in your deep hypnotic trance but you do not sleep." Dr. Valdemar bowed down to the man, speaking in soft and soothing tones. "Although you feel drowsy you are able to hear my voice clearly and distinctly—and talk to me without waking. You will talk back to me just like a person in his sleep. You are able to answer my questions without waking and without difficulty."

Dr. Valdemar bent to the man more closely.

"Do you feel comfortable?"

"Yes." The man nodded stuporously.

"Although you are drowsy you are able to talk to me. Your eyes are shut tight. You do not want to move your limbs. And although you talk to me you remain very drowsy. You may want to open your eyes or move your limbs as you talk. But you will feel you do not want to do this until I tell you to open your eyes and to move your limbs. Do you understand?"

"Yes." He gave another torpid nod.

"Now let us recall why you are here." Dr. Valdemar stood slightly away from the man. "You complain that you suffer from severe and chronic palpitation of the heart. You have tried numerous treatments and your doctors tell you that it is merely nerves. You have noticed your heart beating irregularly so the idea crosses your mind that you could be seized with heart disease. Your heart palpitation persists and you suffer a severe state of anxiety over what you believe is an incurable heart condition. Is this true?"

"Yes." The man's head tilted to one side, his chin dropped down toward his chest.

"Your whole body feels weak and decrepit," Dr. Valdemar continued. "You feel a lot of lethargy. You feel fatigue weighing you down—tiring you to death. You suffer through the exertion that is part of your regular routine such as walking and climbing stairs. You can take only short walks now and climb few stairs. And you do this with great difficulty since you have such a frail and feeble body. Your heart is unsteady and unsound—its beat irregular, pulsating by erratic fits and starts. You fear you will live a short and sickly life—that you will suffer many physical ailments—and that you will endure severe pain and convulsions. Is this true?"

"Yes." The man turned tense and fidgeted, squirming in his seat.

"I want you to imagine something," Dr. Valdemar continued. "Imagine yourself coming face to face with your fear. Make your fear into something you can see. Now look at it closely and see how strong it is. It is very strong—very strong. You are much weaker than it is—much weaker. You are afraid of it because it is so much stronger than you—much stronger. You are ill at ease—totally ill at ease—and weak. You are frowning because your fear has gained great strength and control even though you do not want it. No. You do not want it. You want it to go away. But you cannot imagine your life without it. You live miserably. You are desperate—very desperate—because you cannot face your fear and you know you are utterly weak and helpless. You feel so afraid you gasp for breath. And you feel a surge of fear inside of you powerful enough to make your heart stand still. You frown harder but your fear only swells and spreads. You are paralyzed—powerless and at the complete mercy of your fear!

"Your fear has been weighing heavily upon you. You have been attempting to imagine it baseless but cannot. Yes, you have been attempting to console yourself with that faulty presumption but you have found to no avail. *To no avail*; because Death—in looming ahead of you—has stalked with his lurid shadow before him—and enveloped his prey. And it was the sorrowful sway of the unseen shadow that induced you to sense—although you neither saw nor heard—to *sense* the presence of your fear within this theater!"

Abruptly Dr. Valdemar turned the man around in his chair, swiveling it sideways so that he faced the far off end of the stage. The man grimaced stiffly, gulping and wheezing for air, tossing his head back and forth as if if were growing dizzy.

"Observe the stage," Dr. Valdemar commanded. "Notice that the curtains are drawn together. Raise your hand when you see this."

Limply the man lifted up and lowered his hand.

"You are curious about what is happening behind that curtain," Dr. Valdemar continued. "Now notice the woman standing on the stage at the far end of the curtain."

Another spotlight fell upon a capped and gowned woman dressed as a scrub nurse holding close to her bosom a glinting surgical instrument—a shiny and keenly sharp scalpel! Unmasked she made a contorted face, looking deathly afraid of some unseen menace.

"She has an expression of extreme fear and horror on her face—as if she sees the most terrifying thing imaginable behind that curtain," Dr. Valdemar continued. "You wonder what this could be. And you absorb this woman's fear. In a moment the curtain will suddenly open and you will see what frightens her. As soon as you do tell me about it without waking. As soon as you see what goes on behind that curtain tell me exactly what you see!"

Across the display device's viewing screen the undulating wave of the man's heartbeat widened and stepped up visibly in both speed and intensity.

"Tell us!" Dr. Valdemar commanded in a raspy whisper. "Tell us the tale of your tell-tale heartbeat!"

"Now, I say..." The man strained every nerve to give utterance to his words. "There falls upon my ears a low, dull, rapid sound such as a clock would make when wrapped in cloth. I know *that* sound well too. It is the beating of my own heart. It deepens my dread..."

As the man raised his voice the throbbing heartbeat boomed over the stage speakers even more loudly.

"Meanwhile the infernal beating of my heart intensifies. It grows faster and faster, and louder and louder each moment. My horror *must* be excessive! It grows louder, I say, louder each instant!—do you mark my words? And then in the dead of night—amidst the frightful stillness of this timeworn theater—so mysterious a sound as this incites me to unbridled horror. But for some moments longer I abstain and sit silent. But the beating grows louder, louder! I felt the heart must burst. Yet for many moments the heart beats on with a stifled noise."

He turned frantic and panic-stricken. Then he calmed himself down.

"But before long I sense myself growing pallid. My head hurts and I imagine a ringing in my ears. The ringing grows more definite: it continues and grows more definite. It continues and attains definitiveness—until at last I discover that the sound is *not* in my ears.

"Doubtless I now grow *decidedly* pallid. But the noise intensifies—but what can I do? It is *a low, dull, rapid noise— much such a noise as a clock makes when wrapped in cloth.* I gasp for a breath of air; but the sound steadily intensifies. Oh God! what *can* I do? But the noise blares above all and continuously intensifies. It grows louder—louder—*louder!* I sense that I must scream or die—and then—once more!—listen! louder! louder! louder! *louder!*—"

Then he shouted—his eyes still squeezed shut as though he were blind.

"Scoundrels!" he screamed. "Pretend no further! Confess the act!—torn out from my chest!—there, there!—it is the beating of my horrible heart!"

By inches the rearward sable stage curtain budged aside, exposing to view a sizable space irradiated by iridescent light. At the sight of the stage set then before it the hushed crowd turned clamorous with people taking in their breaths and shifting in their seats. Taken aback many strained their necks to get a better view, for before their eyes floated a ghastly and grisly scene: an open heart surgery operating room.

Overhead high intensity lights illuminated a centrally set operation table supporting at length a shrouded and blood-stained body. Surrounding it were two more instrument tables bearing shining pieces of operative equipment, gauze sponges, dressings and bandages along with another wildly flashing electrocardiograph and a metallic heart-lung machine. Behind the operation table stood a capped, gowned and masked heart surgeon, holding up high in upturned palms a slimy, blood-red, blood-dripping thing—a living, beating, throbbing, pulsating human heart!

During the same time the man seated suddenly made a wry face and cried out aloud in pain. His eyes rolling upward into their sockets, his facial muscles twitching, his bodily limbs shaking—he convulsed violently, reeling in his chair, heaving and spitting up blood.

"Call the paramedics! This man's having a real attack!" An alarmed stage manager ran out onstage yelling. "Close the curtains!"

Abruptly the stage curtains closed, the house lights came on, the stage players retired from sight. Already Lenore hurried onstage in the thick of the commotion to take a stage microphone.

"Ladies and gentlemen," she announced urgently to a restless, unsettled audience. "For reasons entirely beyond our control we cannot continue with tonight's performance. Although there is no immediate emergency please leave the theater as quickly and calmly as possible by the nearest exit. Thank you for your cooperation."

Once Lenore came back down the stairs I waited for her at the foot of the stage. She looked deeply disturbed, heaving a heavy sigh and shaking her head.

"Are you all right, my love?" I embraced her consolingly.

"It's perverse," she said, lifting up her incredulous eyes to meet mine, "but I couldn't help but recall when the palace was once called San Francisco's valentine."

"Whoever called it that," I said gravely, "never figured on the valentine coming from the likes of Dr. Valdemar."

§

"Hypnosis is never without its possible complications even under the best of conditions." Dr. Valdemar heaved a sigh of disappointment. "It's most disconcerting when something goes amiss and a demonstration comes to such grief."

Together we rounded the outside of the *Exploratorium* building, losing sight of the flashing red lights of the boxlike emergency medical vehicle, surrounded by a crowd of curious bystanders watching paramedics wheeling the portly, ill-fated man aboard on a stretcher.

"From what you told me before I gathered that being a hypnotic subject was a fairly safe proposition," I said, perplexed.

"You can never take anything totally for granted—ever—least of all in hypnosis." Dr. Valdemar held up a dissenting hand. "Everyone who pries into its secrets is at some time in danger of being at the mercy of its pitfalls—few though they may be. It's regrettable—and sometimes disappointing—but hardly ever harmful."

"Then perhaps I should reconsider your proposal?"

"You needn't be discouraged so easily, my young friend," he reassured me. "We can never learn anything of any real value if we shrink from taking a calculated chance every now and again."

Dr. Valdemar led the way through the northern end of the lofty colonnade, taking us to the very brink of the darkish, marshy recess of the tree-shrouded lagoon then being seeped in a fuming fog. Pensively poring over the murky mist-laden waters Dr. Valdemar unexpectedly recited some familiar but unearthly sounding words:

"And I came...*to the precipitous brink of a black and lurid tarn that lay in unruffled lustre by the dwelling...where...there hung an atmosphere peculiar to themselves and their immediate vicinity—an atmosphere which had no affinity with the air of heaven, but which had reeked up from the decayed trees, and the gray wall, and the silent tarn—a pestilent and mystic vapour, dull, sluggish, faintly discernible, and leaden-hued.*"

"Shades of Edgar Allan Poe and the *House of Usher*." I smiled knowingly. "As was your performance."

Taken by surprise Dr. Valdemar turned to rivet his inquisitive eyes on me.

"You're acquainted with the work of Edgar Allan Poe?"

"Academically," I said. "I'm an aspiring writer and Poe's a writer I happen to hold in very high esteem."

"So did Bernard Maybeck the architect." He gestured to

the great rotunda nearby. "When he designed this magnificent masterwork he prefaced a book he wrote about the palace in 1915 with a quote from a Poe poem: *To Helen.*"

Dr. Valdemar ran his eyes reflectively over the darkened lagoon.

"Do you know why Maybeck placed his palace at the edge of a tarn while relegating it to the background of the surrounding landscape?" he asked without waiting for an answer. "To give it a sense of sadness of being an old ruin overrun by vegetation—an infestation which subverts even the most conscientious care."

Dr. Valdemar ran on uninterrupted, rambling eloquently as if lost deeply and profoundly in his own thoughts:

"Maybeck meant his palace to manifest the mortality of human grandeur and the vanity of human ambitions. A grand classical ruin with an arcade enclosing nothing. A colonnade without a roof. Stairs that end nowhere. Trees that burst forth from the walls. He meant his palace to slowly crumble and sink into its own grave—to become its own burial ground. He meant it more to evoke a marked mood than as an academic replica of antiquity. And as the mood deepened with decline and corruption the literal would merge with the allegorical, the factual with the fanciful, the real with the unreal. He imagined this palace in the middle of a pool surrounded by dark, deep, rocky cliffs with the sea's white foam frothing over its marble floor. He conjured up a vision of mysterious fear and even horror—as of something weird and uncanny. Like some starry-eyed visionary he realized and knew full well that when the unreal becomes real anything is possible—even a ruined palace rising like a phoenix from its own ashes."

Speechless and spellbound I riveted my eyes and my thoughts on my mysterious host.

"At first made of a mixture of plaster and fiber known as staff," Dr. Valdemar stated fatefully, "it was over fifty years later before Maybeck's palace was restored and rebuilt in concrete to make the unreal real—to make possible a palace that could withstand and stand up against even the rank infestation that closed in all around it!"

FIVE:

THE
SPIRIT OF PERVERSENESS

"Not long ago, the writer of these lines,
In the mad pride of intellectuality,
Maintained 'the power of words'—denied that ever
A thought arose within the human brain
Beyond the utterance of the human tongue:"—Poe
poem:
To — —

Looming ahead of us on Van Ness Avenue were the towering archways and the massive fluted Doric columns closing in the raised balconies of the *War Memorial Performing Arts Center* building. Along with other patrons strolling toward the entrance to the *Herbst Theatre* Lenore and I passed on, stopping briefly to read a glass-encased signboard set in front of the terra cotta wall lighted up by a tall, black, flickering torch lantern:

Talking at the Herbst:
Dr. Vincent Valdemar on the Spirit of Perverseness,
In Conversation with Dr. Kerwin Usher

"I've a feeling it's going to be quite an interesting evening," I told Lenore.

"I've a feeling you're right." She affectionately took my arm as we passed through the brass lined double-glass doors beneath a tall archway capped by a grand keystone. High up in relief its gaping fanged lion's head glared over us.

Inside we crossed the lofty and vaulted lobby, echoing with the footsteps and voices of people shuffling across its spacious and polished marble floor. Bypassing the line of patrons filing toward the small central ticket booth we went through a set of wooden, gold trimmed double-doors, handing over our complimentary tickets to a gracious theatre usher.

Then we found ourselves milling about in a snug, red-carpeted foyer—its high coffered ceiling hung with flaring torch lanterns, its smooth and stony walls decorated with tall mirrors, little wooden consoles and vinyl-covered benches. Above the middle doorway hung a large painting picturing the signing of the United Nations Charter. Passing on we went through another sidelong doorway and down a falling aisle to take our two seats on one side at the foot of the darkened stage.

"It's so beautiful," I marveled, looking around to take the full measure of the expansive red-seated theatre—two great candelabra chandeliers hanging from its ceiling with tall Ionic columns and eight grand murals adorning its stone tracery walls.

"Yes," Lenore said softly, snuggling up against me. "I love coming here with you."

"Me too."

"Those paintings were meant to portray how the ancient elements of earth, air, fire and water have served humanity," she mused. "I wonder whether Dr. Valdemar will have something to say in the service of humanity?"

"We should soon find out."

The house lights and wall sconces dimmed.

"Ladies and gentlemen," an amplified offstage voice ebulliently announced. "Dr. Vincent Valdemar!"

Circled about by a bright spot of light Dr. Valdemar stepped up to a stage podium wearing a solid poplin tan suit. He momentarily fingered his slate blue and gray paisley silk tie, brushing it down over his blue and white spaced fine-striped broadcloth shirt.

"Reason," he started, speaking in distinct, resonant tones, "would prevail upon criminology to concede—as an impulsive and primeval precept of human conduct—an enigmatical something—which we might label *perverseness* for lack of a more demonstrative expression. In the sense I mean it is indeed a *movement* without motivation. Through its impetus we operate without understandable design; or if this will be construed as a contradiction in terms we might so far alter the premise as to assert—that through its impetus we operate—for the reason that we should *not*. Theoretically no reason could be more unreasonable; yet indeed there is none more powerful. With certain minds—under certain circumstances—it becomes positively overpowering. I am not more positive that I breathe—than that the certainty of the wrongfulness or aberration of any conduct is frequently the sole indomitable compulsion which propels us—and by itself propels us to its pursuit. Nor shall this overpowering proclivity to do wrong for wrong's sake suffer of scrutiny—or sifting into ulterior motives. It is an innate, primeval impetus—fundamental. It shall be asserted, I am cognizant, that when we persist in deeds because we sense we should *not* persist in them—our behavior is but an alteration of that which habitually results from the contentiousness of criminology. But a glimpse shall demonstrate the falsity of this notion. The criminological contentiousness retains for its essentialness the requisite of self-preservation. It is our protection against casualty. Its precept respects our welfare; and so the wish to be well is incited coincidentally with its advancement. It follows that the wish to be well must be incited coincidentally with any precept which will be purely an alteration of contentiousness, but in the instance of that something which I term *perverseness* the wish to be well is not just incited—but an irresistibly hostile sentiment persists.

"Scrutinize these and similar deeds as we see fit—we will discover them springing solely from the spirit of the *Perverse*. We commit them purely because we sense that we should *not*. Beyond or behind this there is no comprehensible precept; and we might in fact regard this *perverseness* a direct perpetration of the foul fiend were it not sporadically recognized to act in the advancement of good.

"And then comes—as if to our ultimate and irreversible downfall—that spirit of PERVERSENESS. Of this spirit learning takes no consideration. But I am not more certain that my own spirit exists than I am that *perverseness* is one of the primeval impulses of the human spirit—one of the indissoluble primal powers, or sentiments, which give predisposition to the nature of Man. Who has not countless times found himself perpetrating some depraved or stupid act for no other reason because he realizes he should *not*? Have we not an interminable predilection—in the face of our best judgment—to contravene that which is *Law* purely because we comprehend it to be such? This spirit of *perverseness*, I contend, comes to our ultimate downfall. It is that inexplicable yearning of the spirit to *torment itself*—to extend violence to its own temperament—to do wrong for the wrong's sake solely—because we realize that in so doing we are committing sacrilege—a fatal sacrilege that would so imperil our imperishable spirit as to put it past the reach of the infinite mercy of the Most Compassionate and Most Awesome God!"

To resounding applause Dr. Valdemar turned to retire from sight—the darkness of the stage enveloping him. Presently a spotlight threw its circle about a strikingly handsome man with pepper–and–salt hair, wearing a solid serge navy blue suit and sitting in an armchair. He lifted up his wide and deep brown eyes, exposing his long face, rounded chin and even, sun-burnished features after a long, expectant pause.

"Dr. Kerwin Usher!" announced the amplifed offstage voice.

With a slight, smiling nod of acknowledgment Dr. Usher tucked his slate and silver gray-figured woven silk tie down along his white silky cotton batiste shirt as the expanding spotlight revealed that Dr. Valdemar had sat down upon a facing armchair directly opposite. Once the clapping of hands subsided to a hush they talked together through tiny microphones hung about their necks, carrying on an amplifed conversation with which to close the presentation—*U.* in the discussion standing for Dr. Usher and *V.* for Dr. Valdemar:

U. "In the observance of the powers and impulses—of the primeval movements of the human spirit—do you contend that criminologists have neglected to make way for a proclivity which, although clearly prevailing as a fundamental, primeval, irreducible sentiment, has been similarly ignored by all the criminologists who have preceded them?"

V. "In the sheer vanity of the logic we have all ignored it. We have permitted its existence to escape our faculties solely through lack of belief—of faith. The notion of it has never presented itself purely because of its benign neglect. We perceived no *need* of the impulse—for the proclivity. We could not see its indispensability. We could not comprehend—that is to say—we could not have comprehended—had the idea of this primeval movement ever insinuated itself;—we could not have comprehended in what way it might be made to advance the aims of mankind—either worldly or unworldly."

U. "It could be disputed that criminology has been erstwhile so contrived."

V. "The rational or reasoning man—instead of the discerning and perceptive man—appointed himself to conceive purposes—to decree designs to God. Having so understood—to his complacency—the designs of God—from these designs he fashioned his immeasurable frame of mind."

U. "For instance?"

V. "Having established it to be God's pleasure that man should perpetuate his race—we realized a member of love—immediately. And so—with contentiousness, with idealism, with causation, with productiveness—so, in short, with every member—whether depicting a proclivity, a virtuous sentiment or a power of the perfect perception. And in the dispositions of the precepts of human conduct—whether right or wrong, in part or on the whole—have but succeeded—in principle—the footsteps of their predecessors; deriving and deciding everything from the predetermined fate of man—and upon the basis of the designs of his Deity."

U. "Could there have been an alternative arrangement?"

V. "It would have been wiser—it would have been safer—to organize—if organize we must—upon the ground of what man normally or abnormally did—and was invariably abnormally doing—instead of upon the ground of what we took at face value the Deity meant him to do. If we cannot understand God in His conspicuous works—how then in His incomprehensible considerations—that bring the works into being? If we cannot comprehend Him in his extraneous creations how then in His appreciable temperaments and aspects of creation?"

U. "Is the perfect response to the equivocation just detected a plea to one's own spirit?"

V. "No one who confidently confers and carefully disputes his own spirit will be inclined to doubt the undiminished essence of the proclivity in dispute. It is not more unfathomable than distinguishing."

U. "There exists no man who at some time has not been tortured by a determined wish to tempt a listener by verbosity. The speaker is conscious that he dissatisfies; he has every intention to satisfy; he is normally concise, accurate and clear; the most succinct and lucid language is straining for articulation upon his tongue; it is but with difficulty that he restricts himself from giving it fluidity; he dreads and denounces the animosity of him he addresses; but the thought strikes him that by certain convolutions and insertions this animosity might be generated. That solitary thought is sufficient. The impetus escalates to a fantasy, the fantasy to a want, the want to an unrestrained craving; and the craving—to the bitter disappointment and vexation of the speaker and in defiance of all aftereffects—is gratified."

V. "It will be construed that I speak of coincidences and *nothing more*. What I have stated about this subject must suffice. In my own spirit there resides no belief in the phenomenal. That Nature and its God are two no man who reflects will dispute. That God, creating Nature, can at will control or change it is likewise indisputable. I state *at will* for the matter is of will and not—as the lunacy of logic has presumed—power. It is not that the Deity *cannot* change His laws but that we outrage Him in conceiving a conceivable need for change. In their source these laws were formulated to encompass *all* possibilities which *could* rest in the Future. With God everything is *Now*."

Dr. Usher uncrossed his legs to rise, gesturing for Dr. Valdemar to return to the podium.

"Then, sir, we shall indeed favor you to have the final say on this material subject," he said invitingly in his soothingly resonating voice. Once more Dr. Valdemar took up his place at the podium.

"We have a duty ahead of us," Dr. Valdemar concluded, "which must be expeditiously discharged. We realize that it will be disastrous to defer. The most crucial calamity of our time demands prompt effort and execution. We are spent with earnestness to undertake the task—with the expectation whose illustrious effect our entire spirits are ablaze. It must—it will be embarked upon today—and yet we postpone it until tomorrow; but why? There is no explanation except that we sense *perverseness*—utilizing the term with no understanding of the precept. Tomorrow comes and with it a more restive anxiety to discharge our duty; but with this rise in anxiety comes likewise an unnamed, a decidedly frightful because inexplicable desire for delay. This desire intensifies as time flies. The final hour for action is upon us. We shudder with the turmoil of the struggle inside us,—of the precise with the imprecise—of the substance with the shade. But if the conflict has progressed so far it is the shade which predominates,—we strive to no avail. The pendulum swings and is the death toll of our welfare. At one fell swoop it is the chanticleer-note to the spirit that has so long daunted us. It flees—it fades—we are liberated. The past intensity returns. We will toil *now*. Alas, it is *too late!*"

§

Cramped and carpeted in red the narrow stairway led the lecture reception crowd down three short flights to the spacious and low-ceilinged basement spread beneath the *Herbst Theatre*. Small circles in the ceiling threw light down upon the round tables and chairs situated about the room's wooden floor. And on all sides shiny wall mirrors reflected the theatergoers already gathering and going up for drinks at the bar set up in the room's right rear.

Arm and arm Lenore strolled with me into the forepart of

the room. Across the mingling crowd we caught sight of Dr. Valdemar standing with a glass of water in a corner of the room at the far facing wall. Then we picked out Dr. Usher standing alongside, conversing with him. Discreetly we stepped up to eavesdrop on their conversation.

As Dr. Valdemar continued to dissertate, or rather recite, we discerned the perturbation of Dr. Usher instantly intensifying. At last he blurted out; volunteering some exception taken to a point emphasized by Dr. Valdemar, and explaining his arguments in detail. To these Dr. Valdemar retorted at length—yet retaining his extravagant tone of sentiment and closing—in what we felt was poor taste—with a scoffing and a jeer. Dr. Usher's final expressions we clearly recall.

"Your views," he declared, "permit me to say, Dr. Valdemar, although on the whole accurate, are in many fine points disreputable to yourself and to the academy of which you are a member. In some respects they are even undeserving of serious rebuttal. I would say more than this, sir, were it not for the fear of adding insult to injury. I would say, sir, that your views are not the views to be expected from a scholar."

And there Dr. Usher simpered mildly.

As Dr. Usher concluded this equivocal expression all eyes were directed to Dr. Valdemar. He turned pallid, then extremely red; then we caught sight of his face. It was sparkling with the sprightly aspect which was its essential nature, but which I had never discerned except when we were by ourselves together. In a moment afterward he faced Dr. Usher; and so complete a change of complexion in so brief a time I surely never discerned before. For an instant I even imagined that I had misperceived him and that he was in deadly earnest. He seemed to be suffocating with rage and his countenance was white as a corpse. For a brief period he stayed still, seemingly struggling to control his fury. Having at length apparently prevailed he held out his glass tightly clutched.

"The parlance you have felt fit to use, Dr. Usher, in accosting yourself to me, is offensive in so many details that I have neither mood nor time for stipulation. That my views, though, are not the views to be expected from a scholar is an assertion so expressly reprehensible as to permit me but one course of action. Some civility, nonetheless, is owed to the attendance of this audience and to yourself at this instant as my host. You will forgive me then if upon this stipulation I digress slightly from the conventional practice amongst scholars in similar situations of personal insult. You will pardon me for the mild strain I shall put upon your imagination and attempt to contemplate for a moment the reflection of your person in that mirror as the breathing Dr. Usher himself. This being done there will be no perplexity whatever. I shall throw this glass of water at your reflection in that mirror and so satisfy the full spirit—if not the strict letter—of indignation for your affront—while the need of physical violence to your actual person will be precluded."

"You do have a particular point to make." Dr. Usher smiled sardonically.

"An image to evoke—a vision to conjure." Dr. Valdemar gestured sedately to a wide mirror covering a wall panel behind them. "Imagine yourself as being one of those poor hapless souls suffering from a deathly fear of fear itself. Imagine yourself as being powerless in all situations—as being totally ineffectual in all aspects of your daily life. Whenever you feel you are losing control you always wish you possessed the power with which to regain it. You pause, relax, breathe deeply and you feel that shield which surrounds you—that shield which protects and preserves you from fear. No fear can penetrate or pass through that shield—or so you dare suppose. When it strikes to possess or obsess you the fear just melts away. It just dissolves and flows away. Only it doesn't flow away. It penetrates and petrifies you—utterly and totally. It pierces your shield and runs through it—and impales you—because something has punctured and melted your shield—something

85

caustic and cutting—something nitric and sulfuric. Yes—a powerful acid has breached your shield—an acid that burns, corrodes and corrupts all of your skin until it is you—and not your fear—that fades and flows away—leaving no trace!"

With those words he forcefully flung the glass—full of water—against the mirror which overhung directly opposite Dr. Usher; splashing the reflection of his person with ample accuracy but *not* fracturing the glass into fragments! Everyone watching the watery liquid dribbling down the wall in distorted streams was taken abruptly back—unable to trust their own senses: for where Dr. Usher's face was before reflected in the mirror a gaping, charred and smoldering hole then defaced and disfigured the wall!

Also in attendance—but unrecognized and unknown to us—was another prominent and engrossed onlooker—an older gentleman of a considerably fanciful, melancholic temperament whose demeanor at those moments was passionless and speculative; his eyes were empty of expression: he was the Chevalier C. Dupin—the retired detective chief inspector of French extraction of the San Francisco Police Department.

SIX:

THE PITLESS PENDULUM

"Take this kiss upon the brow!
And, in parting from you now,
Thus much let me avow—
You are not wrong, who deem
That my days have been a dream;
Yet if hope has flown away
In a night, or in a day,
In a vision, or in none,
*Is it therefore the less **gone?***
***All** that we see or seem*
Is but a dream within a dream."—Poe poem:
A Dream Within A Dream

Hovering high in sight of the quiet neighborhood crossing of *Fillmore* and *Vallejo* Streets the lofty Gothic-style house looked curiously misplaced among the other fashionable houses of *Pacific Heights*. With its steeply set roof, pointed arches and carved canopy molding the house shot up in rebellious defiance to the more uniform shapes of its imminent surroundings. As I stepped up to the house I lifted up my eyes to survey its dark and somber facade. Above me a three-sided bay projected from its third story—a dim, hazy blue light showing through the netting of the thin sheer-glass curtains hung closest to the panes of tall, narrow, pointed windows—these being edged by dark, pointed, forest-green shutters carved with misshapen demons. Then I cast my eyes on the polished brass oval-shaped plate bolted directly in front of me onto the facade's dark, walnut-colored stucco siding and engraved with the titled name: *Dr. Vincent Valdemar*. Finally I climbed a short flight of railed steps to set foot on a balustraded portico facing a doorway set inside a pointed arch—the door itself arched to fit the dark molded frame. Hesitantly I reached out to rap the door's shiny hinged brass knocker and waited with bated breath. A diamond-latticed oval of iridescent leaded glass lighted up above the entry as I heard the grating sound of a solid lock unbolted from the opposite side of the wood-paneled door. As the creaking door budged gradually ajar Dr. Vincent Valdemar peered out from behind it only partly exposed to view. His wary expression turned stiffly sociable as he stepped into full view, wearing a gray suit and dark gray wool tie over a white yellow and black tattersall-check shirt.

"Hello," I greeted him. "Dr. Valdemar."

"Good afternoon, my young friend, and welcome." He graciously pressed my hand. "Do come in."

Immediately he stood aside, beckoning me to step inside the very sedate and sober looking foyer and hall, closing the door behind me. Slipping in I curiously glanced around the entry and stair-hall. At the foot of the straight staircase a newel-post lamp having a vase-shaped body topped with an opaque glass shade shed dim light on the white-tinged, charcoal gray-colored foyer. By the door stood a hall tree for holding hats. Underfoot was spread a carpet of garlands surrounding a crooked pattern of flowers and leaves. Along the hallway were set a large console varnished in a painted floral motif, a serpentine-shaped settee covered with a chintz cotton fabric in a gold paisley pattern on a black gold-fringed background—together with a tall, pendulously ticking long-case clock.

Out of nowhere from the lurid dark of the foyer unexpectedly emerged another man who was in no respect more strange than in his particular aspect. He was exceptionally tall and slender. He stooped a lot. His limbs were extremely long and gangling. His forehead was wide and low. His color was perfectly sallow. His mouth was big and supple; and his teeth were more freakishly uneven—although unbroken—than I had ever before beheld teeth in a human head. The aspect of his smile though was by no means disagreeable as might be surmised; but it had no divergence whatever. It was one of deep despondency—of a chronic and ceaseless melancholy. His eyes were singularly big and globular like those of a cat. The pupils also upon any rise or reduction of light experienced contraction or dilation just such as is perceived in the feline race. In moments of stimulation the globes turned bright to an extent almost unimaginable; appearing to emanate luminescent beams—not of a mirrored but of an inherent sheen as does a taper or a star; but their usual state was so utterly dull, filmy and lifeless as to impart the notion of a long-entombed corpse.

"Permit me to introduce—before he leaves us—a remarkable gentleman in every respect," Dr. Valdemar pronounced politely, "whose casual acquaintance I made some months ago and who inspired in me a deep curiosity and intrigue: Mr. Augustus Bedloe."

Mutely and grimly Mr. Bedloe bowed and I nodded just a

slight acknowledgement.

"Between us," Dr. Valdemar added, "there has developed step by step a most definite and profoundly marked *rapport*—or hypnotic relationship."

At the same instant Mr. Bedloe had departed as abruptly as he had appeared.

§

"Let's go upstairs to the drawing room where we can chat comfortably," Dr. Valdemar invitingly suggested.

He led the way up the stairs which were overlaid with a fringed oriental carpet runner. Stepping up I noticed the hall's rising wallpaper assuming the form of a geometric design in a crimson color on a dark burgundy background.

"And the Master of the Macabre welcomes you as well."

He gestured with a knowing nod to a small wall-niche midway up the stairs holding a bare piece of sculpture draped in a veil of gauze.

"Pay your respects to a famous friend of ours!"

He paused to ceremoniously cast off the gauze and unveil a polished bust of Edgar Allan Poe!

"A cultivated choice of artwork," I complimented him.

"I thought you would find it in good taste." He smiled approvingly. "Come."

On the landing at the top of the stairs we passed by a tall wood-framed mirror before stepping up to a pair of double sliding doors with shadowy geometric motifs etched into their frosted glass panels. Dr. Valdemar pulled apart the doors, opening up to view a spacious drawing room. An ebonized and gilded pedestal holding up a silver-plate calling card tray stood at the threshold and was irradiated by a glow of lapis lazuli light flaring down from a triple lamp fixture hanging overhead—one lamp at each end and another in the middle with scrolls connecting the horizontal bar with the vertical support.

We passed on into the expansive drawing room overtopped by a high-plastered ceiling carved into disk-shaped medallions circled with plain-beaded moldings and painted in deep crimson and purple. A medallion set in the middle of the ceiling circled the mount of a hanging chandelier—its curved and branching arms of polished brass cockleshells sprouting from carved crystal pendants formed of pairs of brass globes shaded with frosted glass and connected by spiral-fluted arms. On all sides the room's walls displayed high, steeply scaled baseboards, maroon oval-patterned hardwood paneling, a projecting chair rail molding at their midpoint and a raised, plaster bas relief cornice topping them off in a carved, gilded crown molding, projecting onto the ceiling and forming a band between it and the wall surfaces. Above the chair rail the walls were marbled in light gray paper. And spread over the room's stained hardwood floors of striped oak with walnut were an assortment of colorful oriental rugs. Hung from brass poles around the line of the front bay windows over a lace under-curtain were straight-dropped, blueblack velvet drapes embellished with braided and tassellated festoons and looped swags. Topping those was a stiffened decorative valence. Indoor plum-red shutters were folded into recesses in the window frames. On the facing side of the room was a chimney-piece of heavy black marble mounted by a mahogany mantelshelf holding a clock in a carved oak case under a glass dome flanked by brass candlesticks. In front of the chimney-piece was a black-leaded register grate along with propped pokers, tongs, brushes and coal scuttles.

"Ha! ha! ha!—ha! ha! ha!"—laughed aloud my host, gesturing me to a seat as I stepped inside the room and flinging himself back at full length upon an ottoman.

"I see," he declared, discerning that I could not instantly reconcile myself to the singularity of so unusual a reception—"I see you are astounded at my apartment—at my decoration—at my ornamentation—my creativeness of invention in design and upholstery—positively intoxicated, eh? with my elegance? But forgive me, my dear sir, forgive me for my ungenerous laughter."

There his tone of voice fell to the very soul of geniality.

"You look so *absolutely* astounded. Besides, some things are so utterly ridiculous that a man has *got* to laugh or die. To die laughing has got to be the most splendid of all splendid deaths!"

"But in the current case," he continued with a peculiar change of expression and demeanor, "I have no right to be jovial at your expense. You might well have been astonished. San Francisco cannot fabricate anything so refined as this— my little stately closet. My other apartments are by no means of the same class; sheer extremes of refined mediocrity. This is superior to style—is it not? Yet this is but to be perceived to follow the fashion—that is, with those who could manage it at the expense of their entire estate. I have guarded though against any such sacrilege. With a select few exceptions you are the sole human being besides myself—and my brother—who has been admitted inside the secrets of these imperious confines—since they have been emblazoned as you see!"

I nodded in accord; for the overwhelming sense of magnificence, along with the unforeseen idiosyncrasy of his expression and demeanor, precluded me from articulating—in words—my gratitude for what I might have interpreted as a compliment.

"Here," Dr. Valdemar announced with a portentous tone, "we'll try our hand at hypnosis together and put certain hypnotic theories to the test."

"What kind of hypnotic experiment did you have in mind?" I asked expectantly as I paused at the mantel.

"I'll explain everything to you in due time," Dr. Valdemar said. "Just now it's important that you first learn to respond to simple suggestions before you learn to respond to more complex ones which will elicit changes in your feelings and behaviors. So we'll carry on a series of exercises designed to help you learn how to respond to simple hypnotic suggestions."

"You speak as if you've already decided that I'll make a suitable subject."

"I've come precisely to that conclusion," he said, "for most writers have quite a well-developed sense of imagination—a sure sign of hypnotic susceptibility. Hypnosis is nothing magical nor is it something which simply happens to you. It demands your cooperation and participation. Hypnosis is a skill—a skill which follows the laws of habit formation. It becomes easier with repeated sessions. So almost anyone can learn to respond—and with practice—you can improve your skill. And in turn your skill can improve your life."

"How so?"

"Hypnosis can free the creative imagination of a writer like yourself and give you more scope in which to write more fully and effectively."

"How do you develop this skill?"

"You undertake hyponotic skills training," he explained, "for the skill lies in being able to think and imagine along with a suggestion. Hypnosis has to do with concentrating on thoughts and images which are consistent with the goals of a suggestion."

A shiny, circular-inlaid mahogany table standing on a single column upheld on a flat base with three hairy lion paws and surrounded by deep, buttoned-silk upholstered mahogany armchairs was the drawing room's centerpiece. Across the room facing the chimney-piece sat a sofa covered in patterned velvet and piled with heavily stuffed, fringed and tassellated bolsters and cushions. Set up in corners were small tables next to big easy chairs draped with paisley shawls and faced by an occasional balloon-backed chair.

"Come into my parlor."

Arising to cross the room at my side Dr. Valdemar ushered me through an arch of fretwork and drapery and into a cramped and confined parlor lined with built-in bookcases.

"Said the spider to the fly?"

"Said the pilot to the passenger," he corrected me with a suggestive tone of voice, gesturing to a velvet upholstered sleeper sofa with a camel-back styling and rolled arms—in front of which sat an old leather trunk embellished with brass nail heads and a low table set for tea.

"Lie down and relax. Drink if you like. It's not an analyst's couch."

As I easily laid back against paisley-covered throw pillows Dr. Valdemar reached up to yank the pull-chain to a solitary library lamp supported by a U-shaped bar from a horizontal S-shaped scroll hanging from a ceiling chain. A dim and diffuse lapis lazuli light was thrown upon us from clouded glass as he sat down close to me in a heavily carved, rosewood sidechair upholstered in a silk damask.

"I just hope I don't end up being a couch case by the time this is all over.," I said dubiously.

"Now's the time for us to find out," Dr. Valdemar said softly. "Let's discuss it then, shall we?"

§

What follows is the conversation that succeeded—*V.* in the discussion standing for Dr. Valdemar and *N.* for Nicolino:

V. "You're here to consider being a voluntary subject for a hypnotic experiment. How do you feel about being hypnotized?"

N. "It's a strange feeling."

V. "How so?"

N. "I've heard or read stories about people being hypnotized. But I've never been hypnotized myself. Nor have I ever seen anyone else hypnotized."

V. "Are you afraid that under hypnosis I might tell you to do something humiliating or dangerous?"

N. "I don't know. Would you?"

V. "No. Absolutely not."

N. "Really?"

V. "No question. Serious hypnosis is neither a sideshow nor some parlor game indulged in for performing cheap tricks. So I will certainly tell you to do nothing which will embarrass or endanger you."

N. "Good."

V. "Do you have any other ideas or impressions about hypnosis?"

N. "I'm not sure whether it's possible for you to hypnotize me."

V. "How do you mean?"

N. "I just can't imagine myself being hypnotized by anyone."

V. "Why not? What exactly do you think happens when someone is hypnotized?"

N. "I don't know exactly. I suppose you're put to sleep and told to do things against your will."

V. "That's a false notion a lot of people have. For that matter you never enter a state where you lose contact with the hypnotist. You're in complete control of your activity—except that which you choose to feel is happening in spite of yourself. You stay in contact with me at all times and you never lose conscious awareness."

N. "I had the impression hypnosis was a kind of induced sleep."

V. "A common misconception widely entertained. Hypnosis is more typical of the waking state than sleep. Sleep in this instance describes the trance state—meaning hypnotic sleep not ordinary sleep."

N. "What's the difference between hypnosis and sleep?"

V. "Hypnosis and sleep are two altogether different states—however much they may look alike or appear to be the same. Although subjects often expect or fear that they will be asleep or unconscious during hypnosis the hypnotized person is in no sense ever asleep—nor is his physical state ever that of true sleep."

N. "Then why do you hear of hypnotists repeating the word sleep when they're inducing hypnosis?"

V. "Their misuse of the word only aggravates the misconception: for while consciousness is suspended in sleep—it is profoundly present in hypnosis. In fact the hypnotic state is much more like waking consciousness than the sleeping state."

N. "How so?"

V. "During hypnosis vital bodily functions such as breathing, heartbeat and reflexes are more like what is found in the waking state than while sleeping. Hypnosis provokes changes in the electrical and chemical activity of the brain which differ from the activity of either the sleeping or the waking state. In sleep the bodily functions slow down remarkably. Breathing grows slower and deeper. Blood pressure and heart rate slow down. Reflex action slows down. In hypnosis you will sometimes see the slightest of slowdowns—but most of the time none at all. And in deep sleep there is a conspicuous loss of consciousness. This does not happen in hypnosis. If you test reflex action in hypnosis—such as the knee jerk—you will find it remains quite normal although it lessens in sleep. Breathing does not slow down. Heart rate remains normal. Blood pressure remains normal. So in spite of its appearances it's impossible to confuse these two very different states: the normally functioning body in hypnosis and the slow functioning body in sleep. Although many hypnotists may still suggest sleep—or mention sleep as part of the hypnotic induction process—sleep in hypnosis remains a contradiction in terms. Hypnosis is like sleep as night is to day—and is no more like it than night is like day. So once you set aside all preconceived notions you will find that hypnosis neither looks nor feels like you thought it would. Now what other ideas do you have about hypnosis?"

N. "I have a very strong will. I don't believe I could submit my will to another person."

V. "Do you believe you will lose your willpower in hypnosis?"

N. "I believe I would be expected to surrender my will."

V. "Another misconception which must be corrected. In point of fact you do not lose your capacity for independent action in hypnosis—nor your self-control. Hypnosis does not work on people with weak wills."

N. "I just don't believe I could let myself be hypnotized."

V. "Then you are laboring under a thoroughly false delusion. There isn't a person alive of normal intelligence over the age of two who hasn't been hypnotized. And seeing that you are in your adult years you have been hypnotized many times. Saying you can't be hypnotized is like saying you're a dull, slow-witted person with no power of imagination or concentration whatever. There's simply no such thing as a permanent inability to be hypnotized—although there may be a temporary resistance to enter a trance state—which by employing the proper techniques—can be successfully overcome."

N. "I thought the hypnotist was supposed to take over the subject's will and control it. I don't think I could allow that."

V. "Some of the best subjects I've had were those who believed they could never be hypnotized because they were convinced they could not let themselves be controlled by another person. Although they express a conscious reluctance to let themselves go and relax they may harbor an unconscious desire to be hypnotized and will readily respond to suggestion. So there is no way you cannot help but be hypnotized once you know how to accept and submit to suggestion."

N. "Then I needn't surrender my will in the first place."

V. "Suggestibility is not servility—which would imply a subjugation of the will. In no sense does a hypnotized person ever turn into a puppet wholly at the mercy of the hypnotist. You do not simply obey commands or relinquish your ability to do independent activity."

N. "If you won't control my will then what will you do?"

V. "The will or willing mind has nothing to do with hyp-nosis—except the ordinary willingness to cooperate—and in some cases even this isn't essential. In fact the hypnotist pos-sesses no mysterious power whatever. Nor does he have any sense of imposing his will on his subject. Such a power lies within the subject himself—for the only power present is that of the subject's own imagination. The hypnotist simply pos-sesses the technical skill to direct and guide it. He persuades the subject to use his imagination to its fullest extent by sug-gestion—and it works well. It's the subject who does the work. All the hypnotist does is supply the setting in which this work can be done."

N. "Is there really any difference between directing and controlling a subject?"

V. "A great deal of difference—for there is really no such thing as a hypnotist. As a practitioner of this craft all I can ever do is show a subject how to cross the boundary line from a normal waking state to that special state of mind known as hypnosis. I will never hypnotize you—you will hypnotize yourself. Those of us resorting to suggestion wield no power or control over any subject. There's nothing I do that you cannot learn to do in hypnosis. A more correct term than hypnotist is hypnotic operator. As the operator I guide the subject to arrive at the trance state. And then if the subject is favorably inclined I activate his imagination—acting as his dream pilot. At all times the subject is encouraged to cooperate with the opera-tor—the relationship being that of guide and explorer—not master and slave!"

N. "If hypnosis isn't sleep or subjection of the will then what is it exactly?"

V. "All hypnosis really is is self-hypnosis—for the subject himself knows full well from explanations both in and out of trance precisely what is happening. He knows this from his hypnotist who acts as his medium and guide. Few subjects actually enjoy acting like puppets so they come to appreciate a process where two people are entering into partnership with one another rather than of one dominating the other."

N. "But what is the thing of hypnosis itself?"

V. "Hypnosis is many things—but something which is grossly misunderstood. In short hypnotism is the art and craft of inducing a trance state known as hypnosis. It's also the power of suggestion. But it has nothing to do with sleep since sleep isn't essential for hypnotic suggestion. It's more like the waking state than ordinary sleep. The trance state may be induced by the hypnotist or the subject himself without even any mention of sleep. The degree of trance varies from very light to the very deep somnambulistic state."

N. "How is the subject affected by the trance state?"

V. "Hypnosis is a state of high suggestibility—or hyper-suggestibility—induced by certain manipulated techniques. It's not a super-state. It's simply an altered state of the person being hypnotized. It's an altered state of consciousness. In that state the subject has much enhanced capacity for suggestibility—or acceptivity—and it's this essential capacity that makes possible the transition to this altered state—for it's not the conscious but the subconscious that accepts suggestion."

N. "How can the subconscious accept suggestion?"

V. "The human mind is remarkably suggestible. It's constantly bombarded with suggestive stimuli from the outside together with suggestive thoughts and ideas from the inside. Hypnotism then has to do with the capacity of the mind to selectively ignore those stimuli it considers irrelevant to that which is its focus of attention. So hypnosis is a state of deep concentration. It's like someone paying so much close attention to one thing that everything else is blocked and shut out of the person's mind."

N. "So hypnosis in an induced absence of mind?"

V. "An induced *absorption* of mind. In the ordinary waking state the mind is preoccupied with all kinds of ideas and impressions so that the mind power is scattered and diffuse. So any simple suggestion given in this state literally goes in one ear and out the other. Only a small part of the mind accepts it and so the effect is weak. In hypnosis the mind is concentrated to a degree much deeper than is possible in the ordinary waking state. Almost all the suggestion is absorbed—and accepted— and so the effect is strong. In total concentration or very deep hypnosis there will be no mind power left to devote the mind to anything but what's suggested—and so the subject will be oblivious to anything else. Strictly speaking then hypnosis is a super-concentration of the mind."

N. "How does it feel to enter the trance state?"

V. "Being in a state of highly concentrated attention—focusing on one thing to the exclusion of other things. Although hypnosis is not sleep hypnotic suggestion can be used to induce sleep and relaxation as well as wakefulness and concentration. Even when the trance is induced through suggestions of sleepiness and drowsiness you do not experience a sleeplike state. Subjects experiencing trance usually show signs of relaxed wakefulness—not sleep."

N. "What is relaxed wakefulness like?"

V. "It's a dreamy, drowsy state of partial consciousness—a sort of suspended not–awake–not–asleep state. It's not clear whether you are awake or asleep. This is the normal hypnoidal state—a sort of stopping place along the way to sleep. In this state you can hear, feel, smell, understand, reason, imagine and remember quite actively—as easily and effectively as when you have full consciousness. You are fully aware of what is going on around you. You may be either critical and resistant or compliant and cooperative."

N. "That sounds vague."

V. "That's because during the trance the subject undergoes psychological and physiological experiences which are typical of both waking and sleeping. The amount of waking or sleep traits will depend on how close to either state the person in hypnosis actually is. At one end of the hypnotic spectrum he's close to wakefulness and his behavior—the content and quality of thought processes and the physiological signs—is much the same as the waking state. This is a light trance. As the subject goes into a deeper trance and approaches sleep the thought processes and the physiological signs begin to assume some of the properties of sleep. They are never quite the same as in sleep because hypnosis is not sleep. One person may be in a very light trance that's much the same as being awake. Another may be in a deep trance and look like he was asleep. But both are in a hypnotic state."

N. "Intriguing."

V. "At this point you may perhaps find yourself in one of two states of mind: you wish to participate in hypnosis but you have some misgivings about how or if it'll work for you. Or you may acknowledge that hypnosis may affect some specific part of your life. Either way you're a promising hypnotic subject. As such you're no doubt curious about how the person you are at this very moment can be transported into the field of hypnotic suggestion. Now do you have a desire to be hypnotized?"

N. "Yes."

V. "That's most important because the incentive of simply coming here to be my subject may not be enough. You must feel the need to be hypnotized."

N. "I understand."

V. "Good. Then suppose we now begin to discuss what may actually be demanded of you during this first trance. I should give you just some idea of what things will happen. First you will notice that you begin to relax and that you feel just a little bit drowsy. It's not necessary for you to try too hard."

N. "I see."

V. "Just let things happen as they will. Make your mind restful and relaxed. Then you will become aware of certain things happening as you relax. Concentrate on those. I may even call them to your attention. You may not be able to follow all the suggestions that I give you but don't let that bother you."

N. "I won't."

V. "You may be able to follow some suggestions and not others. You'll be in constant contact with me. And when you come out of it you'll probably remember everything that happened. You may have only a vague idea about certain things and you may perhaps even forget others. But for the most part you'll recall everything that happened."

N. "Should I try to do everything that you tell me to do or should I just be passive?"

V. "Just be *receptive*. It's important not to do things voluntarily. Let things happen as they will."

N. "I will."

V. "Force nothing. Don't push yourself too hard. If things don't happen they simply don't happen. Are you ready?"

N. "Yes."

V. "Excellent. Then let's begin."

§

Unhurriedly Dr. Valdemar arose from his sidechair, moving to an old swivel-desk chair on casters decorated with a soft, loose cushion covered with needlepoint. Once more seated he rolled his chair over to an oak roll-top desk fitted with drawers on either side of the knee-space—pigeonhole spaces at the top with a top shelf holding a photograph in a rich-gilt frame. Above the desk hung an old brass wall clock with Roman numerals. Reaching into one of the pigeonholes Dr. Valdemar pulled out a small, glinting metallic object. Rolling his chair over to me he held out his hand palm upwards but fist clenched. Turning his palm abruptly downward he let fall and dangle from a finger ring a long and thin silver chain. Before my curious face he gently swung the shiny miniature object fastened to the chain's end: a *pendulum*.

"How well do you remember your Edgar Allan Poe?" he asked eagerly.

Only the lower end of this particular pendulum was fashioned into a crescent of glistening metal about an inch long from horn to horn—its horns pointed upward and its lower edge plainly sharp as a razor. I sat up and leaned forward to look over it intently.

"The *Pit and the Pendulum*," I murmured, nodding.

"But in this object lesson," Dr. Valdemar said fatefully, "a pit*less* pendulum—a razor of the mind with which to test your susceptibility to hypnosis."

"Is this the cutting edge of hypnosis?"

"Of hypnosis," he said, deathly solemn, "and perhaps of another world—an infernal region of the mind. Come. Let's see."

SEVEN:

TEETERING AT THE ABYSS

"For, alas! alas! with me
The light of Life is o'er!
'No more—no more—no more—'
(Such language holds the solemn sea
To the sands upon the shore)
Shall bloom the thunder-blasted tree,
Or the stricken eagle soar!

And all my days are trances,
And all my nightly dreams
Are where thy dark eye glances,
And where thy footstep gleams—
In what ethereal dances,
By what eternal streams."—Poe poem:
To One In Paradise

D r. Valdemar stood beneath the draped archway of his parlor waiting for me to get up from the sofa when the gilt-framed photograph on the top of the shelf of his roll-top desk abruptly caught and captivated my eye. From my seat I examined it intently.

"What's so intriguing?" He noticed my rapt attention.

"Excuse me," I said distractedly, "but that picture on your desk..."

"What about it?"

"Am I seeing double—or two of you?"

Dr. Valdemar smiled knowingly and stepped up to the desk to turn on a Rochester lamp with a tall, vase-shaped chimney, a round-metal oil reservoir and a colored, translucent glass shade in the shape of an inverted bowl overhanging the photograph—its bright, plum, swirled flame lighting up the photograph's glass overlay.

"Come and see." He waved me over.

I came up to carefully inspect the photograph and what I saw startled and stunned me: a picture of Dr. Valdemar standing and posing alongside an exact duplicate of himself—a double—the pair wearing different dress suits. Especially conspicuous was the thinness of their persons; but likewise the hoariness of his brother's beard in striking contrast to the blackness of his hair—being very extensively mistaken as a result for a hairpiece.

"That's amazing," I said, dumbfounded. "You look exactly alike."

"My brother," he explained. "Except for a face mole he has on his left temple—and his hair—we're identical twins."

"There's a definite family likeness."

"Yes," he said sullenly. "He's my *William Wilson*."

"Your what?"

"Recall your Poe: like William Wilson's fictional namesake, my brother ventures to contend with me in all explorations but rejects tacit trust in my professions and capitulation to my discretion—in fact to meddle with my capricious dictates in every respect whatever. His defiance is to me a source of considerable embarrassment. In fact his contention, his repudiation and especially his impudent and obstinate opposition to my ambitions are not more direct than personal. He seems to be bereft alike of the aspiration which presses—and of the impassioned strength of mind—which empowers me to excel. He was born on the nineteenth of January—and this is a rather striking coincidence; for the day is exactly that of my own birth."

"His intolerable temper of contradiction must cause you constant anxiety."

"I have already more than once mentioned the insufferable air of condescension which he assumes toward me and his incessant interfering opposition to my discretion. This interference frequently takes the uncourtly nature of unsolicited advice; advice not overtly offered but implied or insinuated… personified in those suggestive whispers…"

"Excuse me for saying so but he sounds like the proverbial thorn in the side," I sympathized.

"Still, a sense of dignity on my part, and a proven pride on his own, keeps us invariably on what are known as speaking terms—though my antagonist has a disability in his throaty organs which prevents him from lifting his voice *beyond a decidedly soft whisper.*"

"Then you can be thankful for small mercies."

"Yes." I watched the intense soreness flush his face. "But I didn't invite you here to listen to me harp upon my family foibles. We have much more pressing matters to contend with. Come!"

§

It has been—or should be observed—that in the bearing of a genuine gentleman we are ever cognizant of a divergence from the demeanor of the vulgarian—without being at the

same time exactly able to decide in what such divergence resides. Granting the observation to have applied in its full effect to the outward deportment of my host I thought it—on
that momentous afternoon—yet more completely pertinent to
his virtuous nature and disposition. Nor can I better describe
that singularity of spirit which appeared to put him so substantially apart from all other gentlepersons—than by terming it a
practice of acute and continuous reflection, permeating even his
most trifling acts—encroaching upon his moments of distrac-
tion—and intertwining itself with his very bursts of mirth.

I could not help though repeatedly regarding—through
the intermingled mood of volatility and gravity with which he
promptly discoursed upon topics of small import—a definite
air of dread—a degree of tense fervor in conduct and expression—a disquiet irritability of behavior which seemed to me
always inexplicable—and upon certain occasions even filled
me with fear. Often, too, stopping in the middle of a sentence
whose onset he had seemingly overlooked—he appeared to be
listening with the profoundest regard—as if either in immediate anticipation of a visitor or to noises which must have had
being in his invention solely.

§

Dr. Valdemar led the way out to the circular table in the
middle of the drawing room.

"Sit down here." He gestured for me to take an armchair as
he settled into one next to it, rubbing at my elbow—the little
pendulum chain clinking in his clasped hand. "It's been long
supposed that hypnosis is mainly a matter of suggestibility—a
state of exaggerated suggestibility in which the subject accepts
the suggestions of the hypnotist. Hypnotic susceptibility on
the other hand has to do with the degree to which a person can
become imaginatively absorbed in everyday life. In fact the
only ability that's consistently related to hypnotic susceptibil-

ity is this ability to become deeply absorbed in activities affecting use of a person's imagination."

"What kinds of activities?"

"Most anything you could preoccupy yourself with, really—even if it's simple daydreaming," he elucidated at length. "Some people become habitually lost in their activities and unaware of other things in their surroundings. Such an ability is essentially childlike and can be compared with the total preoccupation of a child in some game of make-believe—so much so that he's utterly unaware of anything else going on around him, or deaf to adults calling him or oblivious to the flow of time. People possessing this capacity for trance-like preoccupation make good hypnotic subjects—and those who can become lost in this way are the more susceptible. There is however a great disparity amongst people in their ability to experience hypnosis. But contrary to common misconception there is no great disparity amongst hypnotists in their ability to induce hypnosis since it depends more on method than talent."

"What's an exercise in susceptibility?"

"Because hypnotic susceptibility is a highly fixed personality trait people vary in their susceptibility to hypnosis," he explained eagerly. "So there are certain tests of susceptibility that give a good idea of whether a person is likely to make a good subject. People responding favorably to these tests are very likely to make good subjects. Some hypnotists test their prospective subjects for this susceptibility—usually progressing from this directly into a trance state."

"What kinds of tests?"

"Amongst the most conventional is *Chevreul's Pendulum*. This measures your receptivity and responsiveness to suggestion. The greater your suggestibility the more receptive and responsive a subject you will be. A strong response means that you will be a good receptor—and being a good receptor is the first step toward successful hypnotic induction."

"Which is induced by suggestion?"

"Effective hypnotic communication is predicated upon suggestion."

"Which is what exactly?"

"Technically a suggestion is a proposition for belief or action that's accepted in the absence of intervening and critical thought. So when you're hypnotized and in a relaxed state your subconscious is more receptive to suggestion than it is when you're in a full conscious state. The suggestion steers a straight course toward the subconscious—where it easily becomes a belief, alters behavior or elicits an action or effect. Without this component part of belief successful hypnotic communication is impossible. You must have belief for the process to work. How well you can believe then depends on your susceptibility—which in turn depends on how deeply you can become absorbed in living and being alive. Shall we proceed?"

"I'm ready," I said, apprehensive.

"Good," Dr. Valdemar approved, plunking down the little pendulum and chain onto the tabletop. "I thought this would intrigue you since the weight at the end of the chain is normally a ring, a washer or some other nondescript item. But as you see I've radically remodeled my pendulum."

"Very clever. So how do you use it?"

"I'll direct you." He clicked on a switch affixed underneath the tabletop.

Unexpectedly a twirling, phosphorescent green-spiral pattern appeared on the tabletop surface—rotating in a wide circular motion, converging and coming together at dead center like a whirlpool, turning our faces aglow.

"Behold the vortex of the subconscious mind!" Dr. Valdemar announced dramatically.

He instructed me at length and I did what I was told:

"Pick up the pendulum," he said, "holding the finger ring between your thumb and index finger. Hold out the chain in front of you with your arm outstretched so that your elbow does not rest against anything. Let the pendulum hang above the surface of the table. As you hold up the pendulum fix your eyes on the spinning wheel that's turning and twisting on the table. Let your eyes roll and course around the circumference of the circle and keep them moving around in a circle. Just now imagine the pendulum swinging—slowly—back and forth. The pendulum will begin going around in a circle even though you might try to ignore it.

"As you fix your eyes on the pendulum once more think about driving. Imagine yourself driving on the freeway—no particular freeway to no particular destination—just driving along, thoughtlessly, absent-mindedly—in a fog as it were—a San Francisco fog.

"Chances are: at one time or another you've found yourself driving along a familiar freeway past your exit—or perhaps you suddenly become aware of yourself behind the wheel and you wonder where you're going. Happenings such as these are quite common. Let's explore together what makes them possible.

"Everything you've learned up to now is stored in your subconscious. Because you've already learned to drive your driving skill is stored in your subconscious. As you start out on your journey you get into your car, maneuver out onto the freeway, move into a continuous flow of traffic and come to a steady speed.

"Now your conscious mind is free. Because the knowledge for driving exists in your subconscious your conscious mind wanders and goes adrift—letting your subconscious mind become more active. You become so engrossed in your thoughts that you drive in one direction when your destination is in another direction. When your attention is needed to change lanes, steer clear of something in the road, stop at a toll-gate or apply the brake for an off-ramp your conscious mind comes into play again. You may even arrive at your destination and wonder how you got there so quickly.

"Driving is just one automatic activity. Whenever you do anything automatic your conscious mind is distracted from your subconscious mind and you're more likely to go into a hypnotic state such as this one.

"Some of your automatic activities are more apt than others to precipitate daydreaming. Like driving these activities are stored in your subconscious. While you're operating in this automatic manner it's quite easy to drift from an aware state into a different level of consciousness. Daydreaming is the first of several levels in a trance state. I call upon you to daydream for a time:..."

§

"You have now arrived at the peak of the loftiest cliff...

"You can barely look beyond this little cliff without growing dizzy...

"The slippery edge of this little cliff rises—a mere unimpeded drop of dark gleaming rock some fifteen or sixteen hundred feet from the world of rocks below you...

"Now lift yourself up a little higher...and look out—past the band of vapor below you—into the ocean...

"You look giddily—and see a vast stretch of sea whose waters display so black a color...A vista more sadly bleak no mortal invention can devise. To the left and right—as far as your eye can see—there lies outspread—like walls of the world—ranges of dark and bulging cliff—whose nature of melancholy is but the more forcefully embodied by the breakers which rise high up against it—its white and deathly crest shrieking and wailing eternally.

"Of froth there is little except in the imminent proximity of the rocks...

"Do you hear anything? Do you see any alteration in the water?

"You had caught no sight of the sea until it had burst upon you from the peak...Now you become cognizant of a thundering and progressively escalating noise—like the groaning of a huge herd of buffalo upon the grassland at *Golden Gate Park*; and at the same instant you discern that the *choppy* nature of the sea below you is swiftly shifting into a current...Even while you stare this current gains a terrifying swiftness. Every instant adds to its velocity—to its precipitate intensity. In a few minutes the entire ocean is whipped into unbridled turbulence...There the vast surface of the waters—plowed and furrowed into countless contending channels—burst abruptly into furious turmoil—swelling, seething, hissing—wheeling in colossal and uncountable whirlpools—and all twirling and plunging onward with a speed which water never elsewhere gathers except in steep descents.

"In a few moments more there comes over the vista another drastic transformation. The extensive surface turns rather sleek and the swirls—one by one—vanish while monstrous layers of froth became evident where none had been beheld before. These layers—at length stretching out to a vast distance and flowing into fusion—take unto themselves the rotating movement of the abating whirlpools and appear to shape the source of another more immense. Abruptly—very abruptly—this takes on a sharp and explicit being—in a ring more than half a mile in diameter. The brink of the whirlpool is embodied by a broad band of shining spume; but no speck of that slides into the mouth of the terrific shaft whose interior—as far as the eye can plumb it—is a sleek, gleaming and coal-black wall of water slanted toward the skyline at an angle of some forty-five degrees, accelerating giddily round and round with a warping and smoldering movement and scattering to the winds a horrifying clamor—part wail, part howl...

"The cliff quakes to its very bottom and the rock shakes...

"This can be nothing other than the vast whirlpool of the Maelstrom—so it is sometimes called!

"You have a commanding view of the whirlpool now...

"You now ponder the band of breakers that always encircles the whirlpool; and you think naturally that another instant could plunge you into the depths—down which you could only see obscurely owing to the astounding speed with which it spins...

"It may seem like bragging—but what you think is true—you start to contemplate how splendid a thing it is to perish in such a way—and how silly it is in you to mull over so trifling a reflection as your own personal life—in view of so wondrous a display of God's power. You do think that you flush with shame when this notion preoccupies your mind. After a little while you become possessed of the morbid curiosity about the whirlpool itself. You inescapably sense a desire to penetrate its depths—even at the sacrifice you are going to make...

"You pluck up courage and look once more upon the vista...

"Never will you forget the impressions of dread, terror and wonder with which you look around yourself...You gaze upon the innermost surface of a shaft immense in perimeter, vast in depth and whose perfectly smooth sides may well be mistaken for coal but for the perplexing speed with which they turn around—and for the glimmering and fearsome resplendence they shed forth—as the beams of the full moon—from that rounded cleft amidst the clouds—spill in a torrent of golden radiance along the coal-black walls—and far off down into the innermost bowels of the abyss.

"The beams of the moon appear to explore the very bottomless pit of that fathomless chasm; but yet you can pick out nothing clearly because of a dense vapor in which all there is enveloped—and over which hovers a radiant rainbow—like that tenuous and trembling trestle which is the sole pathway between Time and Eternity. That vapor or spume is doubtless occasioned by the colliding of the vast walls of the shaft as they all come together at the bottom—yet the howl that arises to the Heavens from out of that vapor you dare not try to recount.

"You stand upon the edge of this cliff. You gaze into the gulf—you fall ill and giddy. Your first instinct is to recoil from the peril. Inexplicably you stay. Gradually your illness and giddiness and terror become mingled in a fog of nameless sensation. By degrees yet more indistinguishable this cloud takes shape…yet out of this *your* cloud upon the cliff's brink there develops into palpability a shape far more horrible than any apparition or specter of a tale—and yet it is but a notion—although a frightful one—and one which makes one's blood run cold with the ferocity of the rapture of its terror. It is purely the notion of what would be your impression during the sweeping impetuosity of a drop from such a height. And this drop—this surging destruction—for the very reason that it entails that one most hideous and heinous visions of death and misery which have ever suggested themselves to your imagination—for this very reason do you now the most vitally covet it. And because your reason vehemently averts you from the verge *therefore* do you the most impulsively approach it. There is no emotion in nature so infernally impulsive as that of him who, trembling upon the brink of a cliff, thus contemplates a plunge. To wallow for an instant in any attempt at *reflection* is to be inescapably lost; for deliberation but spurs you to indulge and *therefore* it is—you say—that you *cannot*. If there be no hearty hand to restrain you—or if you fail in an abrupt attempt to prostrate yourself backward from the gulf—you plummet and are engulfed.

"Now recall Poe's *Descent into the Maelstrom*…

"Fix your eyes once more on the pendulum. Imagine it still swinging backward and forward—now directly in front of you—then directly across the table. Now imagine it changing direction. Imagine it once more moving clockwise and going round the circumference of the vortex—the whirlpool—the waterspout. Now concentrate and look deep and dead center into the middle of the whirlpool. Fix your eyes onto its shifting eddies and currents—ever changing and erratic—turning and twisting, ebbing and flowing, coming and going—spinning like a top, round and round, in and out—captivating you, enticing you, luring you, drawing you towards it—into it.

"Now close your eyes. Imagine that you're falling forwards—falling right forwards. Imagine yourself falling, falling, falling right forwards. Excellent! There you go now—you
can imagine yourself falling—you can feel yourself falling forwards. That's it! Imagine it! Excellent! You can feel yourself
falling—falling forwards. You're falling right forwards—falling, falling all the time. You can really feel it—falling forwards.

"Now tell me, Nicolino, are you afraid of falling?"

"No," I answered automatically. "I feel drawn towards the
edge. I feel tempted to leap from the cliff. I feel I'm no longer
subject to gravity—that I can glide through the air without
hurting myself. What I fear is not falling dead—but rather it's
the actual falling itself—not the result of it."

"You fear the fall and not the fallout."

"Yes."

"At your own pace then," Dr. Valdemar directed me, "you'll
begin to return to a fully alert, wide-awake state. Begin to
move a little—very slowly and at your own pace—beginning
to open your eyes, returning to an alert state, feeling relaxed,
refreshed and wide awake. You may be quite unaware that
you've made any movement—as when the pendulum swinging
from your hand began to swing from side to side in response to
tiny, unconscious sideways tremors made by suggestion. Now
open your eyes and tell me what you see."

§

Gradually I blinked open my eyes and what I saw startled
and shocked me. Far off below the cold, deep blue waters of
the Pacific Ocean truly did spill against the shore, frothing and
foaming as the rushing rollers ebbed and flowed all along the
rock-bound seacoast! Westward the swiftly setting sun was
throwing its bright light upon the glimmering waters, lighting

up the coast's hilly outlines with a blinding orange glare while northward the haze of a misty gray fog seeped in and settled onto the facing coast, spreading a long and lurid shadow across the spotted *Marin* headlands. And beyond the woodsy bluffs toward the east loomed the lofty twin terra cotta towers of the *Golden Gate Bridge.*

A blustering gust of wind blowing up into my face stirred my blood, arousing me enough to make me realize—with spine-chilling fear—that I was reeling to and fro, my feet slipping at the very gravelly brink of a sheer and soaring cliff overlooking the choppy waters flowing through the *Golden Gate!* Agitatedly I flinched and shrank as I riveted my eyes on a towering rock monolith shooting straight up out of the surging surf far away below. Dr. Valdemar had a fast and firm hold on my arm as he forcibly dragged me backwards to sink down together onto a low, green-painted wooden bench set along the elevated seaside trail!

"God!" I cried. "How in the world did I get here?"

"You drove us here," Dr. Valdemar answered with a cool nonchalance. "In my car."

"No! I can't believe it!"

"Look around you," he ordered. "You have no choice but to believe it. You cannot help but believe it. You took us here—purposely and of your own free will."

"No!" I shook my head madly. "It's too unbelievable! I still can't believe it! I refuse to believe it!"

"Like it or not," he said sternly, "you must. And you will."

"So this is what you have in store for me," I asked, conspicuously perturbed, "putting me in mortal fear of my life as part of some outlandish experiment?"

"Hardly," he said calmly. "What I have in store for you is a rare, exciting, pioneering—and profitable—new experiment. As life-crippling and threatening as any physical danger are the many fears and phobias which plague the human psyche. So what I propose to do is to prove through hypnosis that a person of imagination and invention such as yourself has within himself the wherewithal to conquer his fears—whatever they may be."

"All I have to say," I said, heaving a heavy self-consoling sigh, "is that you have a most grotesque and peculiar way of proving your point."

"Excellent!" Dr. Valdemar exclaimed, congratulating himself. "Then I will take that as a fitting and vindicating tribute to my first test. Shall we return to my parlor then and take the plunge?"

JOSEPH COVINO JR

EIGHT:

MINGLING WITH MYSTERY

"And, veritably, Sol is right enough.
The general tuckermanities are arrant
Bubbles—ephemeral and so transparent—
But this is, now,—you may depend upon it—
Stable, opaque, immortal—all by dint
Of the dear names that lie concealed within 't."—Poe
poem: ***An Enigma***

Back inside the darkened closed-in parlor I was restfully reclined at length on the sleeper sofa as Dr. Valdemar, seated attentively once more in his sidechair, questioned me about my first hypnotic induction—*V.* standing for Dr. Valdemar, *N* standing for Nicolino:

V. "You dozed most of the ride back. How do you feel?"

N. "I still feel a little sleepy."

V. "Describe your feelings to me."

N. "I feel like I've been a very long way away."

V. "Away to where?"

N. "Nowhere in particular. Just far away and wandering."

V. "Tell me what you remember."

N. "More or less everything."

V. "Do you have any ideas or impressions you'd care to discuss with me? You look like you have something on your mind?"

N. "I still feel sleepy."

V. "Did you resent waking up?"

N. "Yes—just a little; or rather where and how I woke up."

V. "Your eyes are still trying to close."

N. "Yes."

V. "You'll wake up soon. Soon you'll be fully awake. You'll feel relaxed. In most cases the drowsiness induced by the trance does not usually persist as long as it has this time. Do you have any other sensation?"

N. "I just feel like I could sleep for a very long time."

V. "It may take a few moments before you wake up completely. I think you'll make an excellent subject. I think I'll be able to train you to enter into a very deep trance state. What do you think?"

N. "Sounds promising—I suppose."

V. "You sound like you have mixed feelings. You must be absolutely certain you wish to continue. What was your first reaction to the suggestions I gave you?"

N. "At first I felt I wasn't hypnotized at all. And then I realized I was."

V. "What made you realize that?"

N. "I was so absorbed by the images you created I got lost in them."

V. "You're not alone. Most people feel they haven't been hypnotized when they come out of a trance. But once they are in a trance state they usually don't want to come out of it."

N. "I didn't feel I was really asleep either."

V. "The feeling you're not really asleep isn't mistaken because you really aren't asleep. You're simply in a mild state of relaxation in which you feel that suggestions have an effect in spite of yourself. Did you feel things happening in spite of yourself?"

N. "Yes I did. When I was falling I thought it wasn't really going to happen like I was dreaming. And then I could feel it."

V. "Feel what?"

N. "Like I was falling—irresistibly—and being sucked into the whirlpool—and the butterflies you get in your stomach from great heights. It really shocked me."

V. "Excellent!"

N. "Why?"

V. "Because even in the waking state suggestion is extremely powerful. A single word or phrase can make a person feel happy, sad, angry or afraid and evoke all the physical symptoms which accompany such feelings. In the waking state however only a very small part of your available mind power is affected by suggestion. If we assume the brain holds so many units of mind power we can imagine them jumping all around like a thousand monkeys in a cage. If we then imagine a stream of suggestion going straight into the brain it will be seen that only a few units will be concentrated in the center by hypnosis then all the units will take a dose of suggestion. You could call it the utmost suggestion."

N. "What would I do with a dose of the utmost suggestion?"

V. "Make the most of it."

§

We stood together at Dr. Valdemar's downstairs threshold, bidding each other goodbye when out of nowhere from the lurid darkness of the foyer emerged another unknown but youthful stranger.

There are some topics upon which I delight in being meticulous. The person of the stranger is one of these topics. In height he may have been below rather than above the average stature: although there would be instants of extreme emotion when his figure actually enlarged and negated the allegation. The light, almost slim symmetry of his frame pledged more prompt vivacity than vibrant strength which he had been known to employ without an exertion upon occasions of perilous crisis. With the mouth and chin of an Adonis—peculiar, impetuous, full, fluid eyes whose shades vacillated from perfect brown to vivid and radiant black—and a profusion of wavy, dark hair from which a forehead of uncommon width shined forth discontinuously all bright and white—his were features than which I have beheld none more gracefully uniform. But his face was nonetheless one of those which all men have beheld at some time of their being and have never afterwards beheld again. It had no unusual—it had no established prevalent expression to be fixed upon the memory; a face beheld and immediately forgotten—but forgotten with an obscure and never-ending wish of recollecting it. Not that the ghost of every swift emotion failed at any time to cast its own explicit likeness upon the mirror of that face—but that the mirror, mirror-like, kept no trace of the emotion once the emotion had retreated.

"Permit me to introduce—before you leave us—another

of my most remarkable subjects who's arriving just now for his session: Mr. Theodore Templeton," Dr. Valdemar pronounced politely. "We share a unique affinity as he suffers his own *William Wilson* syndrome, so to speak, being afflicted with a near exact but unrelated lookalike who rather pompously presumes to be not only his equal, but also his superior in all respects."

Silently the youth smiled with a brief bow and again I nodded a slight acknowledgement. And at the same instant Theodore Templeton had departed up the staircase as abruptly as he had appeared.

§

"Extraordinary!" Dr. Kerwin Usher exclaimed, sitting at ease in an old armchair covered in oatmeal-colored linen but listening intently as I finished recounting my hypnotic induction with Dr. Valdemar. "It just goes to show that hypnosis can evoke uncommon occurrences not possible in the waking state."

Together we relaxed and conversed in the snug ground-level sitting room inside Dr. Usher's four-floor terrace house bordering *Buena Vista Park*. Above us the low ceiling was painted with tree-like images and spotted with gold stars. Around us the stenciled walls looked like faded old silk. Partly the walls were covered in a bright flowered paper with framed watercolor pictures—mostly of gardens and country cottages—hung at angles to reduce glare.

"It all feels a bit theatrical and melodramatic to me." I sat across from Dr. Usher in a facing armchair slip-covered in Old Rose chintz munching mixed nuts from a burgundy and white snack tray. "It seems like he performs these stunts because he enjoys shocking people—but for what I can't figure out. What do you think about Dr. Valdemar's style of hypnotic spectacle?"

"It can be entertaining," he conceded, collecting his

thoughts. "Frankly I find such exhibitions to be an undignified display. Such spectacle is on a par with staging surgical operations for entertainment purposes."

"Voyeuristic entertainment." I put down the snack tray onto the long, polished and low-set coffee table overspread with a length of damask fabric set between us.

"Someone like Dr. Valdemar is concerned more with his own self-glorification than with furthering the craft of hypnotism. But then again many people regard hypnosis as a stage stunt anyway and put it in the category of stage sorcery."

"Like a circus sideshow."

"Have some more brandy." He reached for the partly filled bottle in the middle of the coffee table clutter of ivory and mother–of–pearl boxes, stacked snack trays, a tea set and breakfast china and poured our glasses. "Unfortunately far too many people crave sensation and the mass media are only too happy to pander to their craving. Anyone who can put on a good show and perform astounding feats suddenly becomes some glorified guru whose sensational pronouncements become much more credible to a gullible public than the sober, boring truth. And even if their fallacious pronouncements are challenged and corrected by some competent and qualified authority it's unusual for the truth to be more than obscurely publicized."

Dr. Usher leaned forward to stress the seriousness of his sentiments and an English lamp set next to his armchair threw dim light on his handsomely reddened and sun-burnished features.

"Just remember," he said gravely, "hypnosis is no parlor game to be played at by tricksters."

"Some people will fall for anything I suppose. But aren't we supposed to take what our so-called experts say on trust?"

"That depends of course on the expert and your point of view," he said. "Unhappily hypnosis has been associated with charlatanry and quackery for so long that it's still steeped in superstition and secrecy. In the minds of many people it continues to be associated with the mysterious and magical. In the minds of others it's a useless and sometimes dangerous exercise."

"Then perhaps it should make more sense to the superstitious though I'm tempted to think it's something magical myself."

"The person who believes in superstition has in fact hypnotized himself for he has bypassed the critical faculty of his mind—his sense of judgment—and has implanted, unknowingly perhaps, a process of selective thinking. He has bypassed his sense of judgment and put selective thinking in its place."

"Do you think Dr. Valdemar's a charlatan—or a quack?"

"Far from it," Dr. Usher said with a dismissive shake of his head. "He's quite a distinguished and well-respected practitioner in his field—hypno-analysis—though some of his theories and practices have been considered unconventional and unorthodox to say the least."

"What do you think of him personally?"

"That's harder to say. But many hypnotists tend to be rather curious characters anyway, myself included—downright eccentric, as it were. When hypnotizing others they sometimes try to gratify the innermost impulses of their own peculiar personalities. Some have an incurable craving—though cunningly concealed—for power and control over other human beings. Some may try to indulge a morbid curiosity or vicariously experience a subject's state—frequently with *perverse* implications—to coin a phrase. This may manifest itself in many ways—ranging from an overt, relentless tyranny to a more subtle scheme through which he contrives to foster a dependency in his subject. His more deeply hidden desire may be to indulge certain compulsions in himself: this he may do vicariously as well by means of identifying with his subject through his subject's idiosyncrasies."

"Are these professional practices?"

"It depends on the practitioner and his purposes," he explained. "In hypnosis there's a paradoxical need for both distance and intimacy at the same time. This need to foster an intimate and connecting relationship with another human being must be kept within strict and safe bounds."

"What if the relationship has no bounds?"

"A hypnotist who believes that anything and everything is possible may become overanxious and overly ambitious," he warned ominously. "In the process he will try to exert boundless influence and control over his subject. The goal of his hypnotic induction then becomes the subject's complete compliance—with the hypnotist's motives distorted by a quest for personal aggrandizement. Should the hypnotist harbor some hostile or sinister intent the induction process becomes fraught with danger."

"Can hypnotic experiments be dangerous then?"

"Deeply distorted if not dangerous."

"Distorted how?"

"Hypnosis can be used as an effective means of exploring complex aspects of mental activity and unanswered questions about thinking, feeling and behaving," he clarified. "But it must be used with humility—and with the understanding that there are troublesome problems inherent in any experiment bearing upon the human mind—for a biased experimenter can prejudice his own test results. And a hypnotic experimenter may possess so compelling a need to prove his own theories that he will consciously or unconsciously choose submissive subjects—or suggest to them his own solutions to the tests which he subjects them to."

"Thank you." I sipped some more brandy, sloshed gently in my glass, which I raised slightly to my gracious host. "I'm most grateful for your time. So many things have crossed my mind since my last outing with Dr. Valdemar that I'm not exactly sure what to make of the situation or what to do about it."

"Then why don't you ask your questions," he suggested,

"and we'll take it from there."

§

What follows is the conversation that succeeded—with *U.* in the discussion standing for Dr. Usher and *N.* for Nicolino:

N. "Could I be exposed to any danger by taking part in Dr. Valdemar's hypnotic experiment?"

U. "Danger—or the potential for danger—can be found in almost anything—to say nothing of hypnosis. A subject could fall asleep at some pre-arranged signal in response to some post-hypnotic suggestion. So it should scarcely strain the imagination to see how a serious catastrophe could easily result should the subject be an airline pilot, a bus driver or an ordinary roadway motorist."

N. "Could my participating in this experiment do me any sort of serious harm?"

U. "Hypnosis is intrusive to the subject's mental state and is not harmless. In some ways it's like a powerful and potent drug. Used properly—in proper doses—it can be beneficial to the subject. Used improperly—in excessive doses—it can do considerable harm."

N. "What kind of harm?"

U. "An overdose of hypnosis could give one person almost complete control over another. Theoretically, at least, a hypnotist could—if he had a mind to—do a great deal of moral, psychological or even physical harm to the subject. The moral harm comes if a subject is compelled to commit acts he would not normally do if he were awake. There could be psychological harm if he did not really desire to be hypnotized or was not consciously aware he was even being hypnotized. And should a hypnotist be overly careless his subject could carry certain frightening hallucinations from the hypnotic into the waking state."

N. "What immediate dangers should I guard against?"

U. "Hypnosis and hypnotic induction can elicit all kinds of temporary aftereffects—drowsiness and confusion being among the most prevalent short-term effects. Other symptoms a subject can be afflicted with can include headaches, dizziness, nausea and tremors. Sometimes perceived body-image and self-image can be distorted. Sometimes these symptoms disappear when the hypnotic induction or sessions ends. Sometimes they persist—for they may be a continuation of hypnosis rather than a sequel to it. So they can be of long duration. Depth of trance can relate remotely to their intensity."

N. "None of that sounds too terribly ominous."

U. "Since hypnotic suggestions can have uncommonly powerful effects some subjects can easily develop some quite severe and disabling effects at some later time—the most chronic ones complained of being those of psychotic states and tendencies. A subject may start to suffer unpleasant sensations or recurring trances due to foolish or carelessly given suggestions. And because of these inexplicable occurrences the subject starts to fear damage to the mind and—in an emotional panic—he literally hypnotizes himself. Fear and anxiety provoke even more symptoms and so create a vicious cycle that may bring the subject to the very brink of hypnotically induced psychosis. Now tell me what you think hypnosis is."

N. "I thought hypnosis was just a matter of being put to sleep in a trance by some mysterious process, taking a suggestion and waking up a different person under someone else's influence and control."

U. "A typical misconception. But in spite of the risk of possible adverse aftereffects just remember that a hypnotist is only as skilled as the trance ability of his subject. The hypnotist possesses no mysterious or secret hypnotic power whatever. Such a power lies solely within his subject—the hypnotist simply has the technical skill of how to exploit and manipulate that power."

N. "So the subject is no hypnotic puppet?"

U. "Although the hypnotist continuously defines and so controls outer reality the subject is still himself. He experiences no changes in his personal standards or convictions that won't be violated—whatever the hypnotist may say. The subject still retains his unique character and identity and may refuse to accept suggestions which clash with his own personal preferences. At all times he retains control over what he will do and he may readily reject any suggestions which he perceives as threatening or dangerous."

N. "Hypnosis can put a subject in real danger in some cases?"

U. "True. But the false presumption that there's something of dominance-submissiveness in hypnosis must be corrected. The hypnotist-subject relationship lies in one person trying to influence the behavior, impressions and feelings of another. This relationship focuses on one of the most crucial questions in human life: how much influence will one person permit another to have over him?"

N. "Isn't that domination and control over a submissive person?"

U. "In reality no hypnotist can dominate or control his subject."

N. "So he can't make me do things against my will?"

U. "Correct. The subject in no way gives up his will power. He's free at all times to think and act as he pleases. And even under hypnosis he's not powerless to resist the suggestions of the hypnotist."

N. "If he *wants* to resist."

U. "Right. With hypnosis it's possible to provoke a sweeping change in those patterns of behavior and experience which make up the self—and in those controls of behavior known as volition. But don't confuse this piloting ability with power and control. That the subject is willing and gives consent is imperative. A hypnotist can't give a suggestion unless the subject is willing to take it. At all times and in all depths of hypnosis the subject posesses complete power of choice. So he responds only to suggestions that sound reasonable and agreeable to him."

N. "What happens when a subject is confronted with suggestions which sound unreasonable and disagreeable?"

U. "The subject can and often does refuse to carry out suggestions. You can resist any suggested activity that you truly don't desire to carry out. If you want to resist then you can resist—although resistance can sometimes take a tremendous effort."

N. "Resistance sounds fairly easy."

U. "Easy yes. Effortless no. Simply because the subject is agreeable to suggestions he's not going to allow anyone to dominate or control him. In every stage of hypnosis the subject is in control and can choose the suggestions he will accept or reject."

N. "How does a subject reject suggestions?"

U. "Against truly undesirable suggestions the subject has several defenses. If the crisis of undesirable suggestion arises— or if the situation suggested becomes truly intolerable—the subject can always break off the trance at any time. It's critical for you to remember that: it's your choice to enter the trance state and you can at all times choose and decide to exit it."

N. "Break off the trance how?"

U. "The subject may either wake himself up from the trance state, go into an ordinary sleep or carry on with the trance state but simply refuse to carry out the suggestions. So in all cases one of two things happens when an undesirable suggestion is given: the subject either rejects the suggestion outright or breaks off the trance completely. If he truly doesn't want to go on in the trance state he simply wakes himself up."

N. "Why would it be difficult for a subject to resist certain suggestions?"

U. "Suggestions that sound reasonable and consistent with a subject's personality are usually carried out. Unreasonable or absurd suggestions—and those inconsistent with the subject's personality may not be carried out—even if the subject is a somnambulist. And when the post-hypnotic suggestion is resisted without conscious awareness of the suggestion the subject may complain of certain psychosomatic symptoms like headache and dizziness."

N. "Could a subject ever be overpowered by a hypnotic suggestion?"

U. "In some cases suggestions that are incompatible with the subject's customary conduct or outlook may be carried out with considerable resistance. Often a colossal struggle against compliance occurs with resultant anxiety or emotional disturbance that can take on frightening intensity. This struggle can be traced to a conflict between suggestions given by the hypnotist and the unconscious suggestions of the subject's own conscience that would be violated by the post-hypnotic act. Sometimes this compulsive quality of post-hypnotic suggestions may be so intense that anxiety will force the subject into compliance."

N. "Then the real danger to hypnosis is in the suggestions a subject consciously accepts?"

U. "Exactly. When a literate person is told that he's to be hypnotized he's being told by implication that he's not only permitted but also expected to carry out behavior that he would otherwise inhibit and restrain. Even saying the word hypnosis may send an implied message that when the subject surrenders control of his behavior the hypnotist incurs a responsibility for the results. The real danger occurs when the induction process actually compels a subject to surrender his consciousness along with his will so that he's in more danger of being harmed."

N. "How does this happen?"

U. "Conscious awareness of self is something very distinct from the world that intrudes from without through so many different channels of communication. So from the very start a state is created in which each succeeding sensory stimulus from the hypnotist works less and less as though it reaches the subject from the outside world. Instead the intruding stimuli from the hypnotist become much the same as the self as if coming from the subject's own inner thoughts and impressions. Once the subject has gone under it's only in a purely proximate sense that the voice of the hypnotist is an influence from the outside."

N. "How can the subject determine whether the hypnotist is talking from inside or out?"

U. "Subjectively it's experienced as a projection of the subject's own psychic process. The hypnotist's words are the center of thoughts that the subject is thinking: the hypnotist's suggestions become his own spontaneous purposes. His suggestions don't work as something reaching the subject from without—demanding submission. To the subject they're his own thoughts and purposes—a part of himself."

N. "So the hypnotist's purposes become the subject's purposes?"

U. "In a sense. It's symptomatic of the onset of the hypnotic state that the subject appears to sink into sleep while retaining at least some sensory contact with the outside world. And by the gradual exclusion of other sensory sensations the hypnotist becomes for a time the sole representative of—or contact with—the outside world."

N. "Like the person who sleeps on the *BART* train and wakes up every time the train stops."

U. "Something like. After the induction process is completed the hypnotist no longer acts as the sole channel of communication between the subject and the outside world. Instead he becomes something that the subject carries around inside him—a secret will and purpose; a quiet voice of conscience—an unconscious part of the new personality that's emerged. In this state—the trance state—the connection through which the subject stays tied to the hypnotist becomes hidden. He's led and guided by it but he's not conscious of it—and he filters out all experiences that might force it on his attention."

N. "So it's as if the subject responds to the hypnotist without consciously hearing his words?"

U. "Yes. The hypnotist who starts out as part of the subject is after a time partly disregarded and ignored. At the very same time—on yet a deeper level—the subject is living, thinking, feeling and acting at the suggestion of the secret voice which he carries within him. It's this voice which echoes the spoken words of the actual hypnotist—turning them into the subject's own purposes. So it's not the hypnotist himself but a complex image of the hypnotist which becomes part of the subject. This image acts within the subject: it limits memories and worldly contacts, dictates purposes, inflicts inner rewards and punishments and evokes powerful effects."

N. "What forms does this image take?"

U. "As many forms as the imagination can conjure—for hypnosis is a state of mind. And this state of mind changes constantly and often. The state of mind of hypnosis can be arrived at in a moment—for a state of mind is merely a mood and hypnosis is merely a mood. How many moods have you had since you woke up this morning?"

N. "So the state of hypnosis is more imagined than willed?"

U. "Certainly. The imagination is much more powerful than the will. In any contest between the two the imagination will invariably triumph. In either the waking or the trance state hypnotic suggestion works in the same ways. But because the imagination is more vivid in the trance state—and since the situations impressed on the mind under hypnosis appear more real—the psychological and physicological responses are even more intense."

N. "Then a subject in a trance may be conscious of the hypnotic suggestion but not necessarily where—or who—it comes from? How can this be?"

U. "While it's not reasonable to expect a person to violate his own normal standards of conduct hypnosis can be manipulated to compel a subject to commit an overt act which is inconsistent with his own natural tendencies by temporarily distorting his perception of reality. In the very deepest stages of hypnosis—somnambulism—it's possible to induce visual hallucinations to such a degree that the subject will see unreal objects suggested—or on the other hand—fail to see real objects if it's suggested that he will not see them. Here then lies the power of hypnosis over and above ordinary responsiveness. Totally irrational appeals to accept a desired image as real are somehow especially effective in hypnosis and suggest that it's in fact a unique state of consciousness. But in the waking state we scrutinize, we doubt, we cannot accept the image as real."

N. "How does the hypnotist distort a subject's perception of reality?"

U. "By bypassing the mind's critical faculty and implanting selective thinking in its place."

N. "Critical faculty?"

U. "Yes. Under hypnosis a person has control of more than his free choice or will power. He's in control of all his mental faculties except one. He can hear, see, feel, smell, taste, speak. Although he may sometimes look unconscious he's totally aware and can cooperate. The one exception to this control is the critical faculty. If you give him a suggestion which pleases and satisfies him—and which strikes him as emotionally and morally reasonable—he'll accept it in spite of the fact that under normal circumstances he might consider it an unreasonable suggestion. The critical faculty of your mind then is that part which passes judgment. It differentiates the impressions of hot and cold, sweet and sour, big and small, dark and light. If we can bypass this critical faculty—in such a way that you no longer differentiate such things—then we can substitute selective thinking for conventional judgment-making."

N. "What's selective thinking?"

U. "Selective thinking is whatever you believe in wholeheartedly. If you're led to believe that you can fall from a cliff unharmed—and you believe it wholeheartedly—you'll let yourself fall. Let the slightest doubt creep in and intrude and the selective thinking disappears—the critical faculty is no longer bypassed. Selective thinking disappears not only when doubt intrudes but also when fear does. The instilling of fear induces a defensive reaction which brings the critical faculty back into focus."

N. "How does a subject get to that point where his critical faculty is replaced by selective thinking?"

U. "By means of a certain hypnotic logic. A person who's truly deeply hypnotized can be compelled to see an imaginary person sitting in a chair in front of him with such clarity that he believes the figure to be real—and can describe him in detail. If the subject is asked to describe the back of the chair in which this figment of imagination sits he will do this as well—without showing any surprise that the person while sitting there has gone utterly transparent. This simple acceptance of the impossible is known as trance logic."

N. "So the subject does lose control of himself once his critical faculty has capitulated to selective thinking or trance logic?"

U. "No. Suspension of the critical faculty doesn't change the fact that the subject is in complete control of himself and has complete power of choice. He accepts such an unreasonable suggestion as the transparent person because it's somehow reasonable and agreeable to him—it's in some way of value and benefit to him. But his critical faculty—the doubt that such a fantastic feat like a chair showing through a person's body—is bypassed in hypnosis."

N. "Then the purpose of hypnosis is to ensure that things like doubt and fear don't interfere with selective thinking and trance logic?"

U. "Correct. Negative perceptions can pass through your mind. Conscious doubt, disbelief and skepticism can all interfere with selective thinking and trance logic. That's why doubtful and fearful suggestions are mostly much more effec-

tive while the subject is in a state of hypnosis—for in that state
the critical faculties are almost completely curtailed."

N. "But isn't the subject supposed to forget hypnotic suggestions once the trance has ended?"

U. "It doesn't matter in the least if the suggestions aren't
consciously recalled after hypnosis. It's likely better that they
should be disregarded and ignored at the conscious level—for
then they're immune to critical judgment, doubt and fear."

N. "It's hard to believe that your mind can disregard or
ignore a suggestion it consciously accepted."

§

"And—strange, oh strangest mystery of all," Dr. Usher
abruptly interrupted our original question–and–answer discussion, "you've discovered—in the most ordinary things of
the world—you've derived from numerous entities in the material world a sensation such as you sensed always stirred within
yourself—yet not the more could you define that sensation, or
scrutinize or even steadily study it."

"Exactly!" I blurted out. "I've perceived and sensed it in
the very large and lustrous eyes of my own Lenore!"

"If you've done that," Dr. Usher said forebodingly, "you've
not only put yourself on the threshold of hypnosis—bypassing your critical faculty—but if you really felt like you were
somewhere else then and there—and put yourself there mentally—then you were hypnotized. Sometimes dreams are so
shocking that you awaken yourself. You don't realize it—but
this too is hypnosis. You knew the dream was unreal—yet it
appeared remarkably real to you."

"When the unreal becomes real," I muttered mindfully,
"anything is possible…"

"When the unreal becomes real," Dr. Usher cautioned,
"the danger you asked about—the leap in the proverbial dark;
the stumbling between life and death—becomes all too pos-

sible—even probable. But this is doubtless more true for some people than others."

"How do you mean?"

"There are some people who have a unique ability for looking into the pool of their unconscious. From this pool they may readily draw out latent impulses and compulsions which can come to the fore in either straightforward or symbolic terms. A particular subject may be transported into a kaleidoscopic world of color. Within the limited term of the trance induction he might even act out nightmarish fantasies and flights of fancy. These rare responses are mostly seen in people who possess a singular ability to enter the twilight zone of consciousness—with altered awareness—even in the waking state. When this happens they may conjure up visions or plunge into actions which can inspire extreme fear. Such dreamlike delusions suggest the endless range of thought and emotional processes at work in hypnosis which go beyond the narrow stream of consciousness existing in everyone—but to which only a few have ready access. Under such conditions a curtain is drawn over outer stimuli and inner processes take over. You could possibly be one of these exceptional persons blessed with these special abilities."

"How could I know or find out?" I asked curiously.

"We learn by experience—by keeping the same open-minded attitude of experimentation—accepting no doctrines or dogmas on faith without the strongest supporting evidence. Such an attitude is imperative for anyone who wishes to take part in the advancement of the esoteric arts. Perhaps I'm simply rephrasing the old saying that experience is the best teacher—but I insist that my subjects learn by doing rather than by merely discussing."

"Did you have an experience in mind which I could learn from?"

"An induction."

"By all means."

NINE:

THOSE HAUNTED HEIGHTS

"I have no time for idle cares
Through gazing on the unquiet sky.
And when an hour with calmer wings
Its down upon my spirit flings—
That little time with lyre and rhyme
To while away—forbidden things!
My heart would feel to be a crime
Unless it trembled with the strings."—Poe poem:
Romance

Methodically I carried my thoughts back and re-traced my steps across the tiled walkway lead-ing up to the front door of Dr. Kerwin Ush-er's house. A stained glass window above the door with crest-shaped insets lighted up when he graciously greeted me there on the threshold and bid me welcome, hold-ing out both hands to me and inviting me inside. A globe-shaped lighting fixture hanging from the ceiling brightened the small foyer and I noticed the door and light switch inside were framed in painted marble. And near the door drawings of Gothic stained-glass designs hung above a Gothic chair. Also in the foyer a pair of mother–of–Oriental–pearl lacquer boxes were set out on an altar table—over which a bouquet of dried roses sprouted from a vase set on a wall-hung plaster console.

Along the short, crowded and narrow hall we passed by a burl walnut console, a table bearing two wooden candlesticks, a sculpture resting upon a painted cupboard, a French mir-ror hung above a carved Japanese settee and a Regency butler's bed chest. Dr. Usher showed me the way past a free-standing, pivoting paneled screen separating the foyer from the sitting room, where he invited me to sit down in the more comfortable looking of two armchairs. Reflected in the part of the long, polished coffee tabletop uncovered by damask was a large Irish secretary with a round, convex wall-mirror reflecting the entire room. In the sitting room overspread with a Bokhara embroi-dery was a table upon which stood two lamps with shades made from ordinance survey maps along with some china. Lining the walls beyond were a walnut cabinet, a sofa upholstered in kilim rug fabric and draped with chintz and a chair slip-cov-ered in toile.

§

In a few moments more I was in my room dying. Dr. Usher was horrified by the frightful transformation which the fleet-

143

ing interlude had elicited in me. My countenance displayed a somber complexion; my eyes were utterly lightless; and my gauntness was so drastic that my flesh had been broke open by my cheek-bones. My spittle was extreme. My pulse was hardly discernible. I maintained nonetheless in a decidedly singular way both my mental vitality and a certain extent of physical strength. I spoke with clarity. I was propped up in my death-bed by pillows.

Even as Dr. Usher squeezed my hand it was his opinion that we had not a moment to lose as I was declining rapidly.

Grasping my hand Dr. Usher implored me to declare as clearly as I could whether I was wholly willing that he should carry out the experiment of hypnotizing me in my then state— *in articulo mortis.*

"Yes, I want to be hypnotized"—I answered weakly but audibly, adding instantly afterwards, "I am afraid you have delayed it for too long."

I was already in the agonies of death and Dr. Usher directed his stare totally into my right eye.

By that time my pulse was indiscernible and my breathing was noisy and at interims of half a minute.

That state was almost unchanged for a quarter of an hour. At the end of that time however a spontaneous although a decidedly heavy sigh emanated from my breast and the noisy breathing stopped—that is to say, its noisiness was no longer evident; the interims were unabated. My limbs were of a stone cold frigidity.

The glazed roll of my eye was altered for that look of apprehensive *inward* exploration which is never perceived except in cases of hypnosis and which it is quite impossible to misinterpret. My eye-lids fluttered as in inceptive sleep until they shut entirely and my extremities totally stiffened—after Dr. Usher soothed them in an apparently comfortable position. My legs were at full length; my arms were almost so and relaxed on my death-bed at a reasonable reach from my loins. My head was very slightly raised.

Later on I still lay in the very same position; my pulse was indiscernible; my breathing was easy—barely perceptible except through employment of a mirror to my lips; my eyes were shut naturally; and my extremities were as stiff and as frigid as stone. Yet my prevailing appearance was definitely not that of death.

Dr. Usher resolved to risk some words of dialogue.

"Nicolino," he asked, "are you asleep?" I gave no answer but he observed a quiver about my lips and so was prompted to repeat his question over again. At its third repetition my entire form was convulsed by a decidedly slight shuddering; my eyelids unshut themselves so far as to exhibit a white line of the ball; my lips moved languidly and from between them—in a barely audible murmur—emanated the words:

"Yes;—asleep now. Do not wake me!—let me die so!"

There Dr. Usher felt my extremities and found them as stiff as ever. He questioned me once more:

"Do you still feel pain in your chest, Nicolino?"

My reply then was instant but even less audible than before:

"No pain—I am dying."

Dr. Usher addressed me again, saying:

"Nicolino, do you still sleep?"

As before some moments expired before an answer was given; and during the interim I appeared to be gathering my strength to speak. At Dr. Usher's fourth repetition of the question I said very softly—almost inaudibly:

"Yes; still asleep—dying."

Dr. Usher decided however to speak to me again and simply repeated his question.

While he spoke there came a conspicuous change over my face. My eyes rolled themselves gradually open—the pupils disappearing upwardly; my flesh extensively took on a cadaverous complexion, looking like not so much parchment as ghostly paper; and the rounded agitated blotches, which up to then had been sharply demarcated in the center of my cheek, *blew out* all at once. I employ this wording because the abruptness of their disappearance placed me in mind of nothing so much as the dousing of a candle by a whiff of air. My upper lip at the very same time contorted itself away from my teeth which it had before masked fully; while my lower jaw dropped with an audible snap, leaving my mouth wide open and exposing to full view my blackened and protruded tongue. I suppose that Dr. Usher had been unused to death-bed terrors; but so beyond invention was my appearance at that instant that there was a conspicuous springing back from the area of my death-bed.

There was no longer the slightest vestige of life in me; and deducing me to be dead Dr. Usher was delivering me to the care of the undertakers when a robust vibratory movement was perceptible in my tongue. This went on for maybe a minute. At the end of that time there emanated from my swollen and immovable jaws a voice—such as it would be insanity in me to try recounting. There are in fact two or three labels which may be deemed appropriate to it in part; I may state for instance that the noise was raspy and fitful and unresonant; but the frightful totality is inexpressible for the simple reason that no comparable noises have ever jolted upon the hearing of humankind. There were two details nonetheless which I felt then and still feel may reasonably be asserted as distinctive of the intonation—as well suited to impart some impression of its uncanny singularity. First and foremost the voice appeared to fall upon the ear of Dr. Usher from a remote distance or from some sunken bowels of the earth. Secondly it struck him—I am afraid in fact that it will be impossible to make myself understood—as viscid or viscous substances strike the senses of touch.

I have made mention of both noise and of voice. I intend to state that the noise was one of sharp—of even wondrously, strikingly sharp—inflection. I *pronounced*—plainly in reply to the question Dr. Usher had proposed to me a few moments before. He had asked me it will be recalled if I still slept. I then stated:

"Yes;—no;—I *have been* sleeping—but now—now—I *am dead.*"

Dr. Usher didn't even pretend to contradict or try to suppress the unspeakable, shivering terror which these scant words so spoken were so amply contrived to impart. My own impressions I would not feign to make explicit to the reader.

It lasted in all respects as I have last recounted it with the exception that the mirror no longer provided proof of breathing. The only sure sign in fact of the hypnotic impact was then perceived in the vibratory motion of my tongue whenever Dr. Usher posed to me a question. I appeared to be making an attempt to answer but had no longer adequate will.

My state stayed exactly the same. It was apparent that so far death—or what is normally called death—had been suspended by the hypnotic method. It appeared evident to Dr. Usher that to awaken me would be simply to ensure my instantaneous or at least my rapid disintegration.

All this time I stayed *precisely* as I have last recounted. Dr. Usher finally decided to carry out the experiment of awakening or trying to awaken me. The first sign of recovery was indicated by a partial drop of my iris. It was recognized as especially striking that this falling of my pupil was attended by the copious out-pouring of a yellowish fluid—from beneath my eye-lids—of a putrid and intensely repulsive smell.

Then Dr. Usher suggested a wish to have me posed a question. He did so as follows:

"Nicolino, can you describe to me what are your impressions or desires now?"

There was an immediate recurrence of the agitated blotches on my cheeks; the tongue fluttered or rather vibrated wildly in my mouth—although my jaws and lips stayed stiff as before; and at length the same frightful voice which I have already recounted burst forth:

"For God's sake!—quick!—quick!—put me to sleep—or quick!—awaken me!—quick!—*I tell you that I am dead!*"

"Relish your singular vision for another moment longer," I heard Dr. Usher tell me in a deliberate and low voice. "And then I'll begin to count from one to ten and as I count from one to ten you will begin coming back to full consciousness. And you'll come back feeling refreshed as if you had a long rest. Come back feeling alert and relaxed. Begin to come back now. Begin to open your eyes. Open your eyes and come all the way back—feeling wonderful. Very, very good."

For what actually occurred though it is quite impossible that any mortal could have been ready.

Amidst exclamations of dead! dead! positively *bursting* from my tongue and not from my lips my entire form all at once—within the span of a solitary minute or even less shriveled—corrupted—positively decomposed beneath my own hands. Upon my death-bed before Dr. Usher's eyes there lay an almost molten lump of disgusting—despicable putrescence.

§

"And then," Lenore recounted to me at length, "from the ruin and the abyss of my normal senses there seemed to have emanated within me a sixth—all faultless. In its employment I discovered an untamed *rapture*—yet a rapture still physical insofar as the perception in it had no part. Movement in my carnal form had totally stopped. No muscle fluttered; no nerve tingled; no artery palpitated. But there appeared to have emerged in my brain *that* of which no words could impart to the purely mortal capacity even an imperceptible concept. Let me call it a pendulous pulsation. It was the virtuous incarnation of man's metaphysical concept of *Time.* By the perfect adjustment of this motion—or of such as that—had the orbits of the basic globes themselves been balanced. By its help I appreciated the caprices of the clock upon the mantel and of the watches of the companions. Their ticking fell resonantly upon my ear. The slightest deflection from the true adjustment—and those deflections were omnipresent—moved me just as transgressions against metaphysical truth are given to move the virtuous sense. Although no two of the timepieces in the room struck particular seconds precisely together yet I had no difficulty in keeping firmly in mind the tones and the particular instantaneous inaccuracies of each. And that—that acute, faultless, self-existent sensitivity to time—this sensitivity existing—as man could not possibly have envisioned it to exist—exclusive of any sequence of events—this concept—this sixth sense, uprising from the cinders of the rest, was the first perceptible step of my unearthly spirit upon the threshold of the earthly Eternity.

"It was midnight; and you still sat beside me. Everyone else had left the house of Death. They had placed me in the coffin. The lanterns burned flickeringly; for that I perceived by the fitfulness of the repetitive strains. But abruptly those strains dwindled in clarity and in intensity. Finally they stopped. The scent in my nostrils melted away. Figures touched my eyesight no further. The harshness of the Darkness upraised itself from my breast. A blunt shock like that of electricity permeated my form and was succeeded by the complete loss of the concept of contact. Everything of what man has called sense was fused into the solitary perception of being and in the sole lasting sensitivity to time. My human body had been at length seized with the grip of the mortal *Decay*.

Yet had not all of sensitivity left; for the perception of the sensitivity surviving furnished some of its faculties by a listless instinct. I perceived the ominous change then in conversion upon the flesh and as the dreamer is at times cognizant of the physical presence of one who hovers over him—so I still bluntly sensed that you sat beside me. So also when the noon of the second day arrived I was not uncognizant of those movements which dislodged you from my side, which confined me within

149

the coffin, which placed me within the hearse, which conveyed me to the pit, which lowered me within it, which piled heavily the dirt upon me and which so left me—in darkness and decay—to my sorrowful and somber sleeps with the worm.

"And there—in the cell which has scant mysteries to expose—there wasted away the time; and the spirit watched intently every second as it flew—and without effort—took note of its flight—without effort and without intent.

"My perception of *existence* had become hourly more imperceptible—and that of pure *position* had—to a great extent—usurped its place. The concept of existence was becoming merged with that of *place*. The confined space immediately encompassing what had been my corpse was then becoming the corpse itself. At length—as frequently occurs to the slumberer—by slumber and its world alone is *Death* envisaged—at length as at times occurred on Earth to the deep sleeper—when some darting of light part startled him into awaking—yet left him part enshrouded in dreams—so to me—in the rigid grip of the *Shadow*—arrived *that* light which alone may have had the strength to startle—the light of unfailing *Love*. Men toiled at the pit in which I lay darksome. They upheaved the moist dirt. Upon my rotting bones there dropped *your* coffin.

"And then once more everything was vacuous. That hazy light had been doused. That feeble tingle had vibrated itself into stillness. Profuse *luster* had superseded. Dust had reverted to dust. The worm had fodder no longer. The perception of existence had at length totally left and there ruled in its place—in place of everything—imperious and imperishable—the potentates *Place* and *Time*. For *that* which *was* not—for that which had no shape—for that which had no perception—for that which had no sensitivity—for that which was spiritless yet of which substance composed no part—for all that nothingness—yet for all that deathlessness—the pit was still a shelter—and the corroding hours—companions."

§

Repeatedly and powerfully I kept on plunging myself into Lenore—her legs spread wide open with the backs of her knees hooked over the crooks of my sturdily braced arms—she shrieking lustily with each and every whacking thrust—until we both burst explosively together and collapsed completely spent and breathless into each other's arms on the long and low-set green wooden bench atop *Sutro Heights Park*. While she was discoursing she had abruptly plunged one of my hands up her short skirt, down her silky panties, between her satiny thighs and into her juicy, welling wetness. We had kissed gluttonously as both my hands ran through her jacket and up her blouse and bra to grasp firmly her full and supple breasts. She had gasped aloud when I lunged my body between her legs, dropped my hands, thrust them up her skirt and grasped firmly her wide hips to rashly yank down her nylons.

And then we were enfolded and unhurried in front of the crumbly, crenellated parapet—its crenels connected by steel bars running through its open embrasures—looking out on the expansive Pacific Ocean, watching a great, blazing ball of setting sun sink in a fiery orange glow toward the faraway horizon, throwing its resplendent light upon the choppy blue waters. We were alone together at the park's scarcely visited vista point—a spacious and gravelly but empty, windswept ellipse—sadly bare except for a lone cedar tree standing at its middle. There used to stand the estate of *Adolph Sutro*: the engineering and silver mining German immigrant whose famed *Sutro Baths*—at one time in the late 1800s the largest indoor saltwater swimming pools in the world—also lay in ruins far off below in their now barren but wide open space at the foot of the promontory dividing the Pacific Ocean from the *Golden Gate*: *Point Lobos*. More directly below us but somewhat northward glowed the gold and turquoise lights of the *Cliff House*, standing majestically at the sea's walled edge next to the tall and jagged *Seal Rocks* jutting out before the seashore's rippling breakwater. Southward the *Great Highway* stretched a long way off below us and was astir with the shiny lights of twilight traffic sweeping swiftly along San Francisco's *Ocean Beach*.

§

Ours was the small, white, black-and-gray trimmed two-story house with a single, small-gabled dormer and low, gray picket fence that stood at the east end of a long row of small houses strung together on the crest of *Pennsylvania Avenue* atop *Potrero Hill*. From our long and narrow upstairs bedroom in the rear of the house we could see through undraped sliding-glass doors looking out on Highway 280—then ablaze with glittering lamplight and moving nighttime traffic. And beyond glimmered the lights of the darkened berths and boat basins bordering the southwestern side of *San Francisco Bay*. Just then our rustic room was but dimly lit by the imposing metal frame of a mannequin torso converted into a soft-shaded lamp. Together we lay warmly embraced in bed on our raised sleeping platform beneath a hefty quilt woven in strips of pure white padded cotton. Over our heads hovered a tall Spanish-Mediterranean screen of rope and wood. And a low driftwood table next to a pair of white rug-covered wicker chairs bore the remains of a late-night supper on Venetian glass plates and partly filled wine glasses set beneath burning beeswax candles.

§

Missing the sparkling sheen of Lenore's eyes letters—gilt and glossy—turned more lackluster than lead. And then her eyes sparkled less and less often upon the pages over which mine pored. Lenore fell ill. Her eager eyes burned with a too—too effulgent emanation; her pallid fingers turned into the translucent waxen tint of the pit and the blue veins of her high forehead dilated and contracted unrestrainably with the currents of the most mild emotion. I perceived that she must perish—and I grappled despairingly in spirit with the forbidding Angel of Death. And the strife of my impassioned beloved was—to my amazement—even more intense than my own. There had been plenty in her austere temperament to inspire me with the presumption that—to her—demise would arrive without its horrors;—but not so. Words are powerless to impart any dispassionate concept of the ferocity of defiance with which she struggled with the Shadow. I grunted in anxiety at the pathetic sight. I would have consoled—I would have philosophized; but in the extremity of her fierce lust for life— for life—*but* for life—consolation and philosophy were alike the utmost frivolity. Yet not until the final moment—amidst the most spastic contortions of her ferocious spirit—was unsettled the superficial composure of her bearing. Her voice became more soothing—became more soft—yet I would not wish to harp upon the intemperate import of her softly enunciated words. My head spun as I listened spellbound to a theme more than ephemeral—to suppositions and ambitions which humanity had never before realized.

That Lenore adored me I should not have suspected; and I may have been mildly cognizant that—in a breast such as hers—love would have ruled no unremarkable fervor. But in death solely was I utterly inspired by the power of her passion. For long hours, retaining my hand, would she overflow before me the excess of her heart whose more than impassioned adoration equaled idolatry. How was I worthy to be so blessed by such admissions?—how had I earned to be so cursed with the dispossession of my darling in the hour of her making them? But upon this topic I cannot stand to iterate. Permit me to state merely that in Lenore's more than womanly surrender to a love—alas!—all unentitled, all undeservedly endowed I at length realized the premise of her yearning with so fiercely intense a passion for life which was then flying so swiftly away.

153

It is this fierce yearning—it is this fervent ardor of desire for life—*but* for life—that I have no power to recount—no expression able to articulate.

"God!" squealed Lenore, starting to her feet and stretching her arms overhead with a spastic movement.

And then—as if empty of emotion—she let her ashen arms drop and retired soberly to her death-bed. And as she gasped her last breaths there came merged with them a soft mutter from her mouth.

Lenore bid me to her bedside.

"It is a night of nights," she said as I drew near; "a night of all nights either to live or die. It is a deathly night for the daughters of Eden!"

I kissed her forehead and she went on:

"I am dying yet I shall live."

"Lenore!"

"The nights have never been when you could not love me—but her whom in life you did adore in death you shall idolize."

"Lenore!"

"I repeat that I am dying. But within me is a vow of that devotion—ah, how much!—which you did cherish for me, Lenore. And when my soul leaves shall the daughter live—his daughter and my twin, Lenore's. But your nights shall be nights of sadness—that sadness which is the most everlasting of sensations. For the hours of your bliss are at an end."

"Lenore!" I bellowed. "Lenore! how do you know this?"—but she turned away her face upon her pillow and—a slight shivering came over her limbs—she so died and her voice fell upon my ear no more.

§

Lenore stared down, looking troubled.

"What's wrong, my love?" I gently lifted her chin.

"You really know nothing about Dr. Valdemar." Frowning, she lifted up her anxious eyes to meet mine.

"Only what I learned at our first rendezvous. Why? Do you know him well?"

"Remotely." She looked careworn. "Only what I've gathered while watching him rehearse for his show at the theater..."

"And?"

"I'm not sure." She shook her head doubtfully. "Something about him just strikes me as being very strange."

"He impressed me too—as being more unusual than strange."

"For that matter this proposed hypnotic experiment of his sounds unnaturally strange."

"I'm confident that I can chronicle my hypnotic inductions with Dr. Valdemar and adapt the material I collect into some incredible—and salable—Poe-like prose."

"And I'm convinced that you've read enough of Edgar Allan Poe and that you've seen enough of Dr. Valdemar and plenty to spare. I think he's not only strange but dangerous."

"He certainly resorts to some strange hypnotic techniques. But he's a fascinating man and an eminent expert in his field."

"Peculiar techniques is more like it," she objected, shaking her head. "He comes off as more of a magician than an expert."

"In a way I suppose he is—a magician of the mind." I shrugged indifferently. "Besides, it's only for a few days—about two weeks to be exact."

"Where will it be carried out?" She frowned incredulously.

"I can't tell you that," I said, shaking my head. "Part of the deal that I'm sworn to by contract is strict secrecy about where I'll be and what I'll be doing."

"It sounds like you've struck the proverbial deal with the devil—a devil named Valdemar."

"For the five-figure fee he's paying me—half in advance,

the other half on completion—I can afford to keep my word."

"So you're going through with some cockeyed hypnotic experiment conducted by some dubious quack," she said disparagingly. "Can you afford to suffer the effects of that?"

"Dr. Usher assures me I can take a reasonable risk by going through with it."

"How can he or anyone else know for sure whether it'll be safe?"

"No one can no for sure—not absolutely. But I've decided to chance it. For the next thirteen days and nights—starting tomorrow—I'm going into total seclusion."

"What do you mean by total seclusion?" she asked, looking concerned.

"I mean that as part of my agreement with Dr. Valdemar," I answered ominously, "I must shut myself up completely for about the next two weeks in total isolation—with absolutely no contact whatever with anyone from the outside world—including you."

"Small wonder," Lenore said with an equally ominous solemnity, "my overpowering premonitions of death grow more portentous and foreboding by the hour!"

TEN:

THE BLACKER CAT

"Where dwell the Ghouls—
By each spot the most unholy—
By each nook most melancholy,—
There the traveller meets, aghast,
Sheeted Memories of the Past—
Shrouded forms that start and sigh
As they pass the wanderer by—
White-robed forms of friends long given,
In agony, to the Earth—and Heaven."—Poe poem:
Dream-Land

Another setting sun, ablaze in its fiery orange light, sank slowly onto the faraway skyline—this time shedding its glorious glow across the wondrous and distinctive cityscape of San Francisco. Together with Dr. Valdemar I stood in awe at the brick barricade hedging round the breathtaking vista point atop *Twin Peaks*. High up behind us hovered the three broadcast antennae of the soaring *Sutro* communications tower. Directly below us the winding two-lane boulevard turned and twisted its way round and round the grassy stepped ledges of the lofty peaks. Spreading far and wide beneath and beyond the peaks was the clustered city itself—with *Market Street* cutting its long and slender swath through closely packed, sun bleached buildings and skyscrapers all the way to the tall clock tower of the ferry building terminal on the *Embarcadero* bordering San Francisco Bay.

"Unlucky and enigmatic man!—" Dr. Valdemar rambled exuberantly but inexplicably. "confused in the shrewdness of your own invention—and perished in the blaze of your own youth! Once more in imagination I see you! Again your figure has loomed in front of me!—not—oh not as you are—in the cold valley of the shadow of death—but as you *should* be—wasting away an existence of superb *reaping* in that city of dull dreams—your own San Francisco—which is a star-adored Eden by the bay—and the wide windows of whose opulent mansions stare down with a profound and malignant import upon the mysteries of her still waters. Yes! I repeat it—as you *should* be. There are certainly other worlds than this—other reveries than the reveries of the crowd—other speculations than the speculations of the imposter. Who then will challenge your conduct? who reproaches you for your visionary hours or condemns those pursuits as a wasting away of existence—which were but the outpouring of your unending drives?"

"Are you referring to me or to yourself?" I asked, my curiosity peaked.

"Neither."

"To dream," he went on, continuing the tone of his rambling discourse—"to dream has been the pursuit of my existence. I have accordingly fabricated for myself—as you see—an arbor of dreams. In the heart of San Francisco could I have contrived a better? You look around you—it is real—a melting pot of artificial adornments. Yet the result is irreconcilable to the irresolute alone. Conventions of place—and especially of time—are the hobgoblins which horrify mankind from the pondering of the sublime. Once I was myself an imposter; but that refinement of frivolity has palled upon my spirit. All this is then the more apt for my aims. My soul is squirming in flames—and the dizziness of this view is framing me for the fiercer visions of that place of real dreams for which I am now swiftly leaving."

He there stopped unexpectedly, hung down his head to his breast and appeared to listen to a noise which I could not hear.

"What are your aims exactly?" I felt forced to ask, wavering anxiously against the observation wall.

"The realities of the world move me as visions and as visions solely," he equivocated with a wide wave of his hand, gesturing toward the sprawling city lying so out of reach beneath us, "while the freak concepts of the place of dreams become in turn—not the substance of my ordinary existence—but in very deed that existence wholly and solely in itself."

Dr. Valdemar promptly led me by a few scattered sightseers and tourists and down to a bare, brown, gravelly patch of ground at the foot of the observation wall—leading me straight out to the very edge of the peak looking out on the far off, peaked and twinkling cityscape below. A stormy, frigid gust of wind carried off a lingering layer of fog as if by a wizard's wand.

"This is indeed no dream!" I gestured to the panoramic vista before us.

"Dreams are with us no longer; but of these secrets soon,"

Dr. Valdemar said ominously. "I revel in seeing you looking realistic and rational. The shade of the shadow has already passed on from your eyes. Take heart and fear nothing. Your appointed days of stupor have expired; and the day after tomorrow I will myself induct you into the full delights and marvels of your new existence."

"Really, I feel no stupor—none at all. Yet my senses are perplexed with the sharpness of their perception of *the new*."

"A few days will eliminate all that;—" he assured me, "but I completely sympathize and feel for you. It has been years since I experienced what you are about to endure yet the memory of it hovers over me still. You have now suffered all of discomfort though which you will suffer in San Francisco."

"Most frightfully, frightfully!—this is indeed no dream."

I stared dizzily down the steep slopes plummeting beneath us as Dr. Valdemar abruptly departed from me to deliberately climb the footpath and return to his parked car. I directly followed; but a lone, starkly slender, tall and taciturn but stooped—and darkly hooded—stranger standing at the end of the observation wall suddenly addressed me in a rather raspy but faint voice.

"*Beware!*" he whispered frantically.

Stopping and squinting to rivet my eyes more fixedly upon the strange facial features protruding from beneath the dark hood I immediately recognized the figure's exaggeratedly globular eyes and crooked teeth.

"Mr. *Bedloe!*" I exclaimed under my breath. "This can't be a coincidence. What are you doing here?"

"*Beware!*" he repeated urgently. "I have harbored deep suspicions about the evil-minded designs of Dr. Valdemar for a long time now! Meet me tomorrow night at the *Cafe De La Presse* on Grant Avenue at eight o'clock before you venture to participate in his experiment! You must learn what he is plotting against you—and others—equally gullible! And keep *silent!* Your life could very well depend upon your discretion!"

Fully befuddled I stood aghast, watching Mr. Bedloe depart and recede into the dark, fog-enshrouded distance as silently and abruptly as he had materialized.

§

"There are some mysteries which do not let themselves be told," Mr. Bedloe told me in his raspy whisper. "Men perish nightly in their beds, squeezing the hands of phantasmal priests and staring at them pitifully in the eyes—perish with desperation of spirit and seizure of throat because of the frightful secrets which will not *tolerate themselves* to be divulged. Now and again—alas—the conscience of man takes on a burden so weighty in terror that it can be plunged down solely into the pit. And so the character of all crime is undisclosed."

About the end of that evening in the fall we sat together at the sizable window of the *Cafe De La Presse* on Grant Avenue at the foot of *Chinatown* in San Francisco. I took a sedate but curious interest in everything without. We had then been entertaining ourselves for the better part of the evening in watching the indiscriminate clientele in the room and then in gazing through the hazy panes into the street.

That street is one of the primary avenues of the city and had been very profusely swarming throughout the entire day. But as the night fell the crowd momentarily swelled; and by the time the street lamps were fully illuminated the dense and ceaseless currents of people were hurrying past the entrance. At that particular time of the night I had never before been in a similar state and the turbulent ocean of human heads filled me accordingly with a delectable singularity of sensation. I relinquished at length all concern with things within the cafe and became engrossed in pondering the pageant without—everything pervaded with a rackety activity which jolted harshly upon the ear and imparted a throbbing impression to the eye.

As the night intensified so intensified to me the curiosity of the pageant; for not only did the collective nature of the throng transform but the beams of the street lamps—weak at first in their strife with the dying day—had then at length gained an advantage and shed over all things a spasmodic and gaudy sheen. Everything was lurid yet resplendent.

The freak effects of the light shackled me to an inspection of specific faces; and although the swiftness with which that world of light darted in front of the window precluded me from catching more than a glimpse of each face—still it appeared that in my then strange mental condition I could often interpret—even in that fleeting interim of a glimpse—the chronicle of long years.

With my brow to the pane I was so engrossed in scanning the crowd when unexpectedly there floated before my eyes a face—that of a robust older man—a face which all at once attracted and intrigued my entire attention because of the positive peculiarity of its expression. Anything even remotely resembling that expression I had never perceived before except in the exceptionally peculiar expression of none other than: Dr. Vincent Valdemar! As I strove throughout that fleeting moment of my initial inspection to fashion some study of the significance imparted there emanated perplexedly and preposterously within my mind the notions of tremendous mental strength, of circumspection, of parsimoniousness, of greediness, of calmness, of malevolence, of murderousness, of victory, of mirth, of extreme horror, of acute—of supreme desperation. I felt exceptionally stimulated, stunned, captivated.

"How intemperate a story," I muttered to myself, "is inscribed within that breast!"

Then came a ravening need to keep the man in sight—to learn more of him.

"For your own preservation," Mr. Bedloe gravely admonished me, "you must take the precaution of following Dr. Valdemar to discover his true darker and harsher nature."

And once more Mr. Bedloe departed and was as quickly

and silently gone as he had earlier come.

Hastily putting on my overcoat I found my way into the street and pressed through the throng in the direction I had observed him take; for he had already vanished. With some minute difficulty I at length caught sight of him, drew near and followed him closely yet prudently so as not to attract his notice. And I determined to follow the hypnotist wherever he should go.

It was then wholly night-fall and a dense dank fog hung over the city—before long finishing in a precipitate and op-pressive rain. This alteration in weather had a strange effect upon the throng—the whole of which was set into fresh mo-tion and eclipsed by a world of umbrellas. The wave, the jolt and the drone burgeoned to a tenfold extent. For my own part I did not greatly consider the rain. Holding a handkerchief to my mouth I carried on. For half an hour the hypnotist wormed his way with difficulty along the grand avenue; and I there rambled at his elbow through fear of losing track of him. Never once turning his head to look behind his back he did not see me. In a while he passed on into a cross street, which although solidly packed with people, was not quite so much crowded as the main avenue he had left. There a shift in his bearing became apparent. He wandered more deliberately and with less purpose than before—more reluctantly. He crossed and re-crossed the street monotonously without evident object; and the crush was still so heavy that at every such motion I was forced to follow him closely. The street was a close and long one and his path lay within it for almost an hour—during which the passerby had slowly dwindled.

Another turn led us into the expansive 245-foot granite central plaza of *Union Square*—fringed by Canary Island date palms, radiantly illuminated and overrunning with vitality. In its middle shot up bolt upright the lofty Corinthian column atop which is perched the bronze Victory statue—dedicated in 1903—memorializing Admiral Dewey's victory over the Spanish Navy during the Spanish-American War and modeled after the countenance of a San Francisco benefactress: *Mrs. Adolph de Bretteville Spreckels.*

The past comportment of the hypnotist returned. His chin dropped upon his chest while his eyes flitted fiercely from beneath his furrowed brows in all directions upon those who hedged him in. He pressed his way steadily and persistently. I was stupefied though to perceive—upon his having gone the round of the square's terraced gardens—that he turned and retraced his steps. Still more was I astounded to watch him repeat the same ramble several circuits of the periphery—once almost discovering me as he turned around with an abrupt movement.

Round in circles we went along the stepped sidewalks lined with many-colored flower stands—in proximate sight of glittering and palatial stores: bound by *Brooks Brothers, Saks Fifth Avenue, Tiffany &* Co. and *Gump's* on Post Street to the north, *Macy's* on Geary Street, skirting three tiers of grass with benches and concrete ledges to the south; *Gucci* and *Neiman Marcus* on Stockton Street to the east; and anchored by the grandiose *St. Francis Hotel* on Powell Street to the west.

In this drill he passed another hour—at the finish of which we encountered far less obstruction from passerby than at first. The rain fell fast and furious; the atmosphere grew frigid; and the people were retreating to their abodes. With a gesture of restlessness the rambler passed on into a by-street relatively deserted. Along this—some quarter of a mile long—he hurried and worked his way back and forth.

During the hour and a half or thereabouts which we passed on in this place it demanded ample prudence on my part to keep him within sight without attracting his attention. At no time did he observe that I followed him. With his skittish and blank gaze I was then utterly astonished at his deportment and unalterably determined that we should not part company until I had appeased myself in some degree regarding him.

165

At the same instant at about eleven o'clock I observed a powerful shivering come over his form. He rushed into the street, glanced around him for a moment and then hurried with unbelievable rapidity through numerous winding and unpeopled byways until we emerged again upon the grand avenue from which we had begun—the street of the *Cafe De La Presse*. It no longer bore though the same facade. It was still radiant with lamplight; but the rain fell furiously and there were few people to be perceived. The hypnotist grew pallid. He rambled glumly some steps up the once crowded avenue; then—heaving a heavy sigh—turned in the direction of the theater district and, submerging through a vast variety of deceptive paths, emerged at length in sight of one of the foremost theaters: the *Curran*. It was about being shut down and the theatergoers were surging from the exits. I perceived the hypnotist to gasp as if for a breath of air while he flung himself amidst the throng; but I felt that his acute anguish of his visage had in some degree subsided. His head once more dropped upon his chest; he seemed as I had observed him at first. I discerned that he then shaped his course in which had passed the vast number of the public—but for the most part I was at a loss to understand the waywardness of his wayfaring.

§

Across from the checkered, brown-boothed, all-night diner called the *Pinecrest* a tall, shapely, smooth-skinned streetwalker wearing a long, sable fur coat over a tight-fitting, rump-clutching, red-sequined dress paced quickly back and forth on clicking stiletto heels across the moist sidewalk at the corner of *Mason* and *Geary* Streets not far from *Union Square*. Her long, shiny brown hair blew up in the chilly night breeze as she actively approached passerby—whether on foot or stopped in their cars at the intersection's traffic light. Out of nowhere Dr. Vincent Valdemar stepped up to her, leaning steadily on his rattan cane but keeping silent.

"Would you like some company tonight, sweetie?" the prostitute solicited him mischievously—puffs of breath fuming from her full and luscious looking mouth. "Would you like a date?"

"That depends, my dear," Dr. Valdemar said laconically.

"On what, sweetie?"

"On whether you're a free agent?"

"Whatever do you mean?"

"I'm looking for an independent woman who's her own man as it were. Or in your own parlance—a woman who isn't being pimped or pandered. I don't wish to deal with any middleman."

She jauntily held open her coat to generously display the fleshy, plump curves of her exposed breasts.

"Oh honey!" she squealed, grinning widely. "I'm all man— a real man's man!"

"Are you free then?"

"Free and easy, baby, that's me!"

"Also," Dr. Valdemar added matter–of–factly, "the lady I'm looking for will have to come in a very unladylike costume."

"Costume?"

"Exactly—a…cat–and–witch costume."

"Kinky!" she squealed again, turning stiffly serious. "It'll have to be arranged. And it'll cost you."

"Of course. Permit me to treat you to some refreshment at the diner while you quote your price and we come to terms."

"My price is five hundred bucks."

"I'll gladly double that. I'll pay you half in advance and half when you show up where you're told—alone and in proper costume—or the deal is off."

"Cool, daddy, no problem."

"There's just one more thing."

"What's that, sweetie?"

"This is a lawful and legitimate business proposition," he

said assuredly. "And you should understand quite clearly that I'm in no way soliciting you for sex. I simply want you to put in a brief appearance at a costume party—nothing more. And you will be paid very well for your time—a liberal bonus perhaps."

"Oh I expect to be paid well, sweetie—and in cold hard cash too. I'm no cheap hooker."

"That I can see for myself."

"I'm no cop either—so don't trip."

"So much the better, my dear."

§

As Dr. Valdemar advanced the crowd grew more dispersed and his past restlessness and faltering recommenced. For some time he pursued a narrow and shadowy byway little haunted. The hypnotist halted and for an instant looked lost in thought; then with every symptom of trepidation followed promptly a path which led us to the brink of the *Tenderloin* neighborhood—amidst precincts decidedly distinct from those we had heretofore traversed. It was one of the rankest districts of *San Francisco* where everything bore the worst imprints of the most disastrous privation and of the most incurable crime. By the dull light of the random lamp lofty, antiquated, worm-eaten, wooden slums were seen teetering to their downfall in all directions so numerous and whimsical that scanty the semblance of a path was detectable between them. The pavestone lay haphazardly. Terrible filth festered in the stopped-up gutters. The entire aura swarmed with desolation. Yet as we advanced the noises of mortal existence recovered by deliberate degrees and at length considerable bands of the most forsaken of a *San Francisco* crowd were seen staggering back and forth. The spirits of the hypnotist once more perked up as a lamp which is close to its death-hour. Again he strode forward with a springy pace. Abruptly a corner was turned, a blaze of light burst upon our eyesight and we stood in front of one of the sizable urban sanctums of Intemperance—one of the mansions of the demon: Gin.

It was then almost midnight; and a number of miserable drunkards still pushed in and out of the flashing entrance. With a half howl of mirth the hypnotist pressed a path within, recommenced all at once his earlier demeanor and stalked back and forth without perceptible purpose amongst the mob. It was something even more poignant than desperation that I then perceived upon the face of the peculiar person whom I had observed so perseveringly. Yet he did not falter in his calling but with a fierce drive retraced his steps all at once to the heart of the momentous city. Long and quickly he flew while I pursued him in the fiercest astonishment—resolved not to relinquish an exploration in which I then sensed an interest all-engrossing. And when we had once more arrived at that most mobbed part of the crowded city—the avenue of the *Cafe De La Presse*—it presented a prospect of mortal bustle and briskness barely inferior to what I had beheld only hours before. And there—at length—amidst the momentarily burgeoning commotion did I persevere in my pursuit of the hypnotist. But as usual he rambled back and forth and throughout the night did not pass on from out of the tumult of that street. And as the shadows of the night wore on I grew tired unto death and, halting fully in front of the rambler, stared at him unswervingly in the face. He recognized me not but recommenced his sober ramble while I, stopping to pursue, remained rapt in speculation.

"This hypnotist," I uttered at length, "is the breed and genius of profound crime. He rejects being by himself in a world of his own. He *is* Poe's *man of the crowd.* It will be in vain to pursue; for I shall discover no more of him nor of his deeds."

§

Somewhere in the east *Mission* neighborhood on *York Street*, glistening beneath lamplight from fog-steeped mist and wetness, Dr. Valdemar drove me to the dull, two-story, white-washed brick warehouse loft with the single, shaded glass-block window. He opened up the front door—part of a ground–to–roof metal gridiron framework—gesturing for me to step inside ahead of him. A lone, cane-backed settee stood in the small entry foyer. Going the round of a corrugated, curved, galvanized steel wall we stepped onto a metal grating laid down on a narrow strip of gravel. Grinding underfoot the walkway ran down a lengthy entry corridor dimly lighted by marine supply fixtures projecting in line along the walls. Where it ran out at the corridor's end we stepped across a short foot-ramp and passed through a raised, keyhole-shaped, aluminum-sided entry and into the main loft space. Opening up before us was an expansive, high-ceilinged room buttressed at intervals by a mixture of ornate, cast-iron and plain white columns. Fringing the solid red-brick walls were continuous rows of radiators and lengths of exposed white-painted pipes. From the ceiling high up protruded a structural network of exposed gray- and red-painted steel beams. And spread out beneath to all sides were the room's bleached, waxed and buffed maple wood floors painted in a marbelized checkered pattern.

"Welcome to your new home," Dr. Valdemar invited me, ushering me proudly into the room, "temporarily at least."

"Very impressive." I glanced around—spellbound.

Round a sandblasted cement column and a painted brick gas–and–coal fireplace was centered the loft's main living space: a wide and low platform raised above the room's high-gloss wood floors, covered in gray industrial carpeting and sup-porting a low partition which hedged about a big, black-leather Lota sofa, a coffee table finished in black lacquer and a pair of Transat chairs with red lacquered frames. All around the loft's main floor was divided by a train of folding screens set onto an industrial track making a long, movable, zigzagging partition wall. A blue-painted metal spiral stairway rose to mezzanine and second-story level catwalks and floors.

"Here," Dr. Valdemar announced portentously, "we will give full play to the imagination and together explore the stuff dreams are made of."

Going the round of another curved, circular wall with a glass-block inset Dr. Valdemar budged aside a pivoting, pale, pink-painted partition wall and led the way into a closed-in space dimly lit by wall sconces and furnished with a black Empire daybed and a pair of small modular slip-covered chairs. He budged another pink-painted sliding partition into place at the foot of the daybed. From the brick wall above the partition bulged a slightly spinning industrial fan blowing a gentle current of air.

"Lie down and relax here," Dr. Valdemar directed me, gesturing to the daybed. "I'll show you the rest of the loft and your living quarters upstairs a little later on. Just now we should set to work for we have much to devote ourselves to."

Obediently but comfortably I reclined upon the daybed with outstretched legs.

"Since you're interested in treating phobias," I thought out loud, "I gather then that you intend to induce certain phobias in order to deal with and hopefully do away with obsessive fears."

"As always, my dear Nicolino, you are as perceptive as ever." He sat down on one of the nearby modular chairs.

"How do you expect to go about it?"

"Through a strict search of the creative imagination."

"In particular my creative imagination."

"Creative thought is itself a mental disturbance," he elucidated. "There's very little real difference between the person in the mental hospital who believes he's *Jack the Ripper* and the hypnotized subject in the session room who thinks he's the very same villain. The hypnotized subject can quickly be brought back to normal because he's under the hypnotist's protective control. But the disturbed person in the hospital has in effect hypnotized himself—and is then most difficult to de-hypnotize."

"So you propose to hypnotize a somewhat sane person into becoming somewhat insane?"

"Or rather a somewhat imaginative person into becoming a very visionary person," he clarified, "for imagination is the impression of what does not actually exist—or at least of what does not exist to the degree imagined—and the firm conviction that this impression comes out of reality."

"The impression that the unreal becomes real."

"Exactly," he declared. "Just as the imagination makes existing impressions more perceptible—and existing sensations more vivid—it's equally potent in its effect on those impressions which arise spontaneously from no outside source. So it's quite common for the mind to dwell upon its own innermost suggestions—those offshoots of memory tempered perhaps by illusive impressions—until it believes they were prompted by some outside source which in reality never intervened at all."

"Are you convinced that I'm as imaginative as all that?"

"Among so-called sane people there's something of the visionary in all of us," Dr. Valdemar said encouragingly.

"How then do you liberate the visionary mind to give it full and free play?"

"There's something known as the brain barrier," he explained, "which hypnosis must break through. This barrier is the most chronic and relentless attribute found in those mentally disturbed. It's a very real and unyielding barrier. It restrains a subject from doing what he really wants. This explains why a subject will claim that his reason tells him that he should *not* do something—that he wants to do something but cannot. Such a subject has literally hypnotized himself—accidentally in most cases. He has accidentally induced his own brain barrier and is in fact in rapport with himself. And while his mind concentrates on his own self-made impressions he is unable to concentrate on those of others."

"Like those of his hypnotist?"

"Precisely."

"Then it's preferable for the subject to be in strong rapport with his hypnotist?"

"It's essential," he emphasized, "for as the process of inducing the hypnotic state reaches its goal—however defined—a remarkable and highly crucial change occurs: the subject once more becomes able to communicate freely and at will with the outside world. He redraws the boundary lines of his psyche— those between him and everything and everyone—including his hypnotist. At the same time the hypnotist becomes partly immersed inside him—merged and incorporated into one—a cluster of conscious and unconscious sensations—many highly charged, arising between them."

"It sounds intriguing but very complex."

"No more complex than life or death," Dr. Valdemar said fatefully. "The brain barrier can be artificially induced under controlled conditions in the experimental setting. And under these same controlled experimental conditions it can be just as easily demolished."

"So do you propose to induce a brain barrier in me and then demolish it later on?"

"In part," he conceded. "By means of induced hypnotic hallucination I propose to induce a comparatively mild fear of one kind to be cancelled out by a counteracting fear—the first fear being the barrier—the second fear being the symbolic battering ram which punches through and pulverizes it!"

"So you plan on using fear to neutralize fear?"

"Precisely. Whatever the fear or phobia—it can be conjured up in hypnosis with hallucinatory vividness and protracted for as long as needed."

"Isn't that a rather contradictory way of doing things?"

"Using one negative thing as a countervailing force against another?"

"Quite."

"Not at all." He shook his head. "In hypnosis we can fabricate negative hallucinations so the subject experiences things that don't really exist in his surroundings—but because of their special and symbolic significance to him—they can produce positive results."

"How so?"

"Ah!" Dr. Valdemar cut me short and held up a halting hand. "Therein lies the essence of the experiment. Since whatever may be considered a positive or negative result is open to drastically different interpretation we come directly to the crux of the matter: which is to induce through hypnosis an imaginary fear to gain—hopefully—a positive result. It's a simple matter of cause and effect."

"Can such an artificially induced cause have lasting effect?"

"Lasting and worthwhile," he asserted, "for hypnosis doesn't play on any impressions which can't be induced by other means. If a subject is able to see on suggestion a certain vision during a trance—and cannot do so with the same suggestion in a state of complete consciousness—we would be inclined to credit his perceptual proficiency with the hypnotic state. But we would be wrong to assume that hallucination is an exclusive hallmark of hypnosis?"

"Why's that?"

"If the same subject were sealed up in a dark soundproof room with no sensory stimulation of any kind he would sooner or later suffer imaginary impressions—or hallucinations— even though he were fully awake. Or if he were lost in a desert for days—exposed to parching hunger and thirst—he would likely see an oasis in the faraway distance as part of a mirage. In dreams we accept as normal the seeing of audible and visual images of hallucinatory vividness."

"Is it just in sleep or in pain that it's normal to have such hallucinations?"

"Hardly," he explained. "During the waking state even the most normal people can have varying and ever-changing degrees of imaginary visions or hallucinations. Under certain conditions these hallucinations may be experienced in the waking state by either outside suggestion or self-suggestion—whenever the need for such sensory stimulation is strong. So during a seance a person desperately wanting to hear the voice of a dead person may actually be able to hear it."

"What you're driving at then is a kind of hypnotic illusion conjured up by some hypnotic magician?"

"Whether wittingly or unwittingly all the melodramatic maneuvers of hypnosis are designed to concentrate the subject's attention on one field of sensation while deflecting it from all others. And whatever the hypnotic device the purpose is to induce in the subject an emotional state in which it becomes possible for him to abstract himself and—even as Poe believed possible—to let his sensory sentinels rest and show insensibility—as in death."

"How can a person's senses grow insensitive without the whole mind falling into oblivion?"

"In the normal waking state the degree of distribution of sensory information constantly defines the boundaries between mere imagery and hallucination. But in the sleeping state the episodes of dreaming prove that the mind can be partly conscious without being fully conscious—and that dreaming can devote the mind to one or several of the impressions which may be made—without necessarily perceiving them all."

"Then one part of the brain may be asleep while another part is awake?"

"Absolutely," he affirmed. "A person talking in his sleep exemplifies voluntary muscular movement. If he laughs or cries he adds more muscular movement—yet he's not fully conscious at all in the usual sense. His brain or his mind is perceptive of the thoughts which preoccupy him—and to that degree he may be partly conscious—but he's not aware of what's going on around him. By cautiously playing on one particular sense we may sometimes succeed in suggesting ideas—and so waking part of the brain without waking the person. This affects sensation as when pinching a sleeping person prompts movement and an expression of disturbance."

"So the hypnotic effects of the mind on the body are not purely imaginary?"

"Decidedly not," he declared, "although the mental state from which the effects at first grow may be nothing more than imaginary. Sudden fright has induced death. Sudden delight has done the same. And mental emotions less intense have induced and constantly do induce very imaginable effects on the body. Crying from grief, sulks from sadness, sweat from fear—all are common occurrences of the mind's power over bodily excretion. Blushing and a feeling of warmth from shame, paleness and a sense of coldness from terror, beating of the heart and dizziness from rage—these prove the very same power over blood circulation."

"Then how do you intend to treat fear—or phobia—using hypnotic hallucination?"

"By putting to the test what mesmerists of old called the great conceptualizing activity—the very nature and quality of the soul: the human imagination," he stated gravely, turning urgently toward me. "Shall we begin?"

Guardedly I nodded.

§

"You cannot rid yourself of the phantasm of the cat!" he recited in his half-heard and unhurried undertones.

Assiduously I ran my eyes over Dr. Valdemar, sitting unstrained in his tan suit, black tartan shirt and navy silk knit tie—and unexpectedly the blank partition set at the foot of the daybed prominently displayed the distinct and detailed likeness of a colossal cat upon the wall—with a phosphorescent green light thrown upon it from a spot in the ceiling once the wall sconces grew dim—and before my eyes flitted slowly shut:

"One night as you sit—half dazed—your attention is suddenly attracted to some black thing resting upon the top of one of the huge kegs of Gin or Rum which makes up the main furnishings of the tavern. You have been staring steadily at the top of that keg for some time and what then strikes you with wonder is the fact that you had not sooner noticed the thing thereupon. You approach it and pat it with your hand. It is a black cat—a decidedly big one...

"Upon your patting him he instantly arises, purrs aloud, nudges against your hand and seems entranced with your attention...

"You continue your petting and when you prepare to return home the cat displays an inclination to accompany you. You allow it to do so; sometimes stooping and stroking it as you proceed. When it arrives at your apartment it domesticates itself all at once...

"For your own part you directly discover a dislike to it emanating within you. That is just the opposite of what you had expected; but you know not how or why it is—its apparent affection for you rather revolts and irritates. By slow degrees those sensations of aversion and irritation escalate into the bitterness of hatred. You shun the beast; and gradually—very gradually—you come to look upon it with unspeakable loathing and to abscond quietly from its detestable company as from the breath of a plague...

"What adds doubtless to your loathing of the brute is the detection—on the morning after you take it home—it has been deprived of one of its eyes...

"With your abhorrence of the cat though its partiality to you appears to grow. It follows your footsteps with a persistence which it is difficult to make another understand. Whenever you sit it will crouch underneath your chair or pounce upon your knees, smothering you with its offensive nuzzling. If you arise to walk it will get between your feet and so almost trip you down, or fixing its long and sharp claws in your clothes, climb in that way to your chest. At such times—although you yearn to exterminate it with one stroke—you are yet restrained from so doing mainly—let yourself admit it at once—by perfect *fear* of the brute...

"That fear is not strictly a fear of physical depravity—and yet you should be at a loss how else to interpret it...

"You make repeated allusion to the ancient popular superstition which regards all black cats as *witches in disguise!*"

ELEVEN:

THE RAPPING, TAPPING RAVEN

*"And the Raven, never flitting, **still** is sitting, still is
sitting
On the pallid bust of Pallas just above my chamber
door;
And his eyes have all the seeming of a demon's that is
dreaming,
And the lamp-light o'er him streaming throws his
shadow on the floor;
And my soul from out that shadow that lies floating
on the floor
Shall be lifted—nevermore!"*—Poe poem:
The Raven

"**M**y mind was wandering," I told Dr. Valdemar later on. Again I was lying on the black Empire daybed inside the loft's partitioned parlor. "I could hear everything you said."

"Hypnosis is no club which knocks a person out," he said, sitting again nearby in his modular slip-covered chair. "It would be totally useless if the subject couldn't hear what the hypnotist said. You're supposed to be conscious of everything and even hyper-sensitive to stimulation and impression. We're in contact at all times. If you go in deeper your mind may even bounce around from one impression to another."

"Shouldn't I be deeper—more deeply hypnotized?"

"You will be. Once a deeper state is necessary you will be trained to go into it. It takes time for a subject to learn how to go into a deep trance."

"I could've opened my eyes anytime if I wanted to."

"Of course you could have because you were never out of control. But the fact is that you didn't want to open them."

"How can you be so sure I didn't want to open them?"

"Immediately following their first induction most subjects—even those who have gone into a deep somnambulistic trance—will deny having been hypnotized," he explained, grinning confidently. "This may be a defensive reaction against the thought of having given up some control. But it's usually the result of a mistaken impression about the nature of hypnosis—the expectation of something extraordinary. But when they find themselves pleasantly relaxed and capable of controlling their thoughts and reactions they believe they've failed to go into a state of hypnosis."

"Yes," I confirmed heartily. "I was in full control at all times and could've even resisted suggestions."

"Hypnosis is a cooperative, mutual enterprise and I never want you to lose control of yourself. In fact my purpose is to give you a better control of yourself and your faculties so you'll become stronger and more capable of exploiting them."

"When you tell me to do things then should I do them voluntarily and of my own free will?"

"It's not necessary for you to do things knowingly or by design. If you pacify your mind and make it unresistant things will happen in their natural course. Just relax and enjoy the experience of seeing how things come freely out of suggestion. You never have to try too hard."

Again Dr. Valdemar slid the pink-painted partition into place at the foot of the daybed—again dimming the room's wall sconces and projecting onto the blank screen from a ceiling spotlight yet another distinct and detailed image: that of a big black raven! And again he induced in me a hypnotic trance:

"Now I want you to have a dream," he bid me in his subdued but soothing and resonant undertones. "As soon as you have the dream your eyes will open and you will awaken with a start—as if your heart were made to skip a beat. But you will have forgotten your dream entirely. Every time you think about it your mind will go empty. But I will rap on the wall three times and when you hear the third rap the dream will suddenly pop into your head and you will tell me about it. Do you understand what you are to do upon awakening?"

"Yes," I murmured. My eyes fluttered and my breathing grew shallow as my mouth hung partly agape.

"And once you hear the rapping," he continued, "you will carry out the suggestion I give you. Now listen to me carefully. From now on it will no longer be necessary for you to go through the process of hypnotizing each time you come here. When I give you a certain cue or signal—such as this rapping—you will immediately and easily go into a trance state as deep as the one you're in now."

Dr. Valdemar rapped and tapped the nearby curved, circular wall with his signet ring three times.

"Do you understand?"

"Yes," I muttered.

"Now I'm going to awaken you. As soon as I awaken you I'm going to give you the cue-signal. The moment you get the signal you will again fall into a sleep as deep as the one you're in now. Do you understand?"

"Yes."

"Do you understand that you are to go into a deep trance state when I give you the signal?"

"Yes."

"Once upon a midnight dreary, while I pondered, weak and weary," Dr. Valdemar recited forbiddingly from the Edgar Allan Poe poem: **The Raven.** *"Over many a quaint and curious volume of forgotten lore—while I nodded, nearly napping, suddenly there came a tapping, as of some one gently rapping, rapping at my chamber door..."*

Briefly Dr. Valdemar paused to let me fully hear and comprehend the full weird and uncanny eeriness of his words.

"And that is your signal," he said solemnly, "Quoth the Raven, *Nevermore!*"

§

That cat was a singularly big and beautiful brute—wholly black—and shrewd to an astounding degree...

Pluto—that was the cat's name—was my darling pet and playmate. I alone fed him and he accompanied me wherever I went about the apartment. It was even with difficulty that I could stop him from following me through the streets...

Our companionship continued in this way for a long time during which my prevailing temperament and disposition— through the medium of the Demon Intemperance—I had—I blush to admit it—underwent a drastic change for the worse. I became day by day more irritable, more moody, more heedless of the feelings of others. I let myself use vulgar language...My cat naturally was forced to sense the change in my temper. I not only ignored but abused him…And my sickness grew upon me—for what sickness is like Alcohol!—and at length even Pluto—who was then growing old and therefore somewhat disgruntled—even Pluto started to suffer the effects of my bad mood…

One night—returning home very drunk from one of my dens around town—I imagined that the cat avoided my company. I grabbed him; when—in his panic at my violence—he inflicted a slight injury upon my hand with his teeth. The rage of a devil immediately possessed me. I recognized myself no longer. My primal soul appeared—all at once—to take its flight from my body; and a more than demonic malice—gin-nourished—excited every fiber of my form. I took from my coat a pen-knife, opened it, seized the wretched brute by the throat and purposely gouged one of his eyes from the socket! I blush, I seethe, I shiver while I write the accursed outrage…

When rationality returned with the morning—when I had slept off the stink of the night's licentiousness—I suffered a sensation partly of terror, partly of regret for the outrage of which I had been culpable; but it was at best a weak and ambivalent emotion and the spirit remained unmoved. I once more plunged into dissipation and before long drowned in wine all remembrance of the act…

In the meantime the cat gradually recuperated. The socket of the missing eye presented—it is true—a shocking aspect but he no longer seemed to suffer any pain. I went about the apartment as always—but as might be expected—he flew in desperate horror at my approach…And that impression before long gave way to annoyance…that incited me to consummate the outrage I had inflicted upon the inoffensive beast. One morning—cold-bloodedly—I slipped a noose around his neck and hung him from a rafter in the loft—hung him *because* I sensed he had given me no reason for offense…"

§

For a long while I sat soaking in the round, sunken bath-tub hedged about with mosaic tile laid in a wavelike pattern. Nearby a stainless steel sink was set into a granite counter which, along with the toilet, was cantilevered out from aluminum-paneled walls finished in gray lacquered polyester and fitted out with metal industrial shelving. Overhead a ceiling fan whirred softly as heat issued from vents installed flush with the bathroom's tiled floor.

I got up to step dripping wet from the warm bathwater and dry off. Passing by a translucent canvas and tubular steel screen—a long, blue cotton towel wrapped about my waist—I stepped inside the loft's low-ceilinged bedroom, hedged round by walls of unfinished red-painted sheetrock and a series of frosted glass jalousie windows set under the eaves. I crossed the black–and–white checked floor of aluminum sheeting and threw myself prone upon a single, tubular steel-framed and quilted bed edged by small caster-tables—looking again quite curiously at the swollen-red scratch and bite marks on the back of my right hand and gently rubbing them. Reaching for a black column housing a console of digital controls I dimmed the room's lights. Then I turned on a stereo compact disc player set in a sideboard bearing other electronic controls and cords plugged directly into the floor's built-in conduits.

"What you have seen are fantasies," Dr. Valdemar's deeply resonant voice ran in my head and reached my ear as I lay again on the partitioned daybed. "Fantasies are currents of thought that arise from a state of reverie—or trance. They're related to dreams. Dreams for that matter are nothing more than fantasies in a state of sleep. So hereafter: whenever I tell you to dream while you're relaxed you'll let your mind wander and follow a certain train of thought. Or you may have an actual dream. So when I give you the suggestion to dream just let yourself relax deeply enough to allow a series of images to enter into your mind. As you lie there then I want you to enter into a deep trance state and to have a dream—anything that happens to come to your mind. As soon as you have this dream your eyes will open and you will awaken with a start. But you will have forgotten the dream completely. And every time you think of it your mind will go blank. Then there will come a rapping, tapping at your chamber door. And when you hear the third rap, tap, the dream will suddenly pop into your mind and you will tell me about it without waking up. Quoth the Raven…*Nevermore!*"

Three raps—taps—of Dr. Valdemar's signet ring upon the room's curved partition wall again fell upon my ear…

§

Sleep came not close to my bed—while the hours ebbed and faded away. I strove to rationalize away the restlessness which had power over me. I tried to think that a lot if not all of what I sensed was owing to the mystifying sway of the gloom of the room…But my endeavors were unavailing. An uncontrollable trembling slowly permeated my form; and at length there perched upon my very spirit an incubus of reasonless dread. Shuddering that away with a gasp and a struggle I raised myself upon the pillows and, squinting intently within the extreme blackness of the room, listened—I knew not why except that an intuitive spirit incited me—to certain soft and indistinct noises which came at lengthy interims from I knew not where. Overwhelmed by an extreme sensation of terror—inexplicable yet insufferable—I put on my clothes with haste; for I sensed that I should sleep no more throughout the night and attempted to awaken myself from the pitiful state into which I had sunk by pacing quickly back and forth through the apartment…

My extreme exhaustion impelled me to become recumbent; and sleep before long overtook me as I lay…

Upon awaking and stretching out an arm I found beside me a pitcher with water. I was too much fatigued to ruminate upon this situation but drank with voracity...

Trepidation of spirit kept me awake for many long hours; but at length I once more slept. Upon awaking I found by my side as before a pitcher of water. A parched thirst consumed me and I drained the decanter at a draft. I must have been drugged; for barely had I drunk before I became irresistibly drowsy. A deep sleep fell upon me—a sleep like that of death. How long it lasted naturally I know not; but when once more I opened my eyes the things about me were perceptible...

Aside from the tendency to trance though my prevailing vitality seemed to be sound; nor could I discern that it was at all afflicted with the one prevailing morbidity—unless in fact a peculiarity in my normal sleep might be considered *super*-induced. Upon awaking from sleep I could never attain all at once complete possession of my faculties and always remained—for many minutes—in much confusion and mystification—the mental faculties in general but the memory in particular being in a state of sheer suspension...

My next step was to search for the brute which had been the source of so much misery; for I had at length firmly decided to put it to sleep. Had I been able to encounter with it at that instant there could have been no doubt of its destiny; but it seemed that the cunning creature had been frightened at the violence of my prior wrath and shuddered to present itself in my present temper. It is impossible to recount or to conceive the profound, the blissful sense of deliverance which the absence of the beast engendered in my breast. It did not make its appearance throughout the night—and so for one night at least since its penetration into the loft I soundly and peacefully slept; yes, slept even with the weight of mutilation upon my spirit.

And then was I indeed miserable beyond the misery of mere Humanity. And a *brute beast*—whose fellow I had scornfully exterminated—a brute beast to cause for *me*—for me a man, moulded in the image of the Lord God—so much of intolerable pain! Alas! neither by day nor by night experienced I the godsend of Rest any more! Throughout the day the beast left me no instant alone; and during the night I started—hourly—from dreams of unspeakable dread to feel the fervid breath of *the thing* upon my face and its hefty weight—an incarnate Night-Mare that I had no control to shudder off—incumbent eternally upon my *spirit!*

Beneath the burden of tortures such as these the weak vestige of the virtue within me submitted. Wicked thoughts became my sole companions—the blackest and most wicked of thoughts. The gloominess of my normal mood escalated to loathing of all things and of all mankind; while from the abrupt, repeated and uncontrollable eruptions of a rage to which I then darkly surrendered myself, my imperturbable *witch in disguise*—alas!—was the most normal and the most indulgent of companions.

One night she accompanied me into the loft which our experiment obliged us to occupy. The cat followed me all over and—almost tripping me headlong—infuriated me to insanity. Raising an axe and forgetting—in my rage—the superstitious fright which had heretofore restrained my hand—I pointed a stroke at the creature which naturally would have proved immediately lethal had it fallen as I wanted. But this stroke was halted by the hand of my witch in disguise. Driven by meddling into fury more than demonic I disengaged my arm from her grip and sank the axe in her head. She dropped dead upon the spot without a moan.

§

Through small coppery stepping stones streams a surface aqueduct of frothing water cascading gently over a little waterfall flowing into the bottle-green *Lloyd Lake* between *Cross-Over* and *John F. Kennedy Drives* in *Golden Gate Park.* In the rear of the lake on the brink of the concrete embankment—at the terminus of a serpentine moss-grown dirt footpath—stands a solitary, pillar-supported, tree-enshrouded front portico to an opulent Nob Hill mansion destroyed in the disastrous 1906 earthquake—the sole public memorial to the calamity in the city. And then hanging by the neck by a taut creaking rope—between the four nacreous marble columns reflected in the still waters—swayed slightly the decomposing scarecrow-like corpse of the prostitute with the berouged feline face bedecked in a black witch costume: an axe buried in her brain!

Embedded in stones beneath the body's swaying feet was a rusty green brass plaque which reads:

Portal of Residence, California and Taylor Streets, of A.N. Towne, for many years Vice President and General Manager of the Southern Pacific Railroad Company. This relic of the conflagration of April 18, 1906, was obtained through the kindness of Mrs. A.N. Towne.

§

"Remarkable!" Dr. Kerwin Usher exclaimed, sitting back in his black oak Gimson chair behind a small desk tucked in the recess of a bay window at the bottom of an L-shaped drawing room running the length and breadth of the ground-floor level of his four-floor terrace house bordering *Buena Vista Park*. He looked comfortable wearing a blue blazer over a pale blue cotton shirt with a tan coarse-weave tweed tie and natural tan cashmere V-neck sweater. On one side of a glass box cantilevered out from the window behind him, and supporting some bowls and platters, sliding glass doors opened out to a small terrace and glass-covered courtyard of well-worn slate and brown quarry tiles. Past the courtyard spread a small, lush and sloping orchid garden—furnished with a lone, painted wire seat and bench—overlooking the dull and leaden buildings stretching south of *Market Street* far off below to *San Francisco Bay*.

"And this came into your hands just now?" His face was aglow from the light of a Chinese lamp set on a small Malaysian black lacquer table along with some ceramics and lacquer boxes as he put down on the desktop Nicolino's first journal entry from the third day into his secret and secluded hypnotic experiment transpiring in the out of the way *Mission* neighborhood loft.

"In today's mail." Lenore sat in a window seat covered in striped chintz which matched the bay window's chintz curtains and rattan roller blinds. "It's the only contact Nicolino promised to keep with me while he's away. That's why I hurried here to see you after calling. And because he sounded like he respected your judgment a great deal when he spoke of you."

"I thought much of him when we met as well," Dr. Usher affirmed with a nod.

Surrounding them was a room of walnut paneling glazed in varying shades of pistachio green, embossed with red–and–gold wallpaper and hung with festoon draperies made from a damask design printed in aubergine on raw scarlet linen and woven wool tapestry curtains. Real candles burned in a porcelain chandelier hung from the gold ceiling above. And spread underfoot was an oak-mosaic parquet floor painted to look like sisal. Set in a corner nearby was a tortoise shell-painted fireplace adorned with carvings and hedged in by white-painted oak paneling and a brass guard. Centered atop its marble mantelpiece was an antique French gilt clock flanked by candlestick lamps with tortoise shell shades and a vase of fresh flowers. Flanking the fireplace were two Indian Regency ebony chairs set near a book-covered English oak table. Over the mantel a bookcase held old leather-bound books, ceramics and pottery. In other parts of the room were a pair of sofas upholstered in linen and mattress ticking, an open-shelved pine sideboard bearing blue–and–white, flower-decorated china and a red lacquer secretary bearing cabbage-shaped procelains, pottery and tulip-shaped cups.

What follows is the conversation which succeeded—with *U.* in the discussion standing for Dr. Usher and *L.* standing for Lenore:

L. "From his youth Nicolino has been known for the gentleness and humaneness of his temperament. His softness of heart was even so obvious as to make him the sport of his friends. He is especially fond of cats and never is so happy as when feeding and fondling them. This singularity of temperament grew with his maturity and in his adulthood he derives from it one of his main sources of enjoyment. Is it possible he's actually being driven to do the things he's describing in his journal?"

U. "A practiced hypnotist can compel a subject to do all kinds of strange and peculiar things—outright monstrous things. But just how monstrous depends of course on how suggestible and receptive to the hypnotist the subject is."

L. "How suggestible might Nicolino be to Dr. Valdemar?"

U. "Hypnosis is a peculiar psychical state in which the mind is especially susceptible to suggestion. And when an already suggestible subject becomes even more suggestible then that disparity is hypnosis. It's a state of mind in which the so-called critical faculty of the mind is bypassed and selective thinking implanted and put in its place. The degree of suggestibility varies from subject to subject by his existing emotional state, the kind of defense mechanisms he has or his attitude toward his hypnotist. So it takes a combination of both positive and ample attitude to show much suggestibility or undergo hypnosis."

L. "Nicolino has no aptitude for torturing and killing cats."

U. "In the hypnotic state I'm afraid the subject's aptitude is somewhat beside the point."

L. "Why's that?"

U. "Because in the ordinary waking state the subject is most affected by internal inhibiting influences. In hypnosis these influences are dispensed with. And once induced the happenings of hypnosis are involuntary, unthinking and occur on their own."

L. "Then a subject can be forced to do things in hypnosis against his will?"

U. "Theoretically no. In the technical sense hypnosis is not to be equated with compulsion. It's more a matter of a subject's capacity for accepting suggestions. Even so the most receptive subjects are those who can thoroughly convince themselves that they're obliged to do whatever the hypnotist suggests they do."

L. "How could a subject ever be convinced of that?"

U. "Only three things are really essential for hypnosis to occur: the subject's consent; communication between the hypnotist and the subject; and the subject's freedom from fear—or any reluctance to take the hypnotist on trust. And since these are the only demands there's no limit to the many ways a hypnotist can induce a trance or trigger in the subject a desired response."

L. "So suggestibility is mostly a matter of blind trust?"

U. "Partly. The use of suggestion in hypnosis lies in deliberately creating those conditions which are conducive to uncritical compliance and receptiveness to ideas and impressions."

L. "Like what conditions?"

U. "If he's unconflicted about accepting a passive relationship he could become hypnotized to take pleasure in the indulgence of the hypnotist's attentions."

L. "I seriously doubt whether Nicolino would take much pleasure in that since he's not by nature a very passive person."

U. "If his desire for new experience is strong and he's sure of his own powers and ability then he may turn hypnosis into an adventure in which he transforms the hypnotist into his collaborator—leading him into experiences which go beyond the normal, preferably into the super-normal or even abnormal. So no one kind of person—passive or aggressive, willful or weak—is susceptible or insusceptible to hypnosis. And the hypnotic state does not have the same meaning for all hypno-tizable subjects."

L. "How do you mean?"

U. "Hypnosis can play on the mind and body just as po-tently as any drug—since the human body reacts not only to physical and chemical stimulation but also to symbolic stimu-lation—such as words and events which assume some special significance to the subject or which the subject attaches a spe-cial importance to."

L. "Like Nicolino attaches to the works of Edgar Allan Poe?"

U. "Exactly."

L. "How does all this relate to Nicolino's graphic accounts of cat killing?"

U. "During trance induction a hypnotized subject can in-dulge in illusions and intense fantasies!"

L. "You mean hallucinations?"

U. "Of course. Our special senses of vision, hearing, touch, taste and smell can all be hallucinated by hypnotic induction. When told it's perfume the subject will be quite undisturbed by even the fumes of pungent ammonia. In deep hypnotic trance the subject's eyes may be opened and his hallucinations induced."

L. "How can that happen?"

U. "When the subject's world of experience becomes re-stricted almost entirely to what the hypnotist is telling him. And when the hypnotic trance is well developed this stream of words tells the subject what he will experience in the trance with all the clarity of a vivid dream. And when the hypno-tist tells the subject he will now have a dream then dream he does—drawing on his own stream of inner stimulation in the place of the hypnotist's stream of words, which is then sus-pended. In this way hypnosis can open up areas of psychic ac-tivity habitually under repressed control. Mystifying fantasies and hallucinations—derivatives of the unconscious—are then made accessible to further exploration. And the unconscious has a definite use in hypnosis."

L. "Which is?"

U. "In hypnosis the mind and body are equally suggestible—working as a harmonious unit. And hypnosis makes an impression on the unconscious mind as well as on the autonomic nervous system. So when you pilot a subject into a suggestible state his impressions will be physical as well as mental."

L. "How do you go about piloting someone into such a state?"

U. "By giving ample play to the imagination. Our brain has two sides—the left side and the right side. The left side controls what we feel and imagine. The right side controls how we reason and think rationally. When a subject is hypnotized the left side of his brain is in control. That's why the subject under hypnosis is able to recall, feel and imagine more than he normally does."

L. "Is the imagination really so powerful?"

U. "All kinds of fabulous and fantastic wonders can be conceived by an excited—even perverse—imagination."

L. "Could a perverse imagination force Nicolino to do things which go strongly against his good nature?"

U. "It depends. In hypnosis the mind and body can be manipulated to an incredible degree. Reason and perception are no longer trustworthy. An affected subject first deceives and deludes himself—and then others—about the sources of impressions and courses of action which—since they depend on imagination—are at first themselves imaginary. So the firm conviction of someone so affected—however reliable and intent upon telling the truth he is—and who has surrendered himself to be hypnotized with good faith and an excited imagination—cannot always be considered positive proof of the real source of what he's experienced."

L. "Could a manipulated imagination make Nicolino do

something so sadistic and cruel as killing a harmless cat—or worse?"

U. "Supposedly no hypnotist can compel a subject to do something he truly believes is wrong or bad. There are limits to what a subject will or will not do under hypnosis. So it's unusual for a subject to commit an act he truly considers immoral or evil. But..."

L. "But?"

U. "Hypnosis is a very special state of consciousness. And although a subject in a deep trance state is prepared to carry out only those suggestions that are consistent with his own personal standards and preferences—harmful and even criminal acts could be perpetrated by means of the hypnotic state—and hypnosis could be exploited to induce a subject to commit anti-social acts for anti-social aims. So it is in fact quite capable of inducing him to engage in very dangerous and very atrocious behavior."

L. "How could that be?"

U. "Harmful or criminal acts could best be contrived by deliberately deluding the subject rather than by trying to corrupt his moral or ethical values."

L. "Delude how?"

U. "A subject could be deceived or misled into anti-social acting out. Such a subject would be highly suggestible or believe that hypnotic suggestion is irresistible and overpowering. If a subject believes that hypnosis is a state of helpless automatism—and that the hypnotist can make him do whatever he pleases—harm could result—not from the hypnotist's control but from the subject's own self-suggestions. So either through ignorance or maliciousness on the part of the hypnotist hypnotism could in fact be misused to do harm."

L. "Dr. Valdemar doesn't strike me as being an ignorant man. But it all sounds too incredible to be true."

U. "Why? All kinds of anti-social—and even criminal—acts are perpetrated regularly in the waking state without benefit of hypnosis. There are many people so submissive to authority that they will do whatever is demanded of them—even though such acts are foreign to their better nature. In time of war many men in combat—who were raised and brought up to love their fellow man—willingly go about the slaughter and carnage of war at the beck and call of their chauvinist masters—and then expect to be decorated rather than punished. Intimidation, lying, deception—every type of treachery and duplicity has been resorted to from time immemorial to incite anti-social conduct. Appealing to the worst in men through bribery and blackmail—and to the best in them by appeals to their patriotic and political indoctrination—has always induced the worst outrages from the most ordinary kinds of people."

L. "Then Nicolino could be manipulated through hypnosis to commit a harmful or criminal act?"

U. "If properly and effectively hypnotized he could capitulate to a command to commit an act harmful to himself or to someone else. Theoretically at least it's possible for a deeply hypnotized subject—a somnambule who can open his eyes without coming out of a trance—to commit an anti-social act or to perpetrate such an act through post-hypnotic suggestion even after the trance state has ended. The essential element for success is of course motivation."

L. "Why motivation?"

U. "Nicolino or any subject would have to be motivated—and manipulated—into anti-social acting out through hypnosis—perhaps through induced hypnotic hallucination. Only then could the subject rationalize and justify carrying out hypnotic commands which went against his personal values and beliefs."

§

"What would motivate Dr. Valdemar to manipulate his

subject in such a way?" Lenore asked worriedly.

"It's a curious fact," Dr. Usher remarked, amused, "that often the most obstinate people in positions of power are prone to the most foolish schemes—especially if they promise them even more power."

"You mean Dr. Valdemar is on some sort of power trip?"

"It's not easy to repudiate accepted beliefs, the dogmas of your own education, the successes of your youth, the reputation you've made growing old." Dr. Usher heaved a pensive sigh. "In their way all of these things make up a play for power."

"What kind of power play might Dr. Valdemar be making?"

"That's difficult to say," Dr. Usher conceded. "But bear in mind that whatever else he is Dr. Valdemar is first and foremost an academician. And for the high-brow academician the usual, almost universal method of fabricating a theory is to dream up some darling, pet explanation for it—or rather some speculative explanation—and then to very gratuitously put it to the test by experiment. Experiments of course never fail to bear out his pre-conceived brainchild. How can they fail when vanity and conceit are the driving forces behind whatever speculation he's putting forth? Having then dug up some half-baked facts and truths mere arrogant presumption alone is needed to prove itself. So we have rationales and self-styled theories as endless as the so-called facts on which they're based—quite as contradictory and just as absurd."

"Like the theater of the absurd—with which I'm well familiar. Then will you go with me to see Dr. Valdemar about Nicolino?"

"Not to see Dr. Valdemar but I will go along—as a prudent precaution—to wait out of sight close by while you go in to see him."

"I'll be very grateful for that—but as a precaution against what?"

"Against the evil that men do," Dr. Usher said sullenly. "If

Dr. Valdemar is doing something questionable or improper then he's not likely to admit it if I'm there. So I'll do something for you even better—and more beneficial—than being your chaperon."

"Such as?"

"Come with me please."

Getting up from behind his desk Dr. Usher showed Lenore the way through a curtain of cashmere crewel-work hung on a rail above a nearby doorway and into a small room overlaid with a Scottish carpet and dimly lit by a bronze standing lamp. Its only furnishings were a marble console table, a sharkskin daybed and an armchair covered with a piece of old carpet.

"Relax there please," he invited her, gesturing to the daybed and sitting down himself in the armchair.

"May I ask what for?" Lenore asked reluctantly.

"To demonstrate a few mental techniques you might use to block out any negative thoughts or images should Dr. Valdemar try for some reason to hypnotize you."

"Hypnotize me?" She looked aghast as she plunked herself down onto the daybed.

"Absolutely." Dr. Usher nodded seriously. "If Dr. Valdemar is doing something unscrupulous—then possibly to protect himself from discovery—he could very well try to hypnotize you to cover up whatever mischief or villainy he was up to."

"Then by all means," Lenore consented, "go right ahead."

"Very well." Dr. Usher proceeded to explain further. "Since hypnosis has to do with concentrating the mind on thoughts and images which are consistent with the goals of a hypnotic suggestion the subject's skill in hypnosis lies in being able to think and imagine along with that suggestion. So it's not only important to concentrate on those thoughts and images which will elicit the desired result, but it's also important to block out any negative thoughts or images which might interfere with your ability to either respond—or to resist—suggestion."

"Then I'd be very interested in learning how to resist suggestion."

"Good." Dr. Usher approved, pausing to look expectantly at her. "Are you ready to go then?"

Clearing her throat Lenore roused herself from the restful and relaxed state she had lolled into and looked at him in earnest.

"Let's do it."

JOSEPH COVINO JR

TWELVE:

THE PENDULUM'S RETURN

"Let none of earth inherit
That vision on my spirit;
Those thoughts I would control,
As a spell upon his soul:
For that bright hope at last
And that light time have past,
And my worldly rest hath gone
With a sigh as it passed on:
I care not though it perish
With a thought I then did cherish."—Poe poem:
Imitation

Later on that evening Dr. Kerwin Usher sat alert in his car parked curbside beneath a tree in *Pacific Heights*, watching vigilantly as Lenore stood anxiously awaiting across the street on the balustraded portico of the Gothic-style house of Dr. Vincent Valdemar. She took in a deep, shuddering breath as the front door opened up slowly and exposed to view the elegant older gentleman, wearing a navy blue suit and red plaid madras tie over a pink oxford shirt and looking like the very image of Dr. Vincent Valdemar—his exact and identical twin-double—except for a small skin mole spotting his left temple.

"Hello, my dear," the man whispered, holding out his hand to gently press hers. "You must be the young lady who called."

"Yes," she said unshakably, lifting up her eyes though hanging down her head. "I'm Lenore."

"How do you do?" the man whispered again faintly, murmuring everything under his breath in a soft and low voice as he introduced himself. "I am Dr. Milos Valdemar—Vincent's brother. Please bear with me but I cannot raise my voice—a defect in my voice box. Please come in."

"Thank you," Lenore said, looking aghast but steadfast and feeling sorry for the frail, older man.

"Permit me to introduce—before he leaves us—a distinguished patient of my brother's: Mr. Augustus Bedloe," M. Valdemar pronounced politely.

Out of nowhere from the lurid dark of the foyer unexpectedly emerged the strange and peculiar looking man who, mutely and grimly, bowed and nodded his slight acknowledgment, departing as abruptly as he had appeared.

"As I told you over the telephone," M. Valdemar repeated reassuringly, inviting her to step more deeply inside the foyer and hall and showing her the way up the straight staircase to the spacious upstairs drawing room, "I'm afraid my brother Vincent can neither be reached nor found. But I will gladly help you in any way I can."

"I would appreciate that," Lenore said politely, silently suspicious.

M. Valdemar led her straight across the drawing room through the draped arch and into the snug bookcase-lined parlor, turning on the lone library lamp.

"Rest there," he invited her, gesturing to the velvet sleeper sofa and tea service. "Take some tea if you like. Shall I pour?"

"Nothing for me, thank you."

He settled himself into the parlor's side-chair, staring at her curiously. She smiled slightly but kept silent.

"In any event," M. Valdemar went on after an uncomfortable lull, gesturing to a single, solitary letter resting atop the sizable level writing-table of the nearby roll-top desk, "my brother Vincent left his house in my strictest care—with clear and explicit instructions—to tell anyone asking or looking for him that he would be absent for the full duration of his thirteen-day hypnotic experiment with your gentleman friend, Nicolino. And under no circumstances, he stressed, should be be reached or disturbed in that time."

That letter was profusely sullied and rumpled. It was ripped almost in two across the middle—as if a decision in the first case to rip it completely up as valueless had been changed, or checked, in the second. But then the *extremity* of these disparities; the dust; the stained and ripped state of the paper; so expressive of a purpose to deceive the viewer into an impression of the valuelessness of the letter.

Into a trumpery filigree card-rack of paste-board M. Valdemar shoved the letter casually—and even as it appeared scornfully into one of the rack's upper partitionments.

"Then they're nowhere to be found."

"I'm afraid so." He nodded sympathetically, noting her conspicuous disappointment.

"And you have no idea where they might be?"

"That's correct. I'm sorry."

"Forgive me for prying," Lenore said unflinchingly, "but I gathered from Nicolino that you and your brother were not on the best of terms with one another."

"That's essentially true," he conceded, "although we are on little better than speaking terms, personally, my brother Vincent does call upon me, professionally, for help or favors from time to time—especially when he has some pressing need of me or it's expedient and suits his purposes."

"Then there's nothing really substantial that you can do to help me."

"Only to reassure you that your gentleman friend, Nicolino, is quite safe and sound in my brother Vincent's care."

"How could you possibly know that for certain?"

"Because I know my brother—all too well. Although I may take issue with him at times and side against him professionally I know him to be quite competent and capable in his field. And I feel quite certain—as sure as death—that your friend, Nicolino, will remain quite secure and unharmed in my brother Vincent's experienced hands."

"Don't you mean under his power and control?" Lenore asked skeptically.

"I assure you—as I'm sure my brother has already assured Nicolino—that hypnosis has absolutely nothing whatever to do with one person having any kind of hold over another."

"Forgive me, doctor, if I have my doubts."

"Quite understandable in the circumstances."

"Not to change the subject," she asked unhesitatingly, "but could we turn up the light in here?"

M. Valdemar looked at her inquisitively.

"Do you fear the shades and shadows of the dark?"

"Not so much the dark," she confessed, "as its forebodings of the shades and shadows of *death!*—for, you see, I am afflicted with chronic premonitions of my own death and rebirth."

"Perhaps I can do something to help relieve or even eradicate your fears—both of your deathly premonitions and of any imaginary danger posed to Nicolino."

"What do you suggest?"

Very deliberately M. Valdemar got up and reached into one of the desk's pigeonholes, pulling out a small, glinting metallic object. From a finger ring he let the long and thin silver chain fall and dangle from his down-turned palm. Gently he swung before Lenore's curious eyes the shiny miniature object fastened to the chain's end—the *pendulum!*

"Why—a little hypnotism of course."

Lenore looked intently at the small crescent of glistening metal about an inch long from horn to horn—its horns pointed upward and its lower edge plainly razor-sharp—and nodded knowingly.

"Of course."

§

"You must love Nicolino very much to come here searching for him the way you have," M. Valdemar said suddenly, letting the *pendulum* chain fall and coil slowly into his upturned palm.

"Yes." Lenore nodded, lost in thought. "Very much."

"Hypnosis is a lot like love."

"Are you serious?" She looked at him incredulously.

"Deadly serious. And why not?"

What follows then is the conversation that succeeded—with *V.* standing for M. Valdemar and *L.* standing for Lenore:

V. "Poets have long pondered the nature of love. So why not a hypnotist, for there are remarkable similiarities between the state of mind in love and in hypnosis."

L. "Really?"

V. "The person in love appears indifferent to the attentions of others—just as the subject pays close attention solely to the hypnotist. A person in love is easily influenced by the thoughts and beliefs of the loved one in the very same way that the hypnotist can influence a subject by suggestion. Love can change a person's whole outlook and perspective—even the habits of a lifetime. Love can affect a person's breathing, cause blushing, palpitations or even loss of appetite. Hypnosis can cause comparable changes. Love can happen quite suddenly and unexpectedly—as in hypnosis. And just as there can be love at first sight there can also be almost immediate hypnosis in a highly suggestible subject. The spell—or trance—of both love and hypnosis can be broken by an emotional shock of enough strength and intensity. So too can love turn into hatred—just as the subject can break off his rapport with the hypnotist if he objects or takes exception to a suggestion."

L. "I do see your point. But what does it lead up to?"

V. "Simply that the shared element in both love and hypnosis is essentially a super-concentration of the mind. Strong emotions concentrate the mind. So any emotion strong enough concentrates the mind into a state of hypnosis. In love there is this very same intense concentration on the object of affection. And a person in love is in a highly suggestible state similar to hypnosis. So any notion which enters the mind at this time will have the force of a hypnotic suggestion."

L. "I suppose that's what it means to be hypnotized by love."

V. "No question. In love physical changes like blushing or palpitation are elicited through the action of the autonomic nervous system—causing changes in the body's glands and organs when the mind is disturbed by this powerful emotional state. So too in hypnosis there's a heightened control over the autonomic nervous system acting through the emotions."

L. "Hypnotic suggestion can cause these changes?"

V. "Even in the ordinary waking state it's possible to influence the autonomic nervous system by suggestion. It's possible to bring tears to the eyes or make the mouth water. Suitable suggestions can make a person blush or feel angry, sad, happy or afraid and often provoke all the bodily symptoms which accompany these emotions. But of all the things which can be evoked in hypnosis the one that's common to all stages and levels—even the lightest—is heightened suggestibility."

L. "This is all very interesting but what does it have to do with overcoming my fears and premonitions?"

V. "Simply this: a fear—or phobia—is often the result of some severe shock. A painful emotional experience from the past can provoke an irrational fear of that very same situation which induced the fear in the first place. Your conscious fear—or premonition—of death is typical although some fears can be subconsciously suppressed, for it cannot be recalled without arousing alarm and extreme anxiety. Correct?"

L. "Right."

V. "So the goal and purpose of hypnotism is a sense of security which reaches the deepest unconscious levels of the personality."

L. "And just how do I acquire that security?"

V. "By harnessing those great latent abilities we possess but which are often unknown even to ourselves—by making the most of the greatest progressive force that's known: the human mind!"

L. "And I can acquire that from hypnosis?"

V. "Hypnosis can give you nothing—it can only release and set free what already exists within you. Our many inborn abilities are hardly ever put to full use because of the sheltered and protected lives we're so often forced to lead in our over-protective and paternalistic society. The power of hypnosis lies in its ability to stretch us to the limit. It merely opens the door to a more complete point of view and a fresh new way of thinking—which frees us from the limitations and literalisms of our paternalistic intruders. What we really gain through hypnosis is a broader perspective of the reality of the human mind—and its potential for a more greatly enriched range of experience."

L. "But I'm not sure if I can be hypnotized."

V. "Nonsense. Of course you can. Anyone can. In reality we humans aren't quite the rational beings we pretend to be—wavering daily between ordinary sleep and waking consciousness. To a greater or lesser degree some of the basic mechanisms of hypnosis are part of our daily lives—which we may not fully recognize or perceive. In fact you've been in a hypnotic state countless times. You thought little of it because it felt like such a natural state of mind—which it is, for the hypnotic state is natural for everyone."

L. "Why's that?"

V. "Because all of the happenings of hypnosis have to do with your own thoughts and actions. It's always through your own effort and ability that changes occur. You are the controlling part. And you do feel a strong need to be in control of yourself and your situation—do you not?"

L. "Sure."

V. "Then the changes which hypnosis can make in your life can affect you trivially or dramatically—it's all quite up to you. Only those who are really in control can feel secure enough to give up control—temporarily. So if you could give up some control it would show that you're more in control."

L. "What do you want me to do?"

Before her eyes M. Valdemar held out his closed hand and let the long and thin silver chain clink and drop down so the glinting, miniature, sharp-edged pendulum swung back and forth—slowly—in front of her.

"Tell me about your premonitions of death!"

§

In my disturbed condition of half-sleep there were indistinct noises and uncommon movements amongst the draperies in and about the sitting room of our house which I decided had no source except in the infirmity of my imagination—or perhaps in the phantasmagoric impact of the room itself...

I had just awakened from an unpeaceful sleep...

I partly arose and spoke in a solemn soft murmur of noises which I then heard—of movements which I then saw. The draft was wafting hastily behind the draperies...But as I sat up against our curvy, cotton-duck upholstered sofa two conditions of a frightening character attracted my notice. I had sensed that some palpable although imperceptible thing had passed lightly by my body; and I perceived that there lay upon the goldenrod carpet—in the very middle of the vivid sheen shed by the taper—a shadow—a soft, indistinct shadow of spectral shape—such as might be imagined as the shade of a shadow... It was then that I became explicitly cognizant of a gentle foot-fall upon the carpet and close to the sofa...

It might have been the witching hour or perhaps earlier for I had taken no notice of time when a sigh—soft, soothing but most definite—frightened me from my fancy.—I *sensed* that it came from the bedroom. I listened in anguish of superstitious horror—yet there was no recurrence of the noise...Yet I could not have been deluded. I *had* heard the sound, however soft, and my spirit was aroused within me...

An hour so passed when—could it be plausible?—I was a second time cognizant of some indistinct noise emitting from the vicinity of the bedroom. I listened—in utmost terror. The noise came again—it was a sigh...

And once more—what wonder that I shiver while I re-cite?—*once more* there fell upon my ears a soft sigh from the vicinity of the bedroom...

Freak visions darted shadow-like in front of me...I cast my eyes on the pale, stiff and shrouded shape lying upon my bed...

I strained my eyes to perceive any movement in the form—but there was not the slightest discernible...I firmly and un-flinchingly kept my eyes fixed upon the shape...

The better part of that frightful night had passed away and the figure reclining upon the bed abruptly budged—and then again more vigorously than before...The figure, I repeat, budged and then more vigorously than before...

Through a sort of unspeakable terror and dread for which the tongue of humanity has no amply trenchant parlance I sensed my heart stopped beating—my extremities turned stiff where I sat...

Astonishment then strained in my breast with the deep dread which had before ruled there alone. I sensed that my sight grew dull; that my reason rambled...But why shall I detail the unutterable terrors of that night?...

I had long stopped to strain or to stir and stayed sitting siffly upon the sofa—a powerless victim of a turn of rampant sensations—of which utmost marvel was conveivably the least horrible—the least devouring...I could at least doubt no further when arising from the bed, teetering with unsteady steps and with the carriage of one dazed in a dream—the thing that was enshrouded proceeded audaciously and palpably into the middle of the room!...

I shuddered not—I budged not—for a profusion of unspeakable visions combined with the air, the stature, the bearing of the figure surging headlong through my mind had deadened—had petrified me into stone. There was a frenetic disquiet in my thoughts—a turbulence unplacated. Who could it indeed be who confronted me?...What unutterable lunacy afflicted me with that thought? One jump and I had attained the thing's feet! Recoiling from my touch it let drop from its head, unloosed, the deathly shroud which had cloaked it and there flowed forth into the surging air of the room voluminous masses of long, jet-black and disheveled hair...And then gradually opened the eyes of the figure which stood in front of me...

But then there *DID* stand the tall and enshrouded figure of *MYSELF!* There was blood upon my gown and the signs of some violent struggle upon every part of my wasted form. For an instant the thing stayed shuddering and swaying back and forth upon the threshold; then with a soft groaning outcry fell heavily forward upon my person and in its frenetic and then last death-agonies forced me to the floor—and a prey to the horrors I had foreseen.

§

Later on the two stood together at the drawing room's threshold saying goodbye.

"It was truly a pleasure meeting you, Lenore." M. Valdemar squeezed her hand warmly. "Do call on me again."

"It was a pleasure meeting you—and productive too. I believe you helped me a lot."

"Then I'm very glad."

"And it was a pleasure doing what you said," she admitted. "I was so sure I wanted to do what you said that nothing could dissuade me from it. I was just waiting to hear your voice. Whatever you told me to do I would have done it."

"Then you were hearing—and heeding—your own voice for the will to do anything is in you—no one else."

"Thank you again," she said gratefully. "By the way do you have a card you could give me?"

"Not on me." Abruptly he threw up his hands as if awakening his memory. Turning to the ebonized and gilded pedestal supporting the silver-plate calling-card tray standing near the doorway he rummaged through its heap of business cards with a swishing hand.

"Ah!" he announced happily. "Here it is!"

To Lenore he handed over the little white card printed stylishly with an address, telephone number and name which read simply: *M. Valdemar.*

"I leave my cards here to tally my visits to my brother," he joked.

"Thank you again." She grinned a grisly smile. "Goodbye."

Then Lenore looked suddenly surprised—as if something awakened her own memory.

"I left my purse in your parlor," she reported, staring down unsuspectingly at her own person. "I'll go get it."

"No," M. Valdemar graciously offered. "Please allow me to get it for you."

"No!" she insisted. "That's okay. I'll be right back."

And before he could move to object Lenore left him standing there alone at the doorway—open-mouthed and speechless—as she hurried back across the drawing room and into the darkened parlor to snap up the black bag she had deliberately left lying behind at the foot of the sofa. In the same bated breath she stepped up to the card-rack and took the coveted letter envelope—stashing it hastily inside her jacket. Nervously she hurried back to the drawing room doorway when she stopped dead in her tracks, starting at the unexpected sight of the peculiar but personable youth appearing abruptly and directly before her.

"Please permit me to introduce—before you leave us—another of my brother's distinguished subjects: Mr. Edward Stapleton," M. Valdemar whispered politely.

Silently the youth—who unknown to Lenore looked like the very exact and identical twin-double image of Theodore Templeton—smiled with a brief bow; and Lenore nodded a slight acknowledgment and bid M. Valdemar one final and friendly goodbye before rushing down the eternally long stairway—out the front door, onto the street, bounding frantically into Dr. Usher's parked car.

"I think I've found Nicolino!" she cried, heaving a jittery, ebullient sigh.

As she ripped into the letter envelope she stole away with her agitated, excited breath turned abruptly breathless.

"Oh my God!" she gasped.

"What is it?" Dr. Usher asked—his own breath bated. "What's the matter?"

Suddenly sedate, stoical and afraid Lenore dropped down her arms, looking numb and defeated as she let fall limply into her lap the unfolded writing paper from the envelope.

"There's nothing here!" she cried disbelievingly. "It's totally blank paper—except for a newspaper article clipping from the *San Francisco Chronicle!* It's the story about the man dressed as a sailor who jumped off the *Golden Gate Bridge* a couple days ago!"

"May I see that?" asked Dr. Usher, keeping his eyes really riveted upon the letter. Looking perplexed Lenore readily handed it to him.

"In examining the edges of the paper," Dr. Usher explained, "I observe them to be more *abraded* than appears necessary. They reveal the *brittle* appearance which is displayed when a stiff paper, having been once folded and pressed with a folder is re-folded in an opposite direction—in the same folds or edges which had formed the original fold. This revelation is enough. It is plain to me that the letter has been turned—like a glove—inside out, re-folded and re-sealed."

"Is that significant?" Lenore asked, confused.

"If you knew your Edgar Allan Poe, my dear, then you would know precisely what this is," Dr. Usher pronounced deliberately with a faint grunt beneath his breath. "It is none other than the *purloined letter!*"

THIRTEEN:

CITY IN THE CLOUDS

"Lo! Death has reared himself a throne
In a strange city lying alone
Far down within the dim West,
Where the good and the bad and the worst and the
best
Have gone to their eternal rest…
Resignedly beneath the sky
The melancholy waters lie.
So blend the turrets and shadows there
That all seem pendulous in air,
While from a proud tower in the town
Death looks gigantically down."—Poe poem:
The City In The Sea

A steamy, mist-saturated fog abruptly steeped *Pacific Heights* in a surging, billowing cloud until the entire street where the car was parked was wholly enveloped and overspread with a thickly murky haze. And gradually emerging before them from the lowering, looming and lurid gloom was a lone, darkling, shadowy but sluggish silhouette of a man shuffling along the sidewalk and moving slowly but surely toward them from the front. Together they watched aghast and breathless as the solitary and solemn stranger drew nearer by deliberately slow degrees and stepped straight up to the driver's side of the car, rapping and tapping lightly on the glass. Paralyzed with raised apprehensions the two looked on one another curiously and fearfully until the driver gradually rolled down his window—in full view of which the enigmatical stranger stooped slowly to finally expose himself.

"Pardon this intrusion," he excused himself with a courtly countenance distorted by an unearthly mixture of light and shadow. "My name is Dupin—Detective Chief Inspector of the San Francisco Police Department—retired."

Once more the two looked on one another—struck with wonder—with silent incomprehension.

"And you are Dr. Usher and the lady Lenore," he suggested promptly before either could respond.

"Yes?" Dr. Usher volunteered with an intensely inquisitive tone.

"And you are both looking for your friend, Nicolino?"

"Yes?" Dr. Usher rejoined again—more decisively.

"Well," he said, heaving a sympathetic sigh, "so am I."

"In what connection?" Dr. Usher ventured.

"In connection with a known prostitute found hanging in *Golden Gate Park*—with an axe buried in her brain."

Lenore gasped breathlessly.

"What possible connection could there exist," Dr. Usher asked incredulously, looking stupefied, "between Nicolino and some presumably murdered prostitute?"

"A clear thumb print lifted from the axe," Dupin replied solemnly, "matches perfectly that checked out against Nicolino's Department of Motor Vehicles driving record."

§

Together the three retired to the snug seclusion of Dr. Usher's comfortable ground-level sitting room, relaxing and conversing from adjoining armchairs inside his four-floor terrace house bordering *Buena Vista Park.*

"The intellectual attributes spoken of as the investigative," C. Dupin discoursed at length, "are in themselves seldom subject to investigation. We acknowledge them solely in their results. We recognize of them, amongst other things, that they are invariably to their investigator when excessively enjoyed a source of the profoundest gratification. So revels the investigator in that noble endeavor which *unravels!*"

"As in unravels a mystery?" Dr. Usher suggested.

"Exactly. He derives satisfaction from even the most trivial pursuits bringing his skills into play. He is enamored of puzzles, of riddles; displaying in his revelations of each a degree of *discernment* which seems to the ordinary understanding extraordinary. His conclusions, engendered by the very spirit and essence of logic, have in reality the perfect appearance of premonition...yet to foresee is not in itself to investigate...what is merely intricate is misinterpreted—a not uncommon mistake—for what is calculating...Divested of conventional expedients the investigator insinuates himself into the heart and soul of his adversary, identifies himself therewith, and not infrequently ascertains so at a glance the mere means—oftentimes the preposterously simple ones—by which he might entice into miscalculation or rush into misadventure."

"Presumably you have in mind a most particular adversary and misadventure?"

"Indeed I have. Without question there is nothing of a comparable character so powerfully taxing the talent of investigation...the skill in which implies capacity for conquest in all those more critical endeavors where mind grapples with mind...To observe carefully is to recall clearly...and so far the investigator makes a multitude of observations and inferences...; and the disparity in the degree of the evidence gathered lies not so much in the accuracy of the inference as in the excellence of the observation. The essential evidence is that of *what* to observe."

"Evidence about which adversary and misadventure then have you observed?"

"The investigative faculty should not be confused with mere cleverness;" C. Dupin replied, overlooking the question, "for while the investigator is of necessity clever the clever man is often notably inept at detection...Between cleverness and the investigative faculty there prevails a disparity much greater in fact than that between the vision and the invention—but of a nature very precisely comparable. It will be discovered indeed that the clever are invariably capricious and the really visionary never otherwise than investigative...yet observation has become with me lately a breed of obligation."

"Then I repeat:" Dr. Usher persisted, "specifically to which adversary and misadventure do you refer?"

"To the present day," C. Dupin said gravely, "the actual adversary remains unknown. But the misadventure alludes to murders so mysterious and so mystifying in all their atrocious details as to defy the human imagination: I refer of course to the **SCARABUS** serial killings which terrorized the city of *San Francisco* in distant times past!"

"Ah," Dr. Usher nodded his knowing acknowledgment, "those horrendous serial killings committed some several decades ago who's perpetrator appeared inspired—if not obsessed—by the *modus operandi* of murders portrayed in the terror tales of Edgar Allan Poe! To this day the perpetrator of those heinous crimes remains uncaught and at large amongst us."

"Quite so."

"I could only concur with all San Francisco in deeming them an unsolvable mystery. I ascertained no means by which it would be feasible to track the killer."

"We must not consider the means by this facade of an investigation," Dupin said contradictorily. "The San Francisco police—so much celebrated for their discernment are clever but no more. There is no method in their procedure beyond the method of the moment. They make a grand display of steps; but not infrequently those are so ill suited to the purposes presented…The results reached by them are not infrequently unexpected but by and large are attributable to simple application and activity. When these attributes are ineffectual their designs fail. An investigator can be a good guesser and a persistent person. But without enlightened thought he can miscalculate constantly by the very intensity of his investigations. He impairs his sight by holding the thing too close. He might see perhaps one or two angles with uncommon clarity but in so doing he loses sight of the problem as a whole. So there is such a thing as being too deep. Truth is not invariably in a bottomless pit. Indeed—concerning the more crucial insight—I do think that truth is invariably shallow. The depth lies in the valleys where we seek it and not upon the peaks where it is found…By undue depth we confound and debilitate thought; and it is conceivable to make even Jupiter itself disappear from the heavens by an investigation too protracted, too focused or too direct."

"Then you recommend perhaps a more indirect approach?"

"In that which I now recommend," Dupin expounded, "we will abandon the internal aspects of this conundrum and focus our attention upon its surroundings. Not the least common mistake in investigations such as this is the restricting the investigation to the proximate with utter neglect of the circumstantial or collateral aspects. It is the misconduct of the courts to restrict evidence and examination to the confines of evident relevancy. Yet experience has proved—and a true science will invariably prove—that a vast—perhaps the greater—part of truth ensues from the evidently irrelevant. It is through the spirit of this premise—if not exactly through its letter—that contemporary science has determined to *count upon the unexpected*. But perhaps you do not understand me."

"Quite the contrary," Dr. Usher assured him, "I'm right with you. Do go on."

"The history of human insight," Dupin continued, "has so unremittingly proved that to collateral, circumstantial or accidental incidents we are indebted to for the most numerous and most invaluable revelations that it has at length become essential—in imminent view of advancement—to make not merely great but the greatest concessions for innovations that shall ensure by chance—and quite beyond the scope of common expectation. It is no longer speculative to build upon what has been a vision of what is to be. *Chance* is acknowledged as a part of the substructure. We make chance a matter of perfect appraisal."

"Could you elaborate further?"

"I repeat," Dupin nodded his assent, "that it is no more than fact that the *greater* part of all truth has ensued from the collateral; and it is but in keeping with the spirit of the premise implicated in this fact that I would divert investigation in the current case—from the trampled and hitherto unproductive ground of the incident itself to the current circumstances which encompass it."

"To which circumstances do you refer?"

"As for these serial killings," Dupin said seriously, "let us take up some investigations for ourselves before we make up an opinion respecting them. An investigation will provide us diversion."

221

§

Alone I lay supine upon my bed. And I saw lying there, curled up on the black–and–white checked floor in the middle of a bright but smoky spotlight thrown down from the ceiling a shadow—a faint and dim shadow of shapely but spectral form as might be seen from the shade of a shadow. On an undulating form and on a squirming shadow spread upon the wall I cast my agitated eyes. Then my eyes made out only indistinct shades of the shadow. She—or something—was there no longer but she was breathing, rhythmically, repeatedly—a muffled, almost muted whispering whimper—the heaving of a rasping and purring sigh!

Rising slowly at my upturned feet above the end of the bed was the witch's black hat—its tall, pointed tip poking up into view by slow degrees. Wrapped up in a black, high-necked cape the witch's face cropped up and peered out over the bed's edge: a smiling, purring face—very feminine, very feline. Yes, feline—displaying wildly yellow and catty eyes and wiry, bristling whiskers sticking out from her soft cheeks. Slowly the witch of statuesque stature with the cat's face crept and crawled up, climbing onto the bed itself while reaching out to paw, grope and hold tight to my bare legs. Out of her open black vest burst her exposed, curvaceous breasts. Nearer she drew to me, hissing lowly under her breath with a humming purr.

Soon the delicate, meticulous fingers of the stealthily stalking creature stroked me gently between my legs; her moist mouth and lips suckled me and pulled me out; her fleshy, bare thighs—overspread with tight, black, spider-webbed stockings—thrashed about as her juicy wetness oozed out over my groin. Abruptly raised the blow leveled at her head plunged the axe into her brain! Just as abruptly she sprang and pounced on top of me, snarling viciously, hissing and baring at me her sharp fangs!

The sight of that monster rather alleviated than heightened

my horrors—for I then made certain that I dreamed and tried to awaken myself to waking awareness.

You will say then naturally that I dreamed; but not so. What I saw—what I heard—what I sensed—what I thought— had about it nothing of the indisputable peculiarity of the dream. Everything was strictly self-coherent. At first doubting that I was truly awake I undertook a succession of tests which promptly persuaded me that I truly was. Then when one dreams—and in the dream suspects that he dreams—the suspicion *never fails to substantiate itself*—and the sleeper is almost instantly awakened...Had the vision presented itself to me as I recount it—without my suspecting it as a dream— then a dream it might positively have been; but happening as it did—and suspected and tested as it was—I am compelled to categorize it amongst other phenomena.

§

Momentarily paralyzed by shock and fear Lenore fell back slumped against her curvy, cotton-duck upholstered sofa in their rented house on *Potrero Hill*, looking aghast after reading the next journal installment Nicolino—shut up in the out of the way *Mission* district loft—sent her in the mail on another day into his secret and cloistered hypnotic experiment. She sat lost in amazement, surrounded by profuse plants and fresh flowers set in cache pots and crystal vases. On one side of her sofa stood a pine, book-stacked dresser; on the other a Portuguese cupboard filled with sand-cast bronze-shadow vases and Venetian glass plates. Underfoot were spread a pair of geometrically patterned Turkish rugs which padded a few scattered Swedish pine chairs and bamboo stools.

"But," Lenore thought out aloud, "it is pure idleness to proclaim that I have not lived before—that the soul has no prior existence. You dispute it?—let us not debate the matter. Persuaded myself I seek not to persuade. There is nevertheless a recollection of airy shapes—of ethereal and expressive eyes—of noises, melodious yet somber—a recollection which will not be precluded; a remembrance like an umbra, obscure, changeable, indeterminate, irresolute; and like an umbra also in the impossibility of my ridding myself of it while the sunlight of my logic shall exist."

§

Strung straight together in the ceiling above us the row of bowl-shaped crystal chandeliers lit up the way as Dr. Valdemar led me along the dark and drab corridor stretching to the skylift tower inside the *Fairmont Hotel* atop *Nob Hill.* Passing by ebony doors opening up into facing banquet rooms our feet trod a soft and slow path across black carpet emblazoned by its twirling design of fiery red ferns. At length we stepped onto the white tile floor of the skylift foyer at the hall's end. There we stood reflected in arched mirrors set behind potted plants on either side of the tower's polished gold skylift doors. Once the doors flew open in those late early-morning hours we stepped alone together into the snug interior of the tower's exterior, glass-enclosed skylift. With hardly a lurch the skylift started to crawl smoothly and silently up the eastward face of the hotel's 24-story tower.

"Look steadily into my eyes and think of nothing else but sleep and rest," Dr. Valdemar ordered me, switching off the ornamental leaf-shaped light overhead and rapping, tapping three times with his signet ring on the skylift's inner brass handrail. "Relax your muscles all over so your knees bend a little and your legs barely hold you up—*nevermore.*"

In the twinkling of Dr. Valdemar's penetrating eye I felt a distinct limpness and stillness in my limbs as my deep concentration instantly sharpened and intensified.

"You're riding up a long and tall elevator," he said lowly, deliberately, resonantly, "and with each rising floor you're going into a deeper and deeper state of hypnosis. Picture in your mind each and every floor you are passing by. Each floor you pass by helps you to go into a deeper and deeper state of hypnosis. And you can go as deep as you like by going up as many floors as you like—up, deeper and deeper, every floor, taking you deeper. You're riding up farther and farther, becoming more relaxed with each floor. You'll ride up to the twenty-fourth floor and you'll ride this elevator to get up to the very height of relaxation."

Facing right ahead of us the broad and flat roof of a tall building dropped slowly down as the skylift crawled slowly up. Out of the cityscape of lighted buildings and skyscrapers beyond shot up the distinctive *Transamerica Building*, tapering smoothly to its lofty, pyramidal peak. And beyond the cityscape lay *San Francisco Bay*—crossed gracefully by the suspended gray *Bay Bridge*—its two drooping chains of lights broken off in their middle by the dark and bunchy mound of *Treasure Island*.

"You are rising and riding up," Dr. Valdemar went on. "There are twenty-floor floors and they take you to a very special and peaceful and wonderful place. I'm going to count backwards from ten to one and you can feel yourself riding the elevator up. And as you pass each floor you feel your body relax more and more, feeling it just drift, float, hover, glide and fly by each floor—and relaxing even deeper. And as you watch the numbers of the floors passing by you see the numbers ten, relax even deeper, and now the number nine...eight...seven... six...five...four...three...two...one...deeper, deeper."

At the twenty-fourth floor the skylift gently came up to the barred entrance to the *Crown Room* restaurant, topping off the hotel's tower. Dr. Valdemar pressed the red emergency stop button to hang up the skylift there. From the cityscape to the northeast soared the towers of *Saints Peter and Paul Church* on *Washington Square* and the fluted column of *Coit Tower* atop *Telegraph Hill*.

"You're a capable person who can deal very effectively with every situation," Dr. Valdemar told me. "You can enjoy and revel in being alone because then you can do anything and everything you please. You can do all the things you relish most. Solitude is appealing and pleasurable. The stillness, the silence and seclusion are peaceful, restful, relaxing—and you feel relaxed and strong and satisfied by yourself.

"In this silent place—as silent as the tomb—you let yourself think over your plans, dreams and conquests. You let yourself do anything and everything you please. You are completely and utterly contented and at ease. You may indulge, overindulge and plunge yourself into utter *perverseness*. You may amuse yourself, take your pleasure and kill time—or just plain kill.

"Now think of your peaceful and special place. You can see this special place—you can even feel it. You are perfectly contented in this *city of clouds*. You are alone here and there is no one to worry or disturb you. This is the most peaceful place in the world for you…"

§

Wretchedness is multiform. The misery of the world is manifold. Overspreading the vast horizon as the rainbow its hues are as varied as that arc—as clear also yet as closely merged. Overspreading the vast horizon as the rainbow! How is it that from magnificence I have elicited a sort of non-splendor?—from the pact of peace an image of grief? But as in virtue evil is an outcome of good; so indeed out of happiness is sadness born. Either the remembrance of past rapture is the agony of to-day or the anguish which *is* has its source in the bliss which *might have been*.

Berenice!—I call upon her name—Berenice!—and from the drab remains of remembrance a thousand tumultuous memories are stunned at the sound! Ah! vividly is her image before me now as in the early days of her giddiness and delight! Oh! sublime yet fabulous beauty!...but lifting up my eyes I perceived that Berenice stood in front of me.

Was it my own overwrought invention—or the murky sway of the air—or the irresolute twilight of the room—or the drab shroud which dropped about her form—that engendered in it so fluctuating and obscure an outline? I could not tell. She uttered no word and I—not for worlds could I have spoken a syllable. A frigid chilliness perforated my form; a sense of intolerable dread oppressed me; a morbid curiosity permeated my spirit; and lapsing back upon my chair I stayed for some time breathless and motionless—with my eyes fixed upon her person. Alas! its gauntness was extreme...My fervid glimpses at length fell upon her face.

Her forehead was high and very pallid and unusually serene; and her once jet-black hair tumbled partly over it and eclipsed her hollow temples with numberless ringlets then of a vivid yellow and clashing unharmoniously—in their fabulous nature—with the ruling despondency of her visage. Her eyes were lifeless and lusterless and apparently pupil-less and I recoiled instinctively from their glazed glare to the pondering of her thin and shriveled lips. They parted; and in a grin of peculiar expression the teeth of the transformed Berenice exposed themselves gradually to my view. Would to God that I had never seen them or that having done so I had perished!

The closing of a door troubled me and looking up I discovered that Berenice had left the room. But from the deranged room of my mind had not, alas! left and would not be driven off—the white and grisly *specter* of the teeth. Not a speck on their surface—not a spot on their enamel—not a dent in their edges—but what that span of her smile had sufficed to impress upon my memory. I beheld them *now* even more unmistakably than I saw them *then*. The teeth!—the teeth!—they were here and there and everywhere and perceptibly and palpably in front of me—long, thin and extremely white with her pallid lips contorting about them as in the very instant of their first horrible outgrowth.

§

"Then came the full frenzy of your *monomania*," Dr. Valdemar's voice droned on resonantly, "and you strove to no avail against its mysterious and overpowering sway. In the multitudinous things of the outside world you had no thoughts but for the teeth. For those you yearned with a frenzied longing. All other matters and all disparate concerns became engrossed in their sole preoccupation. They—they alone were present to the rational eye and they—in their peculiarity—became the essence of your rational existence. You viewed them in every light. You turned them in every position. You examined their attributes. You brooded upon their idiosyncrasies. You dwelt upon their configuration. You reflected upon the change in their character. I shivered as you ascribed to them in invention a sensitive and sentient power—and even when unaided by the lips—a capacity for righteous expression...ah there was the imbecilic notion that subverted you! ah therefore it was that you craved them so insanely! You sensed that their possession could alone ever restore you to repose in returning you to reason...

"Enjoy your special place for another moment and then I will begin to count from one to ten and you can begin coming back to full consciousness—coming back as if you took a very long rest."

Dr. Valdemar un-pressed the skylift's stop button.

"Begin to come back now," he commanded. "One...two... comingback...three...four...five...six...seven...eight...nine... and ten. Open your eyes and come all the way back, feeling refreshed, revived, reinvigorated—and deadly!"

Slowly the skylift dropped down—the buildings and skyscrapers stepped up, the distinctive cityscape disappeared, my

eyes blinked wide open and my mind sunk into mindless oblivion.

"Excellent!" Dr. Valdemar approved.

§

Towering eucalyptus and evergreens in *Golden Gate Park*
encircle *Fuchsia Dell*, sheltering its extensive triangular lawn
and the fuchsia bushes—abloom with orange, pink, red and
violet blossoms—fringing it from gusty coastal sea breezes.
Slumped upon a solitary green wooden park bench situated
in a crescent of park benches on one side of the lawn, facing
the narrow hedge-lined footpath, was a perfectly listless and
lumpen form of a lifeless blonde female: bejewelled, paint-be-
grimed yet once adept at the awful coquettries of her libidinous
trade and devoured by a rabid desire to be rated the peer of her
elites in vice. But her tortured mouth was a conspicuously gaping, blood-blotted mess from getting every last one of her teeth
twistingly and wrenchingly torn out at the roots!

JOSEPH COVINO JR

FOURTEEN:

DESCENT INTO THE PIT

"I reach'd my home—my home no more—
For all had flown who made it so.
I pass'd from out its mossy door,
And, tho' my tread was soft and low,
A voice came from the threshold stone
Of one whom I had earlier known—
O, I defy thee, Hell, to show
On beds of fire that burn below,
An humbler heart—a deeper wo."—Poe poem:
Tamerlane

JOSEPH COVINO JR

Hung high from the wood-paneled facade of the bar on *18th Street* in the *Castro* was a luminous sign aglow in the dead of night with an abstract, black–on–white design picturing the distinct outline of an open-ended circle bisected by a vertically aligned rectangle—a disk crossed by a shank. Printed beneath the design in an upturned arc of bold black letters was the word: ***PENDULUM.***

Passing by the wide open, pane-less windows beneath the bar's faded blue awning the "effeminate-looking"(as described by Edgar Allan Poe in his *A Tale Of The Ragged Mountains*)white youth skipped up a stone step and sprang through the darkened doorway. And stepping inside the dimly lit entry he eagerly greeted the portly black doorman leaning against the illuminated cigarette machine wearing a pullover shirt and baggy pants. Affectionately the two embraced and kissed each other's cheeks—the white one reaching down behind to grab and squeeze the black one's rump.

"Hi there, fresh," the doorman teased.

"I try to be," the flirty one said, grinning. "Will you stop by the bar later on and rub my back like you always do?"

"I'll do better than that, honey." The doorman reached down in front to gently fondle the other one's crotch. "I'm getting off in a little while. Wait for me and I'll take good care of you."

"You'd be so lucky." The white youth strutted conceitedly into the bar.

"That's why I love you so much!" the doorman called after him. "You're so cocky!"

Inside the long and narrow bar stretched to its darkest and rearmost reaches where a black disk jockey sat behind wood-framed glass in a wood-paneled booth, spinning a record turntable and loudly announcing the pounding pop music he was so rhythmically and relentlessly playing. From the middle of the bar's blue-lighted ceiling hung rows of multi-colored striped flags. Along the rightward wall ran unbroken a low-lying wooden bench. Set at intervals along the wood-panel wall were rectangular mirrors dimly lit up by the soft and shadowy orange glow of evenly aligned, old-style miniature street lamps. And along the leftward wall ran the long wood-panel bar with its wood-rimmed top and shining veneer surface. Shuffling across the red brick tile floor and shouldering his way through the cramped crowd of closely packed bar drinkers the strutting stranger perched himself onto the black seat of a tall, wooden-legged barstool, eagerly ordering himself a drink. Nimbly a lithe and willowy black barman slid the stranger his mixed drink's glass across the slick bartop—straight through erect bedstead posts bolstering the sunken bar ceiling.

"There you are, sweetie!" the bartender greeted him spiritedly. "What are you up to?"

"I'm just looking—as always." He looked around lewdly—a glaring circle in the ceiling shedding a smoky light across his pale and youthful face. "You know how I am."

"You can't get enough, can you?"

"Never."

"As long as you have a good time." He suggestively touched a pair of fingers to his own lips and then to the stranger's lips with a puckered kiss.

Swallowing from his drink the stranger worked his way through the huddled crowd and pushed ahead to the facing wall.

"Is it true?" another stranger asked him in a low, whispering voice.

Surprised the first stranger turned around slowly to run his eyes over another youth dressed from top to toe in black leather, wearing a snug fitting cap pulled down low to his brow over heavy rimmed sunglasses. He was calmly reclined on the raised bench running the length of the wall.

"Is what true?" the first stranger asked, perking himself up with a swaggering air.

"That you can't get enough."

"Depends on how deprived I am."

"You don't go without—not the way you look."

"And how's that?" He showed a lecherous smile.

"Rough and ready."

"That's what I come here for—drinking, dancing and cruising. It's mellow but direct and straightforward."

"Are you looking for something straight and forward to-night?"

"I wouldn't mind grabbing hold of something that cocked up hard and strong."

"Then why look any further?" He laid firm hold of the other's hips and pulled him forward, nudging a knee between his thighs, tightening his own thighs around the other's hips and snuggling up to his groin.

"What's your name?" the leatherman asked, reaching down to lay a hand on the standing one's bulging erection, gently fingering the tip of it through his pants.

"Damien." He put down his glass on the bench and laid his hands on the leatherman's thighs, smoothly rubbing them.

"That's a nice devilish name. Are you as bad as can be?"

"Rotten to the core." He grinned a ghastly but somewhat solemn smile. "Besides, we're all damned and burning in hell anyway."

"Exactly."

"What's your name?"

"Lucifer of course."

"Sounds hot."

"Like the fires of hell. There's only one thing hotter."

"What's that?"

"My bedroom."

"What makes that so hot?"

"Me in bed with another man."

"Perfect."

"Would you like to plunge your pitchfork into my fiery

pit?"

"I'm ready." He looked supremely lecherous. "Let's go."

§

Later on at the two-story, whitewashed brick warehouse with the single, shaded glass-block window on *York Street* in the east *Mission* neighborhood the two newly acquainted strangers stepped out of an idling taxicab and strode together into the expansive, high-ceilinged loft space.

"This is radical!" Damien exclaimed, standing in awe of the room's cast-iron columns, structural steel beams and hard maple wood floors.

"Make yourself at home." The leatherman gestured to the black leather Lota sofa on the raised platform close to the central gas–and–coal fireplace. "I'll make us a drink."

Damien plunked himself down onto the sofa, kicking off his shoes and propping his socked feet on the black lacquered coffee table. After passing behind the curved, circular wall with the glass-block inset the leatherman soon returned carrying two partly poured glasses.

"Rum." He held out a glass to Damien and sat down in a Transat chair alongside the sofa. "I want to keep you fresh."

"And what about you?" He drained his glass in one gulp. "Get comfortable!"

Leaning forward Damien reached out a groping hand between the leatherman's open jacket flaps and fingered the chest hair bristling at the upper fringe of his black tank top.

"Take this off so I can see your chest and shoulders!" Damien demanded playfully. "I can tell they look very nice!"

"You first." The leatherman looked subdued and stoical. "I'm shy."

"I doubt that—but I'm easy."

Hastily Damien stripped off his shirt, stretched out and laid flat on his back, sprawled submissively on the sofa. Slowly pulling down his zipper and unfolding one flap of his pants he laid open his groin. Then he cast silent but lustful eyes on the leatherman sitting beside him.

"Some people would say your behavior is compulsive and *perverse*," the leatherman said impassively.

"Yeah." Damien snickered obscenely. "I'm a compulsive nympho. Besides, there's nothing wrong with being *perverse*. We all are."

"In our way."

Then Damien reached a hand into the crotch of his pants.

"Do you want to see it?" He lifted up his eyes to the stranger to silently court his approval.

"Do you want to show it?"

"No!" Damien persisted. "I want you to tell me if you want to see it!"

"I'm dying to see it." Still the leatherman acted staid and sedate.

"Then it's do or die." Damien smiled shamelessly. Deftly he pulled his phallus out of his pants, stroking it briskly until it stood up—erect and upright—stroking himself harder to stiffen his fleshy and throbbing organ. "I'm horny now."

"I can see that." The leatherman sounded slightly solicitous.

"You can touch it if you want to," Damien offered.

"Won't that burst if it doesn't cool down?"

"No way. Once he's up he stays there until he shoots off."

"Maybe I can lend a hand and give him a lift. How does he like it?"

"I can do you or you can do me—I enjoy it either way," Damien said anxiously. "I love getting it up the ass. And it's a tight ass too!"

Then he patted the sofa, gesturing for the leatherman to join him on top of it. Moving toward him the leatherman shifted and slid himself onto the sofa, stooping at the same time to stroke Damien's phallus and suck one of his nipples.

"Oh yeah," Damien groaned ravenously. "That feels so good."

Suddenly Damien frowned and made a wry face—his brow furrowing deeply as he raised his hands to his forehead, slowly stroking his temples and squirming on the sofa.

"I feel dizzy," he rasped under his breath, moaning, feeling faint from the first deadening effects of the drugged drink numbing his senses. "My head's spinning."

Just as suddenly the leatherman held up in the air a shiny pair of surgical forceps. He curled his lip and sneered, grinning a malicious and malignant smile.

"Now I'm going to make you feel even better." With grisly and grotesque glee he watched as Damien gradually and uncontrollably blacked out. "Profoundly better."

§

One stormy night, awaking from a deep sleep, I stumbled like a madman...into the labyrinth of the woods. A happening so ordinary attracted no special notice, but...the once tremendous and splendid stables of *Golden Gate Park* where I had wandered were found crackling and quaking to their very cornerstone under the sway of a thick and ashen mass of unfettered fire.

As the flames when first observed had already made so horrible a progression through their gray arched colonnades and terra cotta tile shingled roofs that any endeavors to spare any part of the structure would be patently ineffectual, I stood idly by—astounded—with still if not pitiful wonder. But a fresh and frightful thing soon fixed my attention and showed how much more acute is the exhilaration wrought in the emotions by the pondering of human anguish than that brought about by the most appalling phenomena of inanimate matter.

Down the lengthy trail of venerable eucalyptus trees which led from the woodland to the main gate of the *Golden Gate*

Park stables a charger, carrying an unhelmeted and deranged rider, was observed bounding with a boisterousness which outpaced the very Demon of the Storm.

The flight of the horseman was incontestably on his own part out of control. The anguish of his visage, the convulsive strain of his form, bore witness to superhuman struggle: but no noise, except a single scream, emitted from his lacerated lips which were bitten through and through in the acuteness of horror. One moment and the clattering of hooves resonated sharply and shrilly above the uproar of the flames and the screaming of the storm—another and clearing at a single bound the gate-way and the faded green corral the charger leapt far into the teetering stalls and—with the rider—vanished amidst the windstorm of tumultuous fire.

The rage of the storm instantly faded away and a quiet solemnly followed. A white flame still enshrouded the blighted stables like a pall and, drifting away into the tranquil air, shed forth a glow of preternatural light; while a cloud of smoke settled thickly over the stables in the definite stupendous shape of—*a horse—the horse of Metzengerstein!*

§

At *John F. Kennedy Drive* and *36th Avenue* in *Golden Gate Park* is situated the city's sole but abandoned and battered stables—its principal stalls then discovered burned and ravaged by a devouring fire of some unknown arson. And hanging from a solitary, towering but dilapidated pole at the crumbling corral —swaying slightly on a long taut chain—was then found the overturned charred corpse of a male youth burnt to a smoldering, cinder-clotted crisp!

§

Figures of fiends in shapes of menace with skeletal frames

and other more truly frightful likenesses overspread and defaced the walls. I perceived that the outlines of those monstrosities were amply sharp but the hues appeared murky and obscure as if from the effects of a dank air. I then observed the floor also which was of stone. In the middle gaped a rotund pit.

Lifting up my eyes I inspected the ceiling of the loft. It was some thirty or forty feet overhead and fabricated much as the sidelong walls. In one of its slabs a very peculiar shape fixed my entire attention. It was the painted picture of Time as he is customarily portrayed—except that in the place of a scythe—he held what at a cursory glimpse I surmised to be the depicted likeless of a prodigious pendulum such as is seen on antique clocks. There was something though in the aspect of that apparatus which prompted me to examine it more intently. While I stared straight upward at it—for its placement was imminently above my own—I imagined that I perceived it in motion. In a moment afterward my invention was verified. Its sweep was short and naturally slow. I scrutinized it for some moments—somewhat in fear but more with wonder. Tired at length of watching its tedious motion I directed my eyes to other things in the loft.

It might have been half an hour, maybe even an hour—for I could take but deficient note of time—before I once more lifted up my eyes. What I then observed confused and astonished me. The sweep of the pendulum had extended in range by almost a yard. As a natural result its speed was also a lot swifter. But what mainly troubled me was the notion that it had discernibly *descended*. I then perceived—with what terror it is superfluous to say—that its nethermost extremity was fashioned of a crescent of glimmering steel—about a foot in length from horn to horn; the horns upturned and the lower edge plainly as sharp as that of a razor. Like a razor too it looked massy and weighty, tapering from the rim into a solid and broad shape aloft. It was affixed to a heavy rod of brass and the entirety *hissed* as it swung through the air!

§

Situated at *John F. Kennedy Drive* and *35th Avenue* in *Golden Gate Park* is the expansive and artificial but placid *Spreckels Lake*. And hanging from a lofty and scraggly limb, bristling with foliage at its tail end, amongst the woodsy groves of towering eucalyptus, cypress, pine, aspen and magnolia trees hedging round the lake—swaying slightly from two taut creaking ropes overhanging a bend in the stony serpentine footpath—were then discovered the decaying and dismembered halves of a youthful male torso evenly severed and split in two!

§

Once more the three retired to the snug seclusion of Dr. Usher's comfortable ground-level sitting room, reclining and conferring together from adjoining armchairs in his four-floor terrace house bordering *Buena Vista Park*—this time with the current edition of the *San Francisco Chronicle* outspread before them atop the low-set polished coffee table displaying its big bold banner headline: ***COPYCAT SCARABUS KILLER STALKS SAN FRANCISCO!***

"We should keep in mind," descanted C. Dupin, "that generally speaking it is the purpose of our newspapers rather to create a sensation—to make a point—than to advance the cause of truth. The latter aim is only pursued when it appears compatible with the former. The print which simply chimes in with popular opinion—however well-informed that opinion may be—wins for itself no credit with the rabble. The masses of the mob deem as deep only him who insinuates caustic contradictions to the prevailing notion."

"What notion of truth then do you put forth in this case?" Dr. Usher asked him curiously.

"I will not pursue these suppositions—for I have no claim to name them more—since the shadows of speculation upon

241

which they are predicated are hardly of adequate depth to be tangible by my own conception—and since I could not pretend to make them explicit to the comprehension of another. We shall term them suppositions then and speak of them as such."

"And those suppositions consist of what?"

"Four people—two known prostitutes and two apparently homosexual youths—in as many days have been atrociously murdered by Poe-inspired methods reminiscent of the scandalous—albeit uncaught—*Scarabus* killer—and left discarded in different locations in *Golden Gate Park*," Dupin elucidated fatally. "So someone, I fear, has rather morbidly undertaken to replicate—if not imitate—those deplorable murders."

"Presumably the original *Scarabus* killer would be much too old and frail if not decrepit at this late date to perpetrate these rather strenuous crimes alone," Dr. Usher conjectured.

"Quite so!" Dupin readily agreed. "Perhaps the notorious but now declining *Scarabus* killer has rather cunningly appointed—or empowered—a pre-conditioned proxy—or surrogate of death, if you will—to act on his behalf—and to *murder* in his place!"

"By pre-conditioned then you specifically mean *hypnotized* proxy?"

"Of that I have strongly suspected Dr. Vincent Valdemar for some time now."

"I cannot believe my ears!" Lenore abruptly spouted, sitting up stiffly straight in her chair. "You're seriously suggesting that Nicolino is under the power and control of a latter-day serial killer who's conditioned him hypnotically to commit these heinous crimes by proxy!"

"That's precisely," C. Dupin solemnly affirmed, "what I expect and trust my resumed surveillance of Dr. Vincent Valdemar to ultimately and conclusively prove."

FIFTEEN:

SCOURGE OF THE RED DEATH

"And Darkness and Decay and the Red Death held illimitable dominion over all."—Poe,
The Masque of the Red Death

Wrapped up from top to toe in a long, flowing blood-red hood and robe of sleek and smooth material the tall, imposing figure stepped up to speak—slowly and solemnly as if to deliver a monologue before the footlights to a mass audience. His cloaked arms clasped beneath thick folds in front Dr. Valdemar's distinctive voice issued out resonantly from his hood's darkened face-hole.

"The *Red Death* has long ravaged this city," he soliloquized to his apparent spectators. "No plague has ever been so deadly or so dreadful. Blood is its embodiment and its die—the redness and the terror of blood. There are piercing pains and abrupt vertigo and then copious bleeding at the pores with corruption. The crimson blotches upon the body and especially upon the visage of the victim are the epidemic ban which shut him out from the help and the pity of his fellow creatures. And the entire attack, advance and cessation of the syndrome are the episodes of half an hour."

He gradually drew out his hands from his blood-red robe to gesture demonstrably to his ostensible listeners—exposing to full view the prominent depiction of Time on the front of the robe as he is symbolically portrayed but grasping in place of a scythe the conspicuously razor-sharp *pendulum!*

"I am the *Grim Reaper of souls!*" he pronounced grimly. "And I am felicitous and fearless and shrewd. With my domains half depopulated I have summoned to my presence my *Deputy of Death...Leatherman...*and with him withdrew to the abysmal solitude of this loft...I decided to leave means neither of entry or exit to the abrupt impulses of futility or of fury from within...With such a precaution we might hurl defiance at the pestilence...In the meantime it is frivolity to lament or to think...All this and security are within. Without is the *Red Death.*"

Into full view wearing high biker boots stepped a tall, slender, pale-skinned youth fitted out from head to foot in black leather—a half-hood displaying two small round eye-holes and an inverted V-shaped opening for the mouth masking his pallid face; a slim trooper hat pulled down snug over his head; a decorative slave bow tie circling his neck; and criss-crossing his thin, cadaverous torso an X-banded half-harness which buckled across a scant, front-facing jockstrap. A chrome wrist band glinted in the spotlight as his black-gloved hand gripped tight and snapped a thickset cat–o'–nine–tails flogging whip. He was conspicuously recognizable as one or the other of Dr. Valdemar's twin youth subjects: Theodore Templeton or Edward Stapleton!

"My tastes are *perverse!*" Dr. Valdemar descanted. "I have a refined eye for blood and handiwork. I ignore the decorum of pure style. My plots are daring and wild and my contrivances blaze with sadistic splendor. There are some who would think me mad. My disciples sense that I am not. It is imperative to hear and see and touch me to be *certain* that I am not."

The nebulous and lurid light enveloping Dr. Valdemar blurred, darkening and fading to black, and then brightened again.

With a summoning flourish of his hand Dr. Valdemar waved the Leatherman over. And into the friendly fold of the red-robed figure's welcoming arms the Leatherman stepped up to strike a stately pose.

"And the night closed in upon him so—and then the blackness came and lingered and left—and the day once more dawned—and the fog of another night was then looming ahead—and still he stood motionless in that secluded chamber;" Dr. Valdemar soliloquized, "and still he stood plunged into preoccupation and still the *phantasma* of the teeth retained its horrible predominance—as with the most vibrant and revolting clarity—it drifted about amidst the flittering lights and shadows of the chamber. At length there broke in upon his dreams an outcry of terror and consternation;…It appeared that he had freshly awakened from a confounding and fervid dream. He knew that it was then midnight...But of that dreary interlude which intruded he had no certain—at least no precise conception. Yet its recollection was glutted with terror—terror more terrible from being obscure and horror more horrible from obscurity. It was a frightful page in the register of his being written all over with nebulous and dreadful and incomprehensible remembrances. He struggled to interpret them but to no avail; while ever and soon—like the ghost of a departed sound—the sharp and stabbing scream of a female voice appeared to be piercing his ears. He had done a deed—what was it? He asked himself the question aloud and the murmuring echoes of the chamber answered him: *what was it?*...These things were in no way to be accounted for...He recounted a freak outcry disrupting the quiet of the night...He pointed to his outfit;—it was putrid and curdled with blood. I spoke not and took him gently by his hand;—it was impressed with the imprint of human nails. He drew my attention to some thing...a little casket...which slid from his hand and dropped weightily and fell to pieces; and from it—with a clattering noise—there drummed out some instruments of dental surgery commingled with thirty-two little, white and enamel-looking obects that were strewn back and forth around the floor: the teeth of *Berenice!*"

The nebulous and lurid light enveloping Dr. Valdemar blurred, darkening and fading to black, and then brightened again.

In the dead of night the loft was irradiated by a huge chandelier hanging by a chain from the middle of the sky-light and lowered or lifted by dint of a counterbalance which penetrated outside the vault and above the roof. The chain by which the chandelier usually hung might have been perceived very gradually to descend until its hooked extremity came within three feet of the floor. The Leatherman laid firm hold of the lengthy chain—compassed about the ankles of the supine, "effeminate-looking" youth and *fastened*—at its attachment. There—with the flight of thought—he inserted the hook from which the chandelier was used to hang; and in a moment—by some inconspicuous operation—the chandelier-chain was pulled so far upward as to take the hook out of reach and—as an inescapable result—to hoist the youth's lumpish body upside down.

"Leave him to *me!*" then shrieked the Leatherman—his strident voice making itself readily heard. "Leave him to *me.* I suspect *I* know him. If I can just get a good look at him *I* can soon tell who he is."

Clutching a torch from a wall sconce he scrambled to the middle of the chamber still shrieking: "*I* shall soon discover who he is!"

He abruptly emitted a piercing whistle when the chain shot wildly up for about thirty feet—hauling with it the listless youth and leaving him dangling in mid-air between the sky-light and the floor. The Leatherman thrust his torch up toward him as though seeking to discover who the youth was. He ground and gnashed his teeth as he frothed at the mouth and stared with a look of frenzied fury into the overturned countenance of the youth.

"Ah, ha!" howled at length the incited Leatherman. "Ah, ha! I start to see who this person *is* now!"

With the hefty swab stick clutched in his other hand the Leatherman plastered the youth's suspended body with tar. A thick coating of flax was then plastered upon the coating of tar. There—pretending to inspect the youth more intently— he thrust the torch to the flaxen coating which incrusted the youth—and which instantaneously burst into a shroud of vibrant flame. In less than half a minute the entire youth was burning ferociously. At length the flames abruptly escalated in intensity.

"I now see *clearly,*" the Leatherman wailed, "what species of person this is. He is a celebrated pariah…As for myself I am merely Leatherman the serial killer—and *this is my next to the last killing.*"

Due to the acute inflammability of both the flax and the tar to which it stuck the Leatherman had barely concluded his succinct bombast before his task of killing was consummated. The single overhanging corpse swung on its chain—a putrid, blackened, gruesome and indistinguishable mass. The Leatherman threw his torch at the cremated youth and sedately retired from sight.

The nebulous and lurid light enveloping the corpse blurred, darkening and fading to black, and then brightened again.

Suspended upside down and spread-eagled by chains another "effeminate-looking" youth—the one named *Damien!*—hung heavily from steel beams crisscrossing the ceiling. Manacles clamped down tight around his bruised ankles, pulling long and hard at his sorely strained legs. His manacled arms dangled loosely beneath him. Above him shadowy steel rafters creaked with the strain of bearing the weighty burden of his overturned body, swaying ever so slightly in the stone cold air.

"What good is it," Dr. Valdemar's voice rambled resonantly, "to recount the lengthy, lengthy minutes of terror more than fatal during which he counted the surging swings of the steel!"

Inch by inch—line by line—just perceptible at intervals that seemed eons—down and still down the pendulum came!

"Minutes passed—it might have been that many minutes passed—before the pendulum whisked so closely above him as to fan him with its caustic breath," Dr. Valdemar ran on. "The smell of the sharp steel forced itself into his nostrils…"

The swinging of the pendulum was at right angles to the youth's crotch.

"He saw that the crescent was calculated to cross the region of his groin," Dr. Valdemar ran on. "It would fray the fabric of his breeches—it would return and repeat its performance—again—and again. Nevertheless its terribly broad sweep—some thirty feet or more—and the hissing might of its descent—sufficient to sever those very walls of steel—still the fraying of his fabirc would be all that for several minutes it would achieve...He compelled himself to contemplate the noise of the crescent as it should pass across the fabric—the strange tingling sensation which the abrasion of fabric produces on the nerves..."

Down—steadily down the pendulum crept.

Down—positively, pitilessly down! It swept within three inches of his crotch! He struggled wildly, fiercely to free his arms.

Down—still unremittingly—still unavoidably down! He choked and struggled at each sweep. He cringed convulsively at its every swing. His eyes followed its outward and upward turns with the anxiety of the most meaningless futility; they shut themselves sporadically at its descent.

But the stroke of the pendulum already chafed at his crotch. It had split the seam of the breeches. It had torn through the linen underneath.

"Twice again the pendulum swept," Dr. Valdemar ran on, "and an acute twinge of pain must have bolted through every nerve..."

Over again the pendulum swung—looming ahead largely and moving menacingly toward the two lone spectators sitting and watching together in the darkened theater. Then a flying splotch of blood-red ooze blacked out the moving picture screen!

§

Two directors of the *Cinematheque* sat alone at the foot of the rising rows of drab plastic seats inside the spacious, wood-paneled auditorium, watching attentively the moving picture before them play out its final frames.

"Cut it!" one director called out aloud to the projectionist inside the long, dark, glass-enclosed booth at the room's upper rear. "Turn up the lights!"

Spots in the creased concrete ceiling illuminated the lecture hall as the projection screen in back of the wide wooden stage in front went white.

"Well?" the other director asked. "Is that supposed to be a snuff film or what?"

"Or maybe an S&M flick," the first director grumbled with a shrug. "Who knows? Let's go talk it over. We've got a problem to discuss—and a decision to make."

Across the expansive, windswept concrete terrace the two directors strolled outside between a long and low concrete–and–glass building—displaying a red diamond-shaped sign lettered in white: *Pete's Cafe*—and the Spanish mission-style structure and tower of the *San Francisco Art Institute* perched high up on *Chestnut Street*. Side by side they stepped up to a weather-beaten metal railing looking far out on *Coit Tower* and the sun-bleached houses scattered far and near atop *Telegraph Hill*.

"So what's the problem?" the second director asked the first.

"An anonymous benefactor has sent us quite a generous donation—never mind for the moment just how generous," the first related dryly. "Suffice it to say: it's a sizable enough donation to tickle the board's fancy and give them reason for rejoicing."

"That sizable is it?" the second said, pricking up his ears. "Sounds heartwarming. So how many strings are attached?"

"Only one really: we get double the donation on the condition that we publicize the film and run it in public."

"It's pretty violent."

"No more violent than the necrophilia films we've run for Halloween."

"How long would we have to run this particular contribution?"

"Thirteen days."

"Most auspicious. How do we justify that? The piece is so

251

blatantly *perverse*."

"We have to figure out a legitimate way to gloss over that aspect enough to warrant making off with the money."

"Seizing the opportunity as it were."

"Exactly."

The second director mused only momentarily.

"There's only one way really that we can make off with that much money and make amends for doing it at the same time," he suggested assuredly.

"Yeah? How's that?"

"By donating a sizable gift of our own from the film's proceeds—a much less sizable gift naturally—to some good, worthy and deserving cause."

"Such as?"

"Such as the community fund to fight and defeat *Perverseness!*"

"Now that's very charitable to say nothing of very devious thinking on your part."

"What can I say?" the second director said arrogantly. "I'm just a *progressive* philanthropist!"

§

Agitated and aghast Lenore scrounged around frantically in the already rummaged, rifled and ransacked room in their house on *Potrero Hill*, looking incredulously through disordered desks and dressers, closets and cupboards, cabinets and consoles.

"I don't believe this!" She sighed resignedly, throwing up her hands in disgust.

Shuddering she sank down onto her springy sofa soundly stunned by fearful shock and surprise. Skittishly she snapped up her cordless telephone receiver from the low-lying table in front of her and furiously punched the telephone keys—listening intently for an answer.

"Dr. Usher!" she cried out aloud finally, fidgeting and cutting her conversation short. "I must see you right away! Someone's broken into our house and stolen Nicolino's journals!"

§

Dr. Kerwin Usher sat back and settled into his black oak chair behind his bay window desk.

"Since the police have proven themselves to be so indifferent and ineffectual," he concluded, "there's nothing left for us to do but to try and find Nicolino ourselves—especially now that the thirteen days of the hypnotic experiment have passed."

Lenore shifted restlessly in the chintz-covered window seat in Dr. Usher's drawing room, looking ill at ease.

"Then you'll try to help me find him?" she asked anxiously.

"Certainly I will. Our problem of course is where to look."

Absent-mindedly Dr. Usher was rapping, tapping upon his desktop the white pocket calling card Lenore handed him which was printed simply with the name: *M. Valdemar.*

"And that's what's been troubling me..." he mused.

"Where to look?"

"Or perhaps whom really to look for?"

"What do you mean?"

Arising slowly from his chair Dr. Usher at length looked out thoughtfully on his small terrace, courtyard and orchid garden—and beyond to the southern part of the glittering city far off below. Then he looked like a startling revelation had abruptly entered his head.

"What a fool I've been not to have come to so obvious a conclusion sooner!"

"What conclusion?" Expectantly Lenore sat up in her seat.

"Have you ever heard of the *shadow self?*"

"Shadow self?"

Eagerly Dr. Usher stepped up to the fireplace and took from the bookcase above its mantel an old, leather-bound book, leafing nimbly through its pages.

"What's that?" Lenore got to her feet to step up alongside him.

"At the threshold of the subconscious mind," Dr. Usher said seriously, "stands the shadow self—the complete and utter opposite of the conscious personality which everybody sees in their everyday lives."

He sat back down behind his desk, gesturing for her to sit back down across from him.

"Beyond the shadow is the anima—or animus in the woman—which is a much more sympathetic but essential part with the traits of the opposite sex." He laid down the open book atop his desktop. "At first such a rarity becomes a personality of their own sex whom they intensely dislike—and then one of the opposite sex who appears to gratify some deep-seated need. Frequently the second figure is much more shadowy and mysterious than the first—but this is no more than a reflection of the fact that the mind is habitually more definite about what it hates than what it loves. Many people do appear to possess diametrically opposed personalities operating within them. The *Jekyll–and–Hyde* fusion is no mere figment of the imagination—but a very real and compelling condition. Only rarely are two equally forceful and opposed personalities conjured up by one person; but whenever they are they can be wildly dramatic to say the least."

"Are you speaking of someone with two personalities?"

"A split personality," he clarified, "which is a mental disorder with the presence of two or more different and distinct personalities in one person. Each personality—or identity—takes over control of the person at different times in certain trigger-situations. Serious trouble comes if a malevolent—or murderous—one takes over control. There's a very real danger of suicide if the dominant personality tries to kill off the other, resulting in the person's death."

"Are you saying that Dr. Valdemar is a split personality?" Suddenly the very same startling revelation appeared to enter Lenore's head.

"We're all born with the will to live," Dr. Usher elucidated. "The law of self-preservation is the primary law of our lives. It's basic. Every doctor who knows how to practice hypnosis is able to change in a normal subject the will to die into the will to live. But Dr. Valdemar, I'm afraid, has a mind to instill in someone the will to kill!"

"In Nicolino?" Lenore looked breathlessly aghast. "How could he possibly do that?"

"Through guided imagery suggestions and induced hallucinations of a certain time and place," he explained. "By creating mental pictures and setting scenes having a specific purpose—such as a rehearsal for programmed behavior. Or by creating an environment in which his behavior could be re-programmed and manipulated. And even though the images conjured up could be very fractional and fragmentary they would likely be richly symbolic."

"Like images from Edgar Allan Poe?"

"Exactly. And especially images of phobic fear—for like a contagious disease a phobic fear can be transmitted from one person to another. This source of a phobia is the easiest to comprehend since it is imposed by some outside force. Anyone you are close to or in close contact with—a friend, relative, companion or even a stranger—can transmit a phobia."

"Why would Dr. Valdemar want to transmit such a phobia to Nicolino?"

"To make him desperate enough in his own mind to want to kill—to do away with the phobia."

"What kind of phobia would he transmit to Nicolino?"

"Perverse-Phobia of course—the morbid fear of *Perverseness!*"

"To do away with that phobia whom would Nicolino have to kill?"

"Whomever Dr. Valdemar imagined had *Perverseness* running in their blood."

"I refuse to believe that Nicolino could be induced to kill against his will," Lenore insisted, shaking her head adamantly. "I refuse to believe he could even be made capable of killing."

"If a suitable subject is compelled to accept certain hypnotically induced hallucinations as reality then he could be made capable of anything—even killing," Dr. Usher disputed her. "And since Nicolino shares somewhat Dr. Valdemar's obvious obsession with Edgar Allan Poe—the rest speaks quite eloquently for itself."

He pushed the open book across the desktop in front of Lenore together with the little white calling card. Then he fingered the page—pointing.

"One of the terror tales of Edgar Allan Poe…Take particular note of the story title and the name on the calling card."

"*The Facts in the Case of M. Valdemar!*" Lenore read aloud, gasping with bated breath. "Dr. *Milos* Valdemar! The initials are the same!"

"The very same," Dr. Usher confirmed. "In the story however the initial M. stood simply for mister—the title of address. But this coincidental likeness is much too striking to be a case of mistaken identity. Dr. Vincent Valdemar and Dr. Milos Valdemar must be one and the same!"

"And Nicolino?" Lenore asked worriedly.

"His whereabouts have likely been sitting here right in front of us for some time."

"You mean the address on the card?"

"Yes," he answered urgently. "A place on *York Street* in the *Mission* district!"

SIXTEEN:

THE FACE OF THE OF THE SHADOW SELF

*"With a wild and waking thought
Of beings that have been,
Which my spirit hath not seen,
Had I let them pass me by,
With a dreaming eye!"*—Poe poem:
Imitation

And then there skulked into my imagination—like a lush lyrical note—the notion of what luscious repose there must be in the grave. The notion came calmly and furtively and it appeared long before it reached perfect appreciation; but just as my soul came at length properly to sense and cherish it the murk of gloom transpired; all sensations seemed consumed in a delirious surging descent as of the spirit into hell. Then stillness, silence and night were all the world.

§

In the rear of the *Mission* district loft building Lenore squeezed and slid herself in behind Dr. Kerwin Usher after he jimmied open the chained but tightly parted double doors with a crowbar. Flanked by stepped storage bins and two radiators set into a curved wall they each wormed and wriggled their way into the darkened, circular corridor—lit only by dim lamplight showing limpidly through small, glass-block windows from the outside. Far off ahead of them—beyond the distant bend in the corridor stretching to the loft's opposite end—muttering voices echoed from a corner erratically shedding light and spreading misshapen shadows. Cautiously, quietly—they moved together along the long, curved wall and headed for its lighted but shadowed outlet. Before long they came up to a cluster of folded, free-standing partitions set up at the open end of the curved corridor—one open-work screen of lacquered wood and a multi-panel screen of chip-board, slate and sprayed bronze. Dr. Usher gestured for Lenore to stay still as they crouched low to peer through the tall, slender cracks creasing the partition folds. A double colonnade of hollow fluted columns separated the lighted studio space opening up beyond them. And from where the light and shadows emanated they looked aghast as they watched a strange and bizarre scene play itself out.

§

Brightly illuminated by quartz floor-stand lamps and base-lights hung high up in the ceiling—mounted in light-weight aluminum scoops with door-like panels attached to their rims—the cleared corner of the loft exhibited small and large sound boom microphones attached to level arms, supported and counter-balanced on the center-columns of both stationary and wheeled stands. And standing tall above that lighting and sound equipment was a digital studio video camera mounted on the tail end of a heavy, tri-rubber-wheeled pedestal-base and crane—a centrally pivoted boom counter-balanced on its height-adjustable column. In the middle of that smooth, level and roomy studio space was sunk a shallow but dug-out and elongated grave heaped around on all sides by lumpish mounds of piled-up dirt and rubble. Plunged into the grave was the peculiarly shaped black coffin: the *oblong box!* Hunched over the grave, thrusting lustily his shiny and sharpened grave-digger's spade into the mounds and scooping out dirt to heave and heap atop the coffin below was the red-robed figure of the *Grim Reaper of Souls!* And he could be half-heard talking together—carrying on a vivacious conversation—with himself!

§

Dr. Valdemar's eyes were riveted fixedly ahead of him and throughout his whole visage there ruled a stony hardness. But there came a severe shiver over his whole person; a sickly smile trembled about his lips; and I perceived that he spoke in a soft, impetuous and gibbering whisper as if unaware of my habitation underfoot. Confined closely beneath him I at length imbibed the frightful import of his words.

"Not hear it?—yes, I hear it and *have* heard it," Dr. Valdemar pronounced in his own deeply resonant and sonorous voice. "Long—long—long—many minutes, many hours, many days have I heard it—yet I dared not—oh, pity me—miserable wretch that I am—I dared not—I *dared* not speak!"

"*We have put him living in the grave!*" he rebutted himself in soft, subdued, whispering tones. "Said I not that my senses were astute? I *now* tell you that I heard his first weak movements in the hollow coffin. I heard them—many, many days ago—yet I dared not—*I dared not speak either!*"

Talking together with himself—back and forth—first in his natural speaking voice and then in his affected and artificial whisper—Dr. Vincent Valdemar made conversation with his imagined, made-up twin brother: Dr. Milos Valdemar!

"Oh where shall I flee? Will he not be here soon? Is he not rushing to reprimand me for my impatience? Have I not heard his pounding on the lid? Do I not discern the heavy and horrible beating of his heart?"

Abruptly the red-robed figure stopped digging, cutting himself short and leaving his spade stuck upright in a mound of dirt.

"*LUNATIC!*" there he shrieked out his raspy syllables as if in the attempt he were giving up his ghost—"*LUNATIC! I TELL YOU THAT HE NOW LIES BENEATH THE GROUND!*"

From the immeasurable images of gloom which so persecuted me in nightmares I designate for record but a lone vision. I thought I was submerged in a somnambulistic trance of more than normal term and depth. Startlingly there came a cold hand upon my brow and an impetuous gibbering voice whispering a word in my ear.

"Arise!" it rasped.

I strained every nerve. The blackness was absolute. I could not discern the figure of him who had awakened me. I could call to mind neither the time at which I had tumbled into the trance nor the location in which I then lay. While I stayed stationary and occupied in attempts to collect my thoughts the frigid hand gripped me ferociously by the wrist, shaking it peevishly, while the gibbering voice whispered once more:

"Arise! did I not bid you arise?"

"And who," I demanded from below, "are you?"

"I have no name in the realms which I dwell," the voice answered sorrowfully; "I was human but am demon. I was pitiless but am pitiful. You do sense that I shiver. My teeth chatter as I speak yet it is not with the severity of the night—of the night without limit. But this frightfulness is intolerable. How can you peacefully sleep? I cannot rest for the outcry of this extreme anguish. These sights are more than I can stand. Get you up! Come with me into the distant Night and let me expose you to the graves. Is not this a pageant of despair?—Behold!"

And the voice once more pronounced as I peered:

"Is it not—oh! is it *not* a pitiful sight?" But before I could find words to respond the figure had stopped to grip my wrist while pronouncing once more:

"Is it not—O God! is it *not* a most pitiful sight?"

§

"Nicolino's being buried alive!" Lenore rasped beneath her breath. "What are we going to do?"

"You're going to the police for help," Dr. Usher calmly insisted. "I'll stay here and try to help Nicolino."

"You're going to confront Valdemar alone?"

"We have no choice. This situation's turning critical. So you've got to go get help."

"No way!" she protested, shaking her head. "By the time the cops get here—whatever's going down will be all over and done with. I'm staying so we can both help Nicolino."

"No," he calmly objected. "It's too dangerous."

"Why? Because I'm a woman? There's supposed to be strength in numbers."

"There's also super-human strength in madness and he could be psychopathic? So there's no telling what he's capable of?"

"In which case we'll have to overpower him to free Nicolino. We'll be better off chancing that together than alone."

"Perhaps."

"Besides," she whispered irately, "the cops are useless anyway. They'd care less about releasing Nicolino alive and unharmed than storm-trooping the place and laying waste to everything in sight—including us and Nicolino if we happen to get in their way. So I'd rather take our chances alone than trust our lives to their siege mentality."

"You don't think very highly of your city's peace officers."

"I just think cave men should stay at home where they belong—in their caves."

Just then—and utterly unknown to the two—the silently and stealthily moving figure of the diabolically glaring Leatherman slid out unexpectedly from behind from between two adjacent partitions—and into full ominous view!

§

For the purpose of walling up people in the chamber the loft was well adapted. Its walls were loosely built and had recently been plastered throughout with an unpolished plaster which the dankness of the air had hindered from hardening. From one of the walls projected a protrusion produced by a false chimney—or fireplace—which before had been filled up and rough-hewn to resemble the rest of the chamber.

Amidst dislodged and displaced brick-work the gagged–and–bound persons of Lenore and Dr. Usher were deposited and propped in their positions against the inner wall!

Within that wall was a still inward niche about four feet in depth, three in width and six or seven in height. It appeared to have been built for no particular purpose but delineated simply the gap between two of the large columns of the roof of the loft—and was braced by one of their encircling walls of solid brick.

Lenore and Dr. Usher were pinioned to the brick. Driven into its surface were two pairs of iron spikes—distant from each other about two feet horizontally. From two of those dangled two short chains; from the others two padlocks. About their waists the links were cast and secured.

§

I wriggled and made spastic efforts to force ajar the lid: it would not budge. And then also there came abruptly to my nostrils the powerful peculiar smell of damp dirt.

Then there were noises engendered by the figure in prying open the oblong box by dint of a chisel and mallet—the mallet being evidently muffled—or stifled—by some fleecy cotton or woolen material in which its top was enveloped.

In this way I imagined I could discern the exact instant when he partially detached the lid—also that I could ascertain when he dislodged it entirely.

Upon my struggling he stooped impetuously low, and grasping me by my arm with a gesture of restive anxiety, whispered in my ear the words: *Vincent Valdemar!*

I became soundly sedate in a moment.

There was that in the bearing of the figure—and in the unsteady tremble of his uplifted finger as he held it between my eyes and the light shed by a hanging helium–and–argon fixture which filled me with unequivocal astonishment; but it was not that which had so impetuously touched me. It was the gravity of sober warning in the peculiar, whispering, rasping expression; and above all it was the nature—the pitch, the *tone* of those few plain and familiar yet *whispered* syllables.

The broad and ponderous lid of the peculiarly shaped oblong box was all at once laid open to its entire extent with a powerful and precipitate impatience that doused—as if by sorcery—all light in the loft. That light—in dousing—enabled me to just discern that the figure had hovered over me snugly shrouded in his cloak. The blackness however was then absolute; and I could merely *sense* that he was standing in my midst. Before I could recuperate from my excessive amazement into which this confusion had flung me I heard the voice of the figure.

"Nicolino," he rasped in his soft, sharp and unforgettable whisper which tingled to the very marrow of my bones. "Nicolino, I make no allowances for this conduct because in so conducting I am but discharging a duty. You are beyond question unaware of the true nature of the individual who has to-night interred you…"

While he spoke so deep was the silence that one might have heard a pin drop upon the floor. In stopping he left at once as unexpectedly as he had come. Can I—shall I relate my impressions?—must I mention that I felt all the terrors of the damned? Most certainly I had little time accorded for deliberation.

After some vocalization light was at length totally restored and as very frequently occurs in similar situations a deep and striking stillness ensued. Breaking open the lid the top of the peculiarly shaped oblong box flew abruptly off and—at the same instant—I sprang up into a seated position directly confronting the figure: the red-robed figure of Dr. Valdemar himself! I glared for a few moments fixedly and mournfully full into the face of Dr. Valdemar; pronounced deliberately but distinctly and penetratingly the words—*"Thou art the man!"*— and then, dropping over the side of the coffin as if exhaustively gratified, sprawled my limbs shudderingly upon the expansive floor covered with two-inch ceramic tiles.

Into full view suddenly emerged the tall, slender, sallow, gangling figure of Mr. Augustus Bedloe—jauntily flaunting and brandishing a long-handled, smooth, shining, razor-sharp axe!

"Oh no, my dear Nicolino," Mr. Bedloe uttered contrarily,

ogling me ominously with his big globular eyes and parting his bulbous lips to display his grotesquely crooked teeth as he grinned his grisly glum grin, "perish the thought: he's not the man—*I* am!" And he too was shrouded in a blood-red hood and robe!

§

Dr. Valdemar stepped up slowly to Lenore and Dr. Usher, sagging still in their fetters within the hollowed recess of the red-brick fireplace blocked out of the facing wall. Lenore slumped in deep slumber. Dr. Usher stared with wide-eyed wonder.

"The thousand affronts of Usher I have tolerated as best I could;" he railed at Dr. Usher in his normal resonant voice, "but when you dared outrage I pledged vengeance. You, who so well know the bent of my spirit, will not presume however that I give voice to a threat. *At length* I will wreak my vengeance; this is a resolve decisively formed—but the very decisiveness with which it is formed precludes the danger of risk. I must not purely punish but punish with impunity. A grievance is redressed when reprisal overtakes its redresser. It is equally un-redressed when the avenger fails to make himself impressed as such upon him who has done the injury.

"It must be understood that neither by word nor deed have I given Usher ground to suspect my good-will. I continued—as is my custom—to smile in his face and he did not discern that my smile was *then* at the thought of his extermination."

Abruptly and roughly Dr. Valdemar ripped the gag from Dr. Usher's mouth.

"Quite a good joke indeed—an excellent jest," Dr. Usher uttered irresolutely. "We will have many a great laugh about it."

"I most assuredly will," Dr. Valdemar retorted solemnly. *"For the love of God, Valdemar!"*

266

"Yes," he rejoined him, "for the love of God!"

"Do not pretend," Mr. Bedloe abruptly interrupted him, "to eclipse from your consciousness the identity of the peculiar person who so persistently interferes with your affairs and plagues you with his intrusive advice. But who and what is this *Milos* Valdemar?—and whence came he?—and what are his designs? Upon neither of these points can you be appeased... You can merely imagine this peculiar conduct to ensue from a consummate self-conceit assuming the unseemly airs of condescension and patronage...his knowing and strangely sardonic smiles...his insufferable insolence...*You flee to no avail.* Your sinful fate follows you as if in triumph and confirms in fact that the exercise of its secret domain has as yet merely commenced...Where with truth have you *not* indignant ground to curse him within your heart? From his inexplicable tyranny do you at length flee—panic-stricken—as from a plague; and to the very ends of the earth *you flee to no avail*...And again and again—in mysterious commerce with your own soul—would you demand the questions—Who is he?—whence came he?— and what are his designs? But no answers are there discovered...Be that as it may you now start to sense the promise of a bright prospect—and at length nurture in your secret thoughts a severe and reckless resolve that you will submit no longer to being tyrannized!"

Mr. Bedloe raised a gangly arm and pointed away with a rawboned hand and gnarled finger.

"Valdemar!" he called out commandingly. "At this very moment your nemesis—your own twin brother, Milos—awaits your pleasure atop the mightiest phallic symbol in all of San Francisco: the *Coitus Tower!* And from there—unless you stop him—he'll unleash a plague of *perverseness* of epidemic proportions which will spread all over to every corner of the city, infecting and perverting everyone in it! You must hurry and go there to stop him—stop him dead!—before it's too late. You must climb the *Coitus Tower* and castrate the phallus before it spurts to infest and fester the entire city with *perverseness.* The *Grim Reaper of Souls* must go to the *Coitus Tower* to overtake and destroy the most powerful and potent carrier of *perverseness*—your brother, Milos! You must go to overpower and castrate him! You must go and do it now!"

"Yes." Dr. Valdemar nodded laconically. "I must lose no time in overtaking him before he sickens everyone with his *perverse* poison."

Saying nothing more Dr. Valdemar reservedly headed out of the studio space, leaving silently in front by a door of roll-down canvas shade. That was when Mr. Bedloe roughly dumped into the shallowly excavated grave alongside me the leaden and lifeless body of the youthful Leatherman—an axe buried in his brain!

"Meet Theodore Templeton—also known by his alias as Edward Stapleton!" Mr. Bedloe pronounced with an introductory gesture. "He was an innocent dupe to the experiment— an enticing youthful mantrap to bait and lure male prey with tempting propositions of *perverseness!* He was also the muscle needed to perform the more strenuous duties. Dr. Valdemar solicited the prostitute victims."

§

"What kind of gallery of horrors is this?" I finally asked pointedly, stirring to get to my feet. "Why are Lenore and Dr. Usher imprisoned here?"

Menacingly Mr. Bedlow wielded his axe with a silent but threatening gesture for me to stay still in my seated position.

"Before I give answer to that," Mr. Bedloe announced ceremoniously, "I cordially invite you to attend for your entertainment a masked ball of the most singular magnificence!"

"I'm afraid I don't find you the least bit entertaining." Disgustedly I glared at him.

"You will," he boasted, smiling maliciously; and with another deft flourish he flaunted jauntily before my expectant eyes a shiny key. "This key unlocks the padlocks confining your friends."

Mr. Bedloe latched the padlock key to a metal ring attached at his hip, patting it emphatically.

"If you aspire to take possession of this key—and you *do* aspire to appropriate it—then you shall promptly attend my magnificent masquerade!"

"By all means," I relented resignedly. "Proceed."

§

It was a sumptuous scene—that masquerade of innumerable posed and positioned but motionless *mannequins!*

Be certain they were bizarre. There were ample garishness, glitter, poignancy and phantasm. There were arabesque shapes with repugnant limbs and appointments. There were frenzied caprices such as the demoniac fashions. There was plenty of the resplendent, plenty of the licentious, plenty of the *grotesque,* something of the horrible and not a little of that which might have provoked repugnance. Back and forth in the expansive chamber there stalked indeed a profusion of nightmares. And those—the nightmares—writhed to and fro, taking color from the chamber and prompting the frenzied music of the electronic orchestra to resound as the reverberation of their stationary steps. And soon there struck an ebony clock which stood in a hall of velvet. And then for an instant everything was silent and everything was still except the chime of the clock. The nightmares were stiff-frozen as they stood. But the echoes of the chime faded away—they have lasted but a moment—and a slight, half-restrained laughter drifted after them as they evaporated. And then once more the music swelled and the nightmares revived and writhed back and forth more mirthfully than ever, taking color from the multi-tinged windows through which shed light from tripods.

But this chamber was thickly crowded and in it throbbed frenziedly the heart of life. And the motionless gala went dizzyingly on until at length there commenced the chiming of midnight upon the clock. And then the music stopped as I have recounted; and the stationary revolutions of the waltzers were stilled; and there was a restive halt to all things as before. But then there were twelve strokes to be rung by the chime of the clock; and so it occurred perhaps that more of thought crept with more of time into the rumination of the introspective amongst those who inactively reveled. And so too it occurred perhaps that before the final echoes of the final chime had utterly subsided into silence there was one person in the crowd who had discovered the deliberation to become conscious of the shrouded figure which had attracted the notice of no lone person before. And the sight of this fresh presence having been caught there emanated at length in my breast a sensation expressive of disapproval and surprise—then finally of horror, of terror and of abhorrence.

In a gathering of phantasms such as I have portrayed it may well be presumed that no unremarkable presence could have inspired such sensation. With truth the masquerade licentiousness of the night was almost limitless. There are chords in the hearts of the most desperate which cannot be struck without sensation. Even with the utterly wasted—to whom life and death are both sport—there are matters of which no sport can be made. I indeed appeared then profoundly to sense that in the costume and carriage of the stranger neither esprit nor propriety prevailed. The figure was tall and gaunt and cloaked from top to toe in the garments of the grave. The mask which veiled the visage was made so closely to resemble the countenance of a rigid corpse that the closest inspection must have had difficulty in exposing the deceit. And yet all this might have been suffered if not appreciated by the motionless revelers around. But the mummer had gone so far as to assume the character of the *Red Death*. His habiliments were splattered in blood—and his broad brow with all the features of the face bespeckled with the crimson terror.

When I first set eyes on that ghostly figure—which with a languid and grave movement as if more consummately to reinforce its role stalked back and forth amongst the motionless waltzers—I was agitated in the first instant with a powerful shiver either of horror or aversion; but in the next my brow blushed with wrath.

"Who dares?" I demanded harshly—"who dares outrage us with this *perverse* parody?"

It was at the threshold of an imperial suite where I stood as I pronounced those words. They made the rafters of the loft ring noisily and clearly—for I am an audacious and vigorous person and the music had become stifled at the passage of his presence.

At first as I bellowed there was a slight surging motion directed toward the trespasser, who at that instant was also close at hand, and then with deliberate and dignified step made impending approach towards me. But from an unnamed dread with which the lunatic presumptions of the mummer had evoked in me I could not put forward a hand to arrest him; so that unhindered he passed with a yard of my person; and while the vast gathering—*seemed* to recede from the middle of the chamber to the walls—he thread his way uninterruptedly but with the same dignified and deliberate step which had distinguished him from the rest.

"A sensation for which I have no label," Mr. Bedloe's voice reverberated audibly throughout the loft, "had taken possession of my soul—a sensation which will admit to no interpretation—to which the parables of by-gone days are insufficient—and for which I'm afraid doomsday itself will present no solution. To a mind constituted like my own that last consideration is a curse. I shall never—I know that I shall never—be appeased with relation to the character of my conceptions. Yet is it not marvelous that these conceptions are unclear since they have their source in origins so utterly unique. A novel sensation—a novel entity is affixed to my soul."

"Why are we here?" I blurted out irritably.

"I have asserted so much," Mr. Bedloe echoed, "that to some extent I may answer your question—explain to you why we are here—that I may ascribe to you something that shall have at least the slight semblance of a reason…Had I not been so verbose you might either have misinterpreted me entirely or—with the mob—imagined me mad. As it is you will readily discern that I am one of the many countless prey of the *Imp of the Perverse!*"

That was when I myself retreated—back to the shallow scooped out grave where the youthful Leatherman's dead body had been so dispassionately dumped—to retrieve the axe buried in his brain! Laying a firm hold of the handle I twisted and wrested it loose and determined then to stalk the deathly specter with a weapon of my own!

SEVENTEEN:

SUITE OF DEATH

"Would God I could awaken!
For I dream I know not how,
And my soul is sorely shaken
Lest an evil step be taken,—
Lest the dead who is forsaken
May not be happy now."—Poe poem:
Bridal Ballad To — —

JOSEPH COVINO JR

There were seven sections in that imperial suite. In many chambers however such suites delineate a lengthy and linear prospect while the folding partitions slide back almost to the walls on either side so that the view of the entire extent is hardly obstructed. There the case was decidedly different; as might have been anticipated from the specter's affection for the *grotesque*. The sections were so irregularly arranged that the prospect encompassed but little more than one compartment at a time. There was an abrupt turn at every twenty or thirty yards—and at each turn a remarkable effect. To the right and left—in the middle of each wall—a tall and narrow Gothic window opened out upon a closed corridor which followed the windings and turnings of the suite. Those windows were of stained glass whose colors changed in conformity with the prevalent colorations of the decor of the compartment into which it opened. That of the extreme entrance was draped in blue—and vibrantly blue were its windows. The second compartment was purple in its adornments and tapestries and there the panes were purple. The third was green throughout and so were its casements. The fourth was decorated and illuminated with orange—the fifth with white—the sixth with violet. The seventh compartment was snugly shrouded in black velvet tapestries that hung all over the ceiling and down the walls, tumbling in thick folds upon a carpet of the same material and coloration. But in that compartment solely the color of the casements failed to correspond with the adornments. The panes there were crimson—a deep blood-red coloration. Then in no one of the seven compartments was there any lamp or candelabrum amidst the multitude of golden adornments that lay scattered back and forth or dangled from the roof.

Through the blue compartment to the purple—through the purple to the green—through the green to the orange—through that again to the white—and even thence to the violet before a decisive movement had been made to seize him—the deathly specter passed uninterruptedly.

There was no light of any sort effusing from lamp or candelabrum within the suite of compartments. But in the corridors that succeeded the suite there stood—opposite to each casement—a ponderous tripod bearing a brazier flame that shed its light through the tinted glass and so gaudily illuminated the compartment. And so were fabricated a profusion of garish and fabulous appearances. But in that extreme or black compartment the effect of the fire-light that spurted upon the black draperies through the blood-stained panes was grisly in the extreme—and fabricated so freakish a look upon the faces of those who trespassed that I was hesitant to set foot within its limits at all.

It was then however that I, maddening with wrath and the shame of my own momentary timidity, hurried headlong through the tortuous and twisting windings and turnings of the six compartments in spite of the deathly horror that had seized upon me.

It was in that last compartment too that there stood against the facing wall a colossal clock of ebony. Its pendulum swung back and forth with a tedious, weighty, monotonous toll; and once the minute-hand made the round of the face and the hour was to be struck there came from the brazen bowels of the clock a cadence which was clear and clangorous and full and extremely melodious—but of so strange a pitch and emphasis that—at each lapse of an hour—a spectator was compelled to pause momentarily in their tracks to listen to the noise; and then—while the chimes of the clock yet clanged—after the lapse of sixty minutes—which comprised three thousand and six hundred seconds of the Time that was flying—there came yet another chiming of the clock at midnight! And then there was the same disconcerting and shuddering pause as before.

I held up high my uplifted axe and had loomed ahead with swift temerity to within three or four feet of the retreating specter when, having reached the extremity of the velvet compartment, turned abruptly and confronted me—his stalker. There was a penetrating outcry—and my axe dropped glinting to the sable carpet upon which instantly afterwards I fell prostrate! Then screwing up the freak courage of desperation I at once got to my feet to fling myself into the black compartment and, arresting the mummer—whose tall shape stood upright and motionless within the shadow of the ebony clock—gasped in unspeakable terror discovering the grave-cerements and corpse-like mask which I handled with so rampant a roughness—inhabited by none other than *Dr. Kerwin Usher!*—uplifting his axe aloft to strike at me and deal the mortal blow!

And then was conceded the pervasion of the *Red Death*. He had come and gone like a thief in the night. And I dropped down in the blood-bespeckled corridor of our masquerade and drowned in the hopeless position of my fall. And the spark of the ebony clock departed with that of the last of the desperate. And the flames of the tripods perished.

Lenore gradually revived, clanking clamorously her chains as she stirred sluggishly to come to her senses—only to blench and look wide-eyed and aghast and then suddenly shriek with petrifying fear as she deliberately directed her terror-stricken eyes to the dead body sagging listlessly alongside her in the red-brick nook: *Mr. Augustus Bedloe!*—an axe buried in his brain!

§

I wavered and fell. A momentary and awful infirmity afflicted me. I squirmed—I choked—I died.

"You will scarcely persist *now*," said Dr. Usher, smiling maliciously, "that the whole of your misadventure was not a dream. You are not ready to declare that you are dead? I only struck you with the blunt end!"

"Proceed!" I at length repeated hoarsely.

For many minutes my sole impression—my sole sensation—was that of blackness and nonexistence with the perception of death. At length there appeared to pass a rampant and abrupt shock through my spirit—as if of electricity. With it came the sensation of resilience and light. That last I sensed— not saw. In a moment I appeared to rise from the floor. But I had no physical, no appreciable, no audible, no palpable presence. Beneath me lay my supine corpse. But all this I sensed—not saw. I took interest in nothing. Even the corpse appeared a thing in which I had no concern. Will I had none but seemed to be propelled into motion and thrust buoyantly out of the suite. When I had reached that last threshold of the suite at which I had confronted the deathly specter I once more sustained a shock as of electricity; the sensation of weight, of will, of existence returned. I came to my original self—but the past had not lost the vibrance of the real—and not then—even for a moment—could I compel my comprehension to deem it a dream.

"Nor was it," declared Dr. Usher with an air of profound gravity, "yet it would be troublesome to state how otherwise it should be termed. It is improbable that any feat could have been wrought with a more painstaking deliberation. For weeks— for months—I brooded upon the methods of these murders. I abandoned a thousand schemes because their achievement entailed a *risk* of detection...But I need not distress you with irrelevant trifles. I need not recount the simple devices by which I hypnotized Mr. Bedloe to in turn hypnotize Dr. Valdemar to in turn hypnotize the Leatherman to assist us in enticing our victims—all so that I could hark back to illustrious times past—and revisit, relive and reproduce my own murders—and reap once more this showcase of souls!"

"Then you are the real original *Scarabus* killer?"

"The one and only—at your service."

"And the puppet-master who manipulated everything and made *black* cat's-paws of all the others to do your evil bidding?"

"Quite so," Dr. Usher gloated boastfully. "Mr. Bedloe—

poor deluded fellow!—actually believed he was me and acted out accordingly!"

"How do I fit into this warped charade?"

"I'll plant your journals here before I depart. You're to be the hapless and unhappy scapegoat framed for committing multiple murders! I never meant to murder you from the beginning!" Dr. Usher boasted then bombastically. "I had left no ghost of a clue by which it would be conceivable to convict—or even to suspect—me of these crimes. It is inconceivable how sumptuous a sensation arose in my bosom as I brooded upon my perfect safety. For a very long time I was used to delight in this sensation. It offered me more true delight than all the mundane gains accruing from my sins. But there came at length an age from which the gratifying sensation grew—by hardly discernible degrees—into a haunting and harassing impression. It harassed because it haunted. I could hardly rid myself of it for a moment...In this way at last I would constantly catch myself brooding upon my safety and repeating in soft under-tones the euphemisms, 'I am safe! I am safe—I am safe—yes—if I be not fool enough to make overt confession!'"

"But you *have!*" intruded the very familiar, very comforting and very welcome voice. "You *have* been fool enough and you *have* made overt confession! And now you are no longer safe! I once told you that a vast if not greater part of the truth ensued from the irrelevant: and I traced the seemingly irrelevant fact that the *Pacific Heights* house in which you purport to live is by deed titled to *Dr. Valdemar! His ornate decors betrayed you!*"

I put forward one arm and shuddered to discover that I stood at the very verge of a rounded pit whose depth naturally I had no way of determining at that instant. Slipping about the masonry just beneath my feet I managed to dislodge a small slab and made it drop into the chasm. For many moments I listened to its rumbling as it dashed against the walls of the abyss in its fall; at length there was a solemn plunge into water followed by full echoes.

I could no longer doubt the doom plotted for me by deadly endowment in torment. My consciousness of the pit had become known to the perverse manipulator—*the pit* whose terrors had been fated for so audacious a nonconformist as myself—the pit symbolic of hell. The plunge into that pit I had escaped by the simplest of mishaps and I appreciated that unexpectedness—or ensnarement into torture—comprised a prominent part of all the *perverseness* of those devilish deaths. Having failed to fall it was no part of the diabolical plot to fling me into the chasm; and so—there being no choice—a different and gentler annihilation awaited me. Gentler! I half smiled in my anguish as I thought over such employment of such a term.

Had I not indeed been living in a dream? And was I not then dying a victim to the terror and the mystery of the wildest of all nightmarish visions?

"Death," I cried, "any death but that of the pit!" Idiot! might I have not known that *into the pit* it was the design of the polished and slippery axe handle—on which I had but a flimsy and precarious grip—to propel me. I struggled no more but the anguish of my spirit found vent in one last, loud and long shout of desperation. I sensed that I teetered upon the brink—I averted my eyes as Dr. Usher looked down his nose at me the full length of the axe handle—the opposite end of which he gripped tightly by its sharp-edged head.

An outstretched hand caught my own as I fell—fainting—into the pit. It was that of C. Dupin. The retired chief detective inspector had infiltrated the loft. The *Scarabus* killer had escaped once more the clutches of his stalker!

EPILOGUE:

FLIGHT FROM COITUS TOWER

"The mystery which binds me still:
From the torrent, or the fountain,
From the red cliff of the mountain,
From the sun that 'round me roll'd
In its autumn tint of gold—
From the lightning in the sky
As it pass'd me flying by—
From the thunder and the storm,
And the cloud that took the form
(When the rest of Heaven was blue)
Of a demon in my view."—Poe poem:
Alone

S tanding bolt upright atop *Telegraph Hill*—a bulging outcrop on the northeastern shore of *San Francisco Bay*—the drab gray fluted concrete shaft of *Coit Memorial Tower* shot up one hundred eighty feet above its huge bowed base. Together with Lenore and C. Dupin I ran into the tower's lower lobby, passing by two miniature fluted columns and phoenix bird carved in relief which flank the massive wide open outer door of heavy solid brass. Once inside the art arcade of oil-painted fresco murals we passed straight on through the arched blue-latticed doorway beneath the watchful eyes of *Old Man Weather* and a mighty high-flying eagle with stupendous outspread wings.

Into the narrow spiral stairway we hurried, picking our way by the winding hand-rail and quickly mounting the reddish brown brass-plated flight of steps. Upward we climbed—round and round the turning and twisting spiral steps, passing by lucent marine port-holes and protruding lamps until we burst into the tower's spacious and shaded belvedere with its eight tall portals looking out all over the city.

A small throng of muttering sightseers and tourists already crowded around but stood clear of the curious lone red-robed figure standing close by the low-lying balustrade circling the outer observation tier. Breezy breaths of air blew up his hooded cape as he paced restlessly up and down the cavernous windwafted floor—talking together with himself and carrying on a conversation alternating back and forth between muted whispering and sonorous speech.

"Men normally grow corrupt by slow degrees," Dr. Milos Valdemar reproached his brother whisperingly. "From you—in an instant—all goodness fell materially as a cloak."

In a perfect fit of fury he turned at once upon himself and clutched himself wildly by the collar.

"Villain!" Dr. Vincent Valdemar upbraided him in a voice raucous with wrath while every syllable he pronounced appeared as fresh fuel to his frenzy, "villain! pretender! accursed scoundrel! you shall not—you *shall not* hound me unto death! Follow me or I stab you where you stand!"

He was wild with every breed of savage frenzy.

Abruptly the agitated red-robed figure drew out from his folded cloak a gem-studded dagger, exposing it with a wavering flourish to everyone's view. Nearby onlookers let out gasps of dismay and stood off as the specter of the *Grim Reaper of Souls* lunged at them with the dagger and kept them at bay. I pushed forward to hold out a pacifying hand to the tortured man shrouded in red.

"I would freely have you believe," I pleaded, "that you have been to a great extent the slave of a situation beyond mortal control. I would wish for you to search out for yourself some small oasis of casualty amidst a freakish mistake. I would have you admit—what you cannot avoid admitting—that although enticement may have before existed as extreme man was never *so* at least enticed before—surely never *so* sank. And is it then that he has never so suffered?"

It was Valdemar; but he uttered no longer in a whisper and he could have imagined that he himself was pronouncing while he recited verbatim:

"You have conquered, and I yield. Yet, henceforward art thou also dead—dead to the World, to Heaven and to Hope! In me didst thou exist—and, in my death, see by this image, which is thine own, how utterly thou has murdered thyself."

Before our very awestruck eyes—and before anybody could move toward him—Dr. Vincent Valdemar shrieked aloud in agony, straining gutturally his throat as he swiftly slid his hands into the lower front folds of his crimson cloak, plunging his dagger deep into his own groin as he fell backward over the low balustrade and plummeted headlong to the very bottom of the lofty tower—his body battering the hard red-brick base below!

§

Yet let me not be misunderstood.—The unjust, intense and morbid preoccupation so inspired by things in their own constitution trivial—must not be confused in character with that speculating tendency common to all mankind—and more especially indulged in by people of fervent imagination. It was not even—as might be at first surmised—an excessive situation or extravagance of such tendency—but principally and substantially disparate and distinct. In one illustration the dreamer—or visionary—being intrigued by a thing normally not trivial indiscernibly loses sight of that thing in a wasteland of inferences and speculations ensuing therefrom—until at the end of a daydream *frequently full of luxury* he discovers the incitement or first source of his speculations wholly evaporated and obliterated. In my case the principal thing was invariably trivial—although assuming through the medium of my distempered vision a deflected and *unreal* significance. Few inferences—if any—were made; and those few persistently reverting in upon the original object as a focus. The speculations were *never* pleasant; and at the termination of the trance the first source—so far from being not in sight—had reached the supernaturally extravagant fascination(or fixation)which was the prevailing peculiarity of the affliction. In a few words the powers of mind more specifically practiced were—with me—as I have stated before—the *preoccupying* and are with the visionary the *speculative*.

"Death approaches;" Lenore said solemnly as we stood together inside the round but roof-less observation deck at the very top of *Coit Memorial Tower*, looking out one of its many arched windows and commanding a far off view of the *Embarcadero* piers and the gray *Bay Bridge* hanging suspended in an overcast mist between its two outstretched necks of land, "and the shadow which precedes him has cast a tempering sway over my soul. I long—in passing through the shadowy valley—for the empathy—I had almost said for the sympathy—of my fellow creatures."

Throughout the brightest days of her unapproached beauty most certainly I had never loved her. In the mysterious peculiarity of my being emotions with me *had never been* of the heart and my passions *always were* of the mind. Through the gray of the early dawn—amongst the trellised shades of the woods at noon—and in the stillness of our bookroom by night—she had darted by my eyes and I had perceived her—not as the living and breathing Lenore—but as the Lenore of a dream—not as a creature of the world—worldly—but as the abstraction of such entity—not as a thing to esteem but to scrutinize—not as an object of love but as the theme of the most esoteric although erratic speculation.

Around the broad and tall base at the southeastern foot of the *Coit Memorial Tower* stretched a spacious clearing. Spread over a wide mound behind and below the tower between two majestic eucalyptus trees was a layered bed of wood chips, shards and shavings. Beyond swept the distant vista of the faraway *Ferry Building* at the foot of *Market Street* and the *Bay Bridge*.

And *then*—then I shivered in Lenore's presence and grew pallid at her approach; yet bitterly deploring her deathly and forlorn condition I called to mind that she had loved me long and—in one wicked moment—I folded her snugly and warmly in my arms and proposed to her marriage.

Postscript: Look for the sequel—in which Lenore and Nicolino will return: **Edgar Allan Poe's San Francisco: More Terror Tales of the City**

FOOTNOTE:

REBUTTING THE(PRETTY

ILLITERATE)CRITICS

*"I started reading the book(**Terror Tales of the City: Prince of the Perverse**)yesterday and I was quite impressed with the depth of thought and creativity that you invested in writing the prologue and the opening chapter."*—former gay gym-mate in a personally hand-written note to the writer dated 20 November 2002

E dgar Allan Poe's San Francisco: Terror Tales of the City is an extensively and heavily revised—and re-worked—version of my original novel titled *Terror Tales of the City: Prince of the Perverse*(2002).

Publication of this first original novel was duly *CANCELLED* and completely *REMOVED* from the retail bookselling market as of January 2005. Any and all further retail trade of so-called unauthorized "new" illicit on-demand editions of this 2002 title is strictly prohibited by the publisher(*Epic Press*)and wholly illegal. This first original novel was a "gay"-themed allegory. Its currently revised successor most absolutely, most certainly, most definitely and most positively is *NOT*. Except for a single "gay" bar pick-up scenario(which I personally field-researched in San Francisco's *Castro* district)that particular "gay" aspect or element has likewise been entirely and totally *ELIMINATED* from the currently revised novel.

I took this rather drastic and extraordinary step of radically revising my novel—which to date I've never, ever taken with any of my other published work—not so much because I was at all disappointed or dissatisfied with my original novel as such—but rather because I myself seriously re-considered and re-examined my work, and because I myself carefully concluded that its "gay"-related element had *ruinously* contaminated and corrupted it, and finally, because I myself resolutely decided that the only way to save and salvage it(as well as to more firmly found its planned sequel)was to radically revise and re-write it. I make these not–so–delicate–or–subtle distinctions to clarify and stress the simple fact—like it or not—that I most categorically did *NOT* submit, succumb or otherwise capitulate to its rather illiterate criticism emanating from certain ignorant, uninformed and unenlightened quarters as my principal and real reason for revising it.

The sole even remotely "gay" allusion Poe makes is to an "effeminate-looking person" in his *A Tale of the Ragged Mountains*.

That clearly stated, I now effectively rebut, defy and challenge my first original novel's rather rampant illiterate criticism *thus:*

• **"Don't bother.** *This book is just dreadful. It purports to be one of the first horror books written from a gay point of view. Wait for the next one. Poorly constructed sentences, stock characters, and a ridiculous plot makes it clear why this book was rejected by "real" publishers. Xlibris is essentially a vanity publisher. No editor has touched this, or would want to. There is much better gay fiction available, and much better horror fiction available."*— "parker reilly"(San Francisco, CA 25 July 2002)

This "review" obviously originates from some extremely self-frustrated pretender of an "editor"(i.e. that of one of San Francisco's "alternate" weekly gratuitous–editorials–subsidized–by–sex–ads rags)who couldn't conceivably hold a "real" editorial position at any really *legitimate* newspaper in the entire country; and yet so pompously presumes("purports")to speak for all other editors on the planet!

The book may very well be "dreadful" but due solely to its "gay"-related content if anything.

First off, this "reviewer" outright *lies*: the book never ever anywhere claimed to be "one of the first horror books written from a gay point of view." In actual fact, it never ever anywhere even claimed to be written *at all* from a "gay point of view." In actual fact, even the word "gay" was virtually never ever even uttered(much less written)anywhere throughout the entire manuscript. In actual fact, its prime "point of view" is that of an allegorically *"straight"* character—though nowhere is that particular distinction ever even overtly made either!

So this particular pretender of an "editor" sorely needs to first learn how to *read* with some small semblance of *literacy* before ever presuming to be capable of reviewing anything coherently.

All the book ever asserted it was "first" at being was a gay–themed *allegory* that exploited the graphic visual and vivid imagery of Edgar Allan Poe to make a strong fictional gay–advocate–or–liberationist statement—without ever once resorting to tedious "gay" terminology.

"Poorly constructed sentences?"(lacking concrete examples)That's really rich coming likely as it does from an "editor" who most creatively and originally starts virtually every sentence in his own "editorials" with the thoroughly–thought–out article *"The!"*

"Stock characters?" Hardly. Every last character in the book was fictitiously taken from an *actual person* in life!

"Ridiculous plot?" Perhaps. But Poe's graphic visual and vivid imagery—neither characters nor plot—was the book's driving device.

This book was never ever anywhere "rejected" by any "publishers"—"real" or un-real—simply because it was never ever even *submitted* anywhere. It was published by my own small *New Humanity Press*—operating since *1990!*—in cooperation with *Xlibris Corporation*. And *Xlibris*–an on-demand publishing service—is not a "vanity publisher"—"essentially" or otherwise.

Editorial distortion was in fact *itself* "rejected" as undesirable.

So "much better" gay or horror fiction may or may not be "available"—that's patently a matter of opinion. But—all petty and resentful misrepresentations aside—this experimental *ALLEGORY* never ever anywhere claimed to be *EITHER*.

• "Whatever his(the writer's)day job was, hope he didn't quit!"—**A reader**(Missouri, 28 August 2002)

Well, I'm *not* from Missouri! And hope is always heartening! But I haven't been stuck like this bitter loser in any "day job" anywhere since 2000!

291

- **"Pretty tedious.** *If ever someone asks you if having an interest in Edgar Allan Poe, a working knowledge of hypnosis and strong feelings about GLBT folks is enough to write a story about, say 'no'. I wish I could have liked this book, but I found it long-winded and tedious. Large sections of the book are done in 'interview' format, and involve the same thoughts being repeated time after time. The action of the book consists of a way to represent every work of Poe in one story, with little else in the way of discernable(sic)plot.*

The characters were shaky at best, and little was done in the way of making the story consistent. For example, the 'hypnotist' started off by completely and utterly taking over a man's senses in the middle of a bridge without any set up, and then began to work harder and harder to deepen the man's hypnotic state. Fine, except that his results got less impressive each time, but the story was built to make it seem like he was doing better and better."—**A reader**(14 April 2004).

Pretty ***ILLITERATE!***
This "reviewer" poses several *SO WHAT?*–questions:
An intense "interest" in Edgar Allan Poe I'll readily admit to—that goes without saying! *So what?* The novel's obviously and unabashedly a *devoted derivative homage* to Poe's works. *Duh? Hel-lo?*
A "working knowledge of hypnosis" I take strong exception to as outright *illiterate* ignorance of my exhaustive near semi-professional research into the subject-matter for purposes of genuine authenticity. *So what? Duh? Hel-lo?*
"Strong feelings about *GLBT*(Gay, Lesbian, Bi-Sexual, Trans-Gender)folks" I object to as equally outright *illiterate!* Even as a gay-themed *allegory* the novel alludes solely to *gay males* and absolutely no other "orientation" whatever—and even then, again, without *at all* overtly resorting to tedious "gay" terminology much less equally tedious "GLBT" termi-

nology! So...*So what? Duh? Hel-lo?*

Not–so–sizable sections of the novel are indeed done—not in "interview"—but rather *dialogue* "format" in keeping with Poe's resort to that device. And since again the novel's a *derivative—and devoted—homage* to Poe's works...*So what? Duh? Hel-lo?*

That particular illiterate comment demonstrates a down-right *glaring* ignorance of Poe's work—in which the *dialogue* device is extensively exploited in several Poe stories—to-wit:

The Conversation of Eiros and Charmion
Three Sundays in a Week
Mesmeric Revelation
The Power of Words
The Colloquy of Monos and Una

And if any *similar* thoughts are "repeated" then it's to different *listeners!*

Doubtless this illiterate critic would prefer—rather than dialogues—resort to the tediously redundant he said-she said device!

Incorporating into my *devoted derivative homage* terrific elements from many if not most of Poe's stories I'll also readily admit to. But again...*So what? Duh? Hel-lo?*

But the eminently discernible plot is indeed readily so to the truly discerning—which this illiterate "reviewer" is decidedly *NOT!*

And again the novel's supposedly "shaky" characters were in their entirety fictitiously taken from actual persons in life!

As for the story's consistency(or supposedly lack thereof)the first actual *hypnotic induction* of the story's principal protagonist never even occurs until the novel's *SIXTH* chapter!

As the novel's "hypnotist" rightly and repeatedly harps upon throughout—from the outset—hypnosis has absolutely nothing whatever to do with mentally "taking over" *anything* much less any hypnotic subject's "senses!"

The "middle–of–the–bridge" incident this "reviewer" deliberately mis-represents is(in the novel's *second* chapter)simply a vivid "guided imagery" which is duly "set up" by the "hypnotist" at the chapter's outset with his recounting of a ghostly *traveler's tale*; it's clearly not portrayed as a hypnotic induction at all.

So again…So what? Duh? Hel-lo?

As for whether this particular "reviewer" actually "liked" the book: frankly, my dear, I don't…well, you know!

* *"Qvamp says:*

"This book is based **heavily** *on the works of Edgar Allan Poe. But the references are pretty heavy-handed and don't necessarily further the plot, which is pretty loose to begin with.*

"I don't recommend this book at all. It focuses on GLBT(Gay, Lesbian, Bi-Sexual, Trans-Gender)folks, but enjoys debating all of the homophobic arguments and making references to Poe and hypnotism than in actually developing a plot or characters."—lame "Queer Horror" website.

Sounds like a *SO WHAT?*-rehash re-worded("GLBT folks")by the very same anonymous sissy!

That my novel's a devoted derivative Poe homage I've already readily admitted to. *So what? Duh? Hel-lo?*

Whether the "references" are "pretty heavy-handed" or whether the plot is "pretty loose to begin with" is yet another pretty *ILLITERATE* and sense-*LESS* comment with absolutely no frame of reference whatever. Heavy-handed or loose in what *sense?*

No one asks much less cares whether the anonymous sissy would "recommend" my novel. That it allegorically "focuses" not on "GLBT folks" but solely "gay" males; that it employs(not "enjoys")the challenging of "homophobic arguments" through the creative and unique fictional medium of vivid hypnotic Poe *imagery* has already been well-established as what the novel's all about. So why would it *NOT* effectively execute all of those things? *So WHAT? Duh? Hel-lo?*

Poe himself frequently resorted to stories treating the subject-matter of hypnotism(or more specifically *mesmerism*)—to wit:

A Tale of the Ragged Mountains
The Facts in the Case of M. Valdemar
Mesmeric Revelation

And few of Poe's stories were ever celebrated or distinguished by "actually developing a plot or characters."

So again, since my novel's a devoted derivative Poe homage...*So what? Duh? Hel-lo?*

Rather habitually—even compulsively—the "gay" community rabidly whines like cry-babies about how the mass media so rampantly and so unjustly mis-portrays and mis-represents them—and how the rest of humanity is somehow obligated to "tolerate" if not "accept" them to do them justice which is evidently their divine "right."

They whined like cry-babies about their supposed mis-portrayal in the excellent film, *Cruising.* They whined like cry-babies about their supposed mis-portrayal in the not–so–excellent film, *Basic Instinct.* They've even whined like cry-babies about their supposed mis-portrayal in the extremely controversial *as–yet–to–be–made* film about gay San Francisco supervisor Harvey Milk which will likely *NEVER* be made owing to all their cry-babyish *WHINING!*

My allegorically gay–advocate–liberationist Poe-inspired novel was my modest but rather under- and un-appreciated attempt to at least empathize against some of the bigotry and prejudice they whine so cry-babyishly and so rabidly about. Rest assured: I won't make that mistake ever, ever again.

• *"Indeed, I did find a reviwer and sent him the book, but after reading Terror Tales, he decided that it revealed a strong **anti-***

gay stance, and he did not, therefore, find it suitable for review in The Edgar Allan Poe Review. I trust the reviewer's judgment, and, therefore, concurred not to review the book."—Dr. Barbara Cantalupo, Associate Professor of English & Editor, **The Edgar Allan Poe Review**, Penn State University

This rude and inconsiderate pseudo-intellectual didn't even do me the common courtesy of this pompous email until some *six months* after receiving my novel for review—proving effectively even the not–so–highbrow academic but equally illiterate mis-representation of my novel's supposed "strong *anti-gay* stance."

Utterly *UNBELIEVABLE!*

Rude obnoxiousness abounded in the not–so–compassionate "gay" reception to my novel:

Bay Area Reporter publisher, Bob Ross, appraised in August 1993 the short story upon which I based my novel's first chapter as "interesting and well-written."

In December 2001 Ross couldn't be bothered(God forbid!)to even *acknowledge* receipt of my novel's review galleys, dispatching his "Arts&Entertainment Editor," Roberto Friedman, to reject its review owing to its origin in "self-publishing concerns like *Xlibris*."

Both Paul Reidinger(Associate Editor, *The San Francisco Bay Guardian*)and Andrea Goode(*SF Weekly*)took reciept of review copies of my novel under the false pretenses of review consideration but neither—unsurprisingly—did me the common courtesy or decency of a follow-up reply.

And these are all the very same cliquish cohorts and cronies who self-proclaim themselves so pretentiously—and hypocritically—to make up the world-saving universal champion vanguard of the so-called "progressive" agenda! Common courtesy and consideration evidently don't figure too greatly in that magnanimous agenda.

• *"Thus we're treated to acres of overwriting and to unbeliev-*

ably long didactic passages, many rendered in the form of Platonic dialogues...Two are dialogues between Peter and Jonna debating whether or not he is right to be terminally peeved that she still enjoys the company(and no more than that)of her ex-lover; after about two paragraphs of Peter's spoilt-brat whinings on the subject one's incredulous that Jonna hasn't long ago hurled him off the Golden Gate Bridge...indeed, one's eager to volunteer to do it for her...Covino enjoys his Grand Guignol effects, again reminiscent of Poe, but these fall late in the book; for many readers perhaps too late, because by then they'll have picked up a different book in preference to this one."—John Grant(***Infinity Plus***, 15 March 2003).

Yeah, well, John: the girl-friend who insinuated herself into my novel, and who(still)wrongly felt it was it was proper to spend interminable lengths of time with her duly dumped "ex-lover"—rather than sensibly *MOVE ON*—has herself long since been *HISTORY* and duly replaced now by some six years by a far more beautiful and bustier model; but even *she* complimented the novel as being "brilliant"—doubtless because she was in it. Rest assured: I won't make that mistake ever, ever again either!

But John: a true writer *is* his characters. And if you really believe yourself capable enough to "hurl" Peter off the *Golden Gate Bridge* then I most heartily welcome you to try if you really think you can: *anytime!*

As for those "Grand Guignol effects" coming too late in the novel, John, perhaps you've never encountered or heard of it before but it's called...*DE-VEL'OP-MENT!*

As for "acres of overwriting," sorry about that John, but I won't *DUMB DOWN* my literature for *any* illiterate critic—let alone you!